Defending Violet

DEFENDING VIOLET

JENNIFER LOUISE JEFFERSON

FIVE STAR

An imprint of Thomson Gale, a part of The Thomson Corporation

Detroit • New York • San Francisco • New Haven, Conn. • Waterville, Maine • London

Set in 11 pt. Plantin.

LIBRARY OF CONGRESS CATALOGING-IN-PUBLICATION DATA

Jefferson, Jennifer Louise.
Defending Violet / Jennifer Louise Jefferson. — 1st ed.
p. cm.
ISBN 1-59414-536-9 (alk. paper)
1. Women lawyers—Fiction. I. Title.
PS3610.E365D44 2006
813'.6—dc22
2006021337

U.S. Hardcover:
ISBN 13: 978-1-59414-536-0
ISBN 10: 1-59414-536-9

First Edition. First Printing: November 2006.

Published in 2006 in conjunction with Tekno Books and Ed Gorman.

Printed in the United States of America on permanent paper
10 9 8 7 6 5 4 3 2 1

To my former colleagues at the
Passaic County Family Court
in Paterson, New Jersey—attorneys,
judges, caseworkers, and staff,
all dedicated to the difficult task of
preserving families and protecting children
and
in memory of my father, Lou Jefferson
(1927–2006),
who always told me to keep writing.

ACKNOWLEDGMENTS

For their participation in the creation of this book, I am grateful to:

My friend Kathleen Reddy, whose insightful critiques and Irish wit got me from first page to last.

My agent Susan Schulman, for her enthusiasm and support.

Hugh Abramson, for his keen editing suggestions.

John Helfers, and the folks at Five Star, for turning a stack of paper into a book.

My husband and sons: Bob, Jason, Matthew, and Luke, for love and home.

My mother, for making sure I had a library card.

PREFACE

In God We Trust is inscribed on signs hanging behind the judge's bench in every courtroom in this state. In the older courtrooms, those that feature high ceilings, mahogany paneling, and grand windows, the words are scripted in gold. The new "temporary" courtrooms, jerry-built from storage rooms to accommodate rising crime rates, have cheap plastic signs stuck to the wall. Everyone in the courtroom, except the judge, has a view of *In God We Trust,* and in quiet moments, boring moments, can stare at it and ponder the phrase and its prominence in a court of law. When I was a rookie criminal defense attorney, I viewed it as a pie in the face of the separation of church and state. Eventually I understood that it represents the bottom line.

For victim and defendant alike, a trial is a free fall, cushioned only by faith and trust. The first landing is faith: faith in the judicial system and the constitutional guarantee of due process, via the safeguards of separation of powers, constitutional rights, the adversary system, rules of evidence, jury of peers, and right to appeal. In other words, faith in justice. If the judicial system fails? The plunge continues into the realm of mercy. And if mercy fails? All that remains between mercy and the pavement is the bottom line: trust in God, or destiny, or some other cosmic concept beyond our control.

And if trust fails?

You hit the pavement.

Because this is the way it works: Despite structure, safeguards, and guarantees, a trial is simply two competing versions of the facts, and it is standard practice for lawyers to manipulate facts to create their rendition of the story. A good lawyer can handle what appears to be hard fact, and it becomes illusive, elusive, and allusive. Conversely, the amorphous can be massaged into fact. Facts are sometimes unwittingly altered when the wrong person is identified, a witness lies or forgets, a false confession is coerced, politics intervene, or power is asserted.

Usually the mechanics of the judicial system run smoothly, and justice prevails. However, every time I take on a new client I feel a flash of fear—maybe this will be the one, the one who takes that leap of faith and tumbles right past justice, past mercy, landing on In God We Trust; hanging on as she waits to hear the words—It was him I saw that night—She is unfit to be a mother—In the best interests of the child—Guilty—Innocent—words that allow the jury to go home, the lawyers to close their files, the judge to clear her calendar and the defendant to go to prison. Or not. And then she loses her grip and continues falling, until she hits the pavement.

★ ★ ★ ★ ★

Part One

★ ★ ★ ★ ★

1

The phone rang and Violet tumbled back into my life. I wouldn't have answered if I'd known where it would lead me, that I would be forced beyond my role as an advocate, into the realms of justice, morality, and mercy; that I would agonize over the true meaning of culpability, and over trying to understand what was truth and what was fact. Violet's case, *State v. Violeta Rosada* in Criminal Court and *In the Matter of the Minor Child T.R.*, in Family Court, took me for a ride to places I did not want to go. But I didn't know that when the phone rang.

It was the last day of winter. My yard was strewn with snowbells and crocuses, and I longed for the sharp breeze lifting off of the bay to infuse me with light, salt, and moral clarity. Winter ended on a bitter note; temperatures skidded around the freezing mark, scattering birds and scorching the green spikes of daffodils that poked out of the ground prematurely. It rained and hailed intermittently, and I was more irritable than usual.

My policy is to not answer the phone when I am with a client. However, I had listened patiently for an hour while Mary Abbott ranted about her husband and her plans to take him for everything he had and to make him feel pain. She was considering hiring me to make him feel that pain. I am a divorce lawyer and licensed to do damage—financial, emotional, and psychological damage, and that is what many clients want to pay me to do.

"I hear you're a real shark," she said, ten minutes into her appointment. I am not a shark, but I didn't tell her that, because I heard the ka-ching! of the cash register when she pulled up to the curb in a silver Lexus that was clearly out of place in this neighborhood of two-decker houses and mom and pop businesses, where the cars are older American models; a neighborhood where it appears that time stopped in 1952, where there is no evidence of the revolutionary 60s, the self-indulgent 70s, the yuppie 80s, or the smug 90s, only of people who value hard work, extended families and high-carb diets.

From the window I watched her walk up the wooden front steps and look left and right as though uncertain she was at the correct address. My private clients are usually straight-up working and middle class; it is rare for me to get one from the Heights, so I was slightly more curious than usual about her. When the buzzer finally rang I ducked into my office and indicated to Marco to answer. After a minute I strode out, right hand extended. "Ms. Abbott? Thank you for coming. I'm Ginger Rae Reddy." My hearty handshake felt crude against her well-moisturized skin. "Please. Come into my office."

Marco lingered in the doorway as we seated ourselves. Mary Abbott arranged her purse and bulging accordion folder of papers just so.

"Would you like some fresh coffee?" Marco asked her. "Or a soda or spring water?"

"Spring water, please." She gave him a pretty smile and stayed focused on him as he left the room. I watched her try to figure out his position in the office—dressed in faded jeans, black polo shirt and tan work boots, he was not a typical receptionist, and since he did the greeting and serving he was probably not an attorney.

I cleared my throat and she turned to me. It was 5:50 and she was almost an hour late. I was getting hungry. When I'm hungry I get cranky. Being cranky is not the way to woo a new client, but I couldn't resist giving her a nudge. "Did you have trouble finding your way here?"

She answered my small zing with one of her own. "I'm late aren't I? I apologize. I got turned around; I don't often come to this part of town."

This part of town. I considered what she might mean. It is a neighborhood of wooden two-family houses with modest front lawns and narrow driveways filled with immaculate Chevys and Fords. Bay Avenue, where my office is, is lined with a mixture of residences and small businesses—diner, produce market, hardware store, that type of thing. Three blocks west is Benny's Friendly Tavern and Go-Go Bar, marking the descent into a neighborhood that is a step down economically—the houses are shabby, the cars dented, and the lawns show more dirt than grass. Five blocks east is the bay, and in that direction the houses become progressively larger and more architecturally complex, so that the final two blocks are lined with Victorians whose wide front porches and large shade trees evoke a sense of history, of grace.

Port Grace benefited from a brief wave of gentrification in the 1980s, when young professionals and college professors bought the Victorians, most of which had previously been converted to rooming houses. They painstakingly restored them, removing dropped ceilings and vinyl floors, sanding, scrubbing and painting the exteriors novel color combinations such as hooker green and pumpkin or lavender and nutmeg. My office is in a modest wood frame two-family that my landlord, Mr. Ziznewski, has owned for forty-five years. He is a retired longshoreman, the self-deputized watchdog of the block, with a bulldog physique and a golden retriever disposition.

That, in a nutshell, is this part of town. I assumed that Mary Abbott was comparing it to the Heights, where the houses are opulent, the driveways circular, and the gardens are perennial borders. This neighborhood is marigolds and petunias. Hers is hollyhocks and delphiniums. She was a pretty woman in her late forties or early fifties, sporting a buttery blond bob, light makeup, and a petal-pink manicure. Although presently fragile, she possessed a cool, innate self-confidence that might have made me insecure under other circumstances; however that day, because I had slogged through three years of law school, I was in the driver's seat and she was wavering between fury and utter loss.

Marco returned with spring water, a glass with ice in it, and a neatly folded napkin that he placed upon the table next to Mary. "Can I get you anything else?" he asked, looking directly at her.

"No thank you."

He gave me a questioning look.

"Go," I said. "I'll see you in the morning." He had a night class and I didn't want him to be late. Today the sign on my office door reads *Ginger Rae Reddy and Marco Tavares, Attorneys at Law.* At that time he was my investigator, paralegal, receptionist, collection agent, and friend, a former cop attending law school at night. He is a solid 5'10", with short, wavy black hair and eyes that are gentle on the surface and steel further down. Like a lot of the men in Port Grace, he looks like he would be comfortable picking olives or mending fishing nets. Mary and I watched him exit. She crossed and uncrossed her legs, smoothed her silky silver-gray slacks. "Is he your . . . ?"

"Investigator," I said. People like the word investigator. It sounds masculine and authoritative, evoking TV cop shows.

Marco was gone and I was alone with Mary Abbott when Violet called. But I am getting ahead of myself. Mary touched the arm of her chair and pointed to framed botanical drawings on the wall. "Your office is pretty." This was throat-clearing, nervousness, as she considered whether I was good enough to be her lawyer. She eyed my black stretch pants, ivory silk blouse and burgundy high heels. I watched the tabulation in her eyes as she analyzed me—working class, reasonably bright, diligent, and rough around the edges.

Enough preliminaries. "Now, Ms. Abbott. Who referred you to me?" I picked up a pen and legal pad. Typically, women like her go to one of the Broad Street firms, to Martin Wolfson or Terry Donahue, men who net six figures thanks to the Mary Abbotts of the world. Wives from the Heights don't often come down to the flats, to offices in old wooden houses next door to a butcher who hangs pigs upside down in his picture window.

"Call me Mary." She paused. "Professor Burns gave me your name. I took his American Culture lecture series at the Jordan."

I nodded. Tommy Burns is my husband. He is an associate professor of American Studies at Winslow College, and I guess that's not enough for him, because every winter he presents a series of lectures at the museum. He makes friends everywhere he goes, so I was not surprised at the leap from lecturer to divorce counselor that Mary implied. "How can I help you?" She pulled papers from her accordion file. Tax forms, deeds, bank statements, stock certificates. A paperback book tumbled to the floor, and as she bent to retrieve it a lapful of documents fell too. "Don't worry about that stuff," I said. "You won't need it today. What's the book?" I wanted to distract her from her concern over the voluminous file she was trying to get control of. She held it out to me. *The Spiritual Divorce.* "Good book?" I asked.

She paused before she replied. "Most of the time I'm just so angry and hurt I want to kill him, but then there's a part of me that knows it would be better to go this way." She gestured toward the book. "You know, transcend the negativity."

"I hope it helps," I said as I returned it to her. "Why don't you put those papers down, and tell me why you're here."

As she spoke, a picture of their marriage slowly emerged—

twenty-three intertwined years of accumulated assets and debts, grief, pleasure, children, forgotten birthdays, burnt toast, carpools, and summer evenings at the lake; all of which must be untwined in the process of divorce. I have never met a client who understands how difficult that will be, particularly in a long marriage like the Abbotts'.

By seven o'clock I was famished. I wanted to go home and have dinner with Tommy, who is an accomplished cook, but I didn't want Mary to feel rushed, because I hoped to get a fat retainer check from her. I desperately needed a cash infusion. Marco isn't cheap, and neither are spring water and high heels.

Her story was one that I've heard many times, and she was starting to repeat herself. "My husband, well, it's not just the girl, but that was the final straw. Our marriage has been bad for years. He's always been emotionally unavailable. Always working long hours or on the golf course, never treating me like I'm special."

The phone rang. I decided to answer it and break up Mary's self-absorbed diatribe. "Sorry. I'm expecting an urgent call." Which was not a total fib because everyone who calls a lawyer believes that their problem is urgent. I picked up the receiver. "Ginger Rae Reddy."

"Ginger? It's Violet. Violeta Rosado." She was sobbing, babbling. Something about Teddy, her baby. Something about jail.

"Slow down, slow down. I can't understand you."

I had represented Violet in a domestic violence case more than a year before, when she was six months pregnant with Teddy, and her boyfriend AJ beat her up. The police referred her to the women's shelter, and they asked me to represent her because I often take their worst cases *pro bono.*

"Teddy, it's Teddy," Violet was saying.

"AJ hurt Teddy?"

"No. Not AJ. They think I did. I'm arrested. You have to help me."

Violet was only nineteen and she had no family support. However, I only take very minor criminal cases, and *baby in the hospital* didn't sound minor. "I'm sorry, but I'm not taking criminal cases. I'll find someone for you. Someone good."

A couple of years ago I decided to limit my practice to what is optimistically called Family Law, which is really about the disintegration of families. My practice is filled with people ripped apart by the divorce process, for whom the stuff of daily life—helping the kids with homework, sorting the recycling, cheering at softball games, Sunday dinners, seasonal chores, family routines—is in disarray. I take the occasional misdemeanor—minor marijuana charges and underage drinking summonses, but nothing that will deal the client more than 364 days in the county jail.

"Please, Ginger." Violet's voice tugged at me: a plead, a whisper, a child's voice, the voice of one who has never been a child.

After law school I worked in the D.A.'s office, seduced by what I perceived as a moral compass and a simple goal: Put bad people behind bars. I prosecuted juveniles who sold nickel bags, prostitutes who sold sex, and vagrants who had nothing to sell. I quit after less than a year and flipped over to criminal defense, where, after four intense years I was fried like an egg on a black car in August.

At first I was dazzled by the possibility of fighting injustice, being a crusader for the oppressed. I was fascinated by the mutable, evanescent nature of facts, and excited by the high stakes in defense work. Predictably, the novelty wore off and I was unable to develop the coping techniques that sustain many defense attorneys: constitutional righteousness, social worker convictions, and Robin Hood heroics. Ultimately I was unable to sustain empathy for my clients, which proved fatal in terms of my career as a criminal defense attorney.

"Okay," I said to Violet. I wasn't heartless enough to tell her to wait until morning, when she would be assigned a public defender who would pick up her case along with twenty others. "I'll be there soon. Don't talk to the police. Tell them your lawyer said you couldn't." I banged the phone into the cradle. Mary had perked up as she tried to piece together the conversation. Confidentiality breach. "I'm sorry," I told her. "An emergency." I remained standing, gave her my closing pitch, and retrieved her Burberry from the closet. She put it on, we shook hands again, and I opened the door for her. It was raining. Too bad Marco wasn't there to walk her to her car holding an umbrella over her head. Now her pretty blond bob would get messed up and she'd blame it on me and hire another lawyer.

I envision catalog copywriters as poets and novelists, who, at the end of a workday encouraging rampant consumerism, will be found in Starbucks pecking away on their laptops. Port Grace landed its first and only Starbucks a year ago. It huddles downtown in a dismal shopping arcade, and is totally unnecessary because this town is filled with Spanish and Portuguese cafes where you can get an espresso or café con leche for half the price and twice the atmosphere.

Officer Decker, who escorted me to the interrogation room, was not familiar; fortyish and portly, he was too old to be a rookie, so he was probably a transfer, demoted from another precinct and resigned to desk work until he'd done his twenty. I tried breaking the ice with a remark about the Mets, but he wasn't interested. As we walked down the hall I saw Eduardo Fortunato coming the other way. He is the best criminal defense attorney in the city, the one who takes the dirty cases—big-time drug dealers and major violent crimes. Everything I know about being a good lawyer I learned from him.

"Ginger Rae!" He leaned in and kissed me on the cheek. "I thought you weren't doing this anymore," he said, the sweep of his arm encompassing pea-soup walls, cracked vinyl floor, and Officer Decker and his duty belt which sagged with the weight of his Glock; two magazines each holding fifteen rounds of 9-millimeter ammunition; radio; mace; sap; flashlight; and handcuffs.

"A former client in distress." I considered asking him to talk to Violet, to take her case, to let me go home and see if Tommy [illegible] something warm in the oven. "I might be calling you."

[illegible] ignored Officer Decker's impatience. "I'll buy [illegible] continued on his way out [illegible] down the

I didn't want to be alone on a cold rainy night in a dirty hall with Officer Decker, on my way to see a client who might have hurt her child.

We stood outside of the interrogation room. Through the one-way glass I saw Violet, sitting with her head on the table. "Did anyone talk to her?" I asked Decker.

He shrugged. "I did the picture and the prints. I might have said 'say cheese,' or 'put your thumb here.' "

"I mean anything resembling an interrogation."

"Not that I heard."

"Why is she being held?"

He shrugged again, not interested in me, or Violet, or in being courteous; maybe he didn't care about anything at all.

"The arresting officer had an emergency and left," he said. "I'll get the Complaint." He closed the door hard, and the odor of metal, fear, sweat, and burnt coffee surrounded us.

Violet was too distraught to speak. "Pull yourself together," I said. "We have to talk." She didn't look up, so I rubbed her back and felt her tremble through the thin cotton shirt that hung off of her youth and delicate bone structure. "What happened?"

She didn't respond. She stopped crying but seemed to retreat deep inside of herself. I closed my eyes and tried to ignore hunger, fatigue, and a desire to be at home in front of the TV with a plate of nachos close at hand.

Finally she crawled out of her cave and started talking. "Yesterday I put Teddy down for his nap around noon. Later I fell asleep on the couch and when I woke up it was [illegible] o' clock. He doesn't usually sleep that long and [illegible] just tired. He was getting over an [illegible] while later I look[illegible] leaving space for her to fill. Eventually she spoke. "They're saying I hurt Teddy."

I kept my voice low. "Did you?"

"No! No!" She looked straight at me for the first time. "I love my baby. I would never hurt him."

"What's wrong with him?"

"The doctor said he's in a coma. Like a deep, deep, sleep. They don't know when he'll wake up."

"How was he before he took his nap?"

"Fine. Like I said, he had an ear infection. But I got him the pink stuff and he was a lot better. He spit up his bottle in the morning. But that just happens sometimes with babies."

"Why did they arrest you? What makes them think that you hurt Teddy?"

"I don't know. I stayed at the hospital all last night and I didn't sleep at all. This morning they did a brain thing on him, and this afternoon the DCW lady came and talked to me. Then the police came."

I felt a ping in my gut. DCW is the Department of Child Welfare. Doctors are mandated by law to call DCW when they suspect child abuse.

"What did the DCW worker say?"

"She just asked a lotta questions. How old am I. Who lives with me. Who is Teddy's father. How was Teddy yesterday. Do you think they'll call AJ?"

"I don't know. Did you tell her about the restraining order?"

"No." She appeared to hesitate, like she was going to say something else, but she didn't.

"I'll call them," I said. "They should know about it. There's not much point in contacting him since he's never even seen Teddy." She didn't respond and I felt that ping in my gut again. "He hasn't seen Teddy, has he?" No answer. I did a quick mental inventory of possible scenarios. "Violet, has AJ been visiting

Teddy?" She nodded slightly. "When was the last time he saw him?"

"A few days ago."

"Where? Who supervised? Did he get a court order?" She shook her head. She wouldn't look at me. More scenarios. "Did you just let him see Teddy?" She nodded. A bolt of anger shot through me. "Jesus, Violet. AJ's dangerous. Why did you do that?" I got tired of her not answering. And I was pretty sure I knew why. I stood up and stretched. In two-inch heels I am over six feet tall. I looked around that smutty room. "Have you been seeing AJ?" I asked. I pictured him the way I'd seen him in court—a solid block of a man, blond brush cut, too much cologne, falling all over himself to kiss the judge's ass; but Violet's bruises made her case easy for me.

"He was being nice to me."

"Damn it Violet, you should have called me."

"Why?"

Why indeed. I took a minute to regroup. "I'm sorry. You caught me off-guard; I know you think he's changed, but I don't trust him." I put my hand on her arm. Gently. "When you were at the shelter, didn't they teach you about the cycle of violence? After they beat you they woo you back, and then it starts all over?" She didn't answer or look at me. "When was the last time you saw AJ?"

"A few nights ago."

"Did he do anything to Teddy that might have caused an injury?"

"No."

"Did he do anything at all with Teddy?"

"No. Teddy was asleep when he got there. It was late. He'd worked a double shift."

AJ was a prison guard at Western State, about eighty miles away. Violet met him when she went to visit her father, who is an inmate, and AJ saw her crying in the parking lot while she waited for the bus back to Port Grace. He bought her a soda and told her he'd look out for her father and one thing led to another.

"So you were asleep when he got there?" She nodded. "And Teddy was asleep?" She nodded again.

The door opened and Officer Decker handed me the Complaint. "I need more time," I said. After he left I scanned the Complaint, an affidavit the arresting officer, Pete DiCicco, signed, detailing why he had probable cause to believe that a felony had been committed, and that Violet had committed it. She'd been Mirandized and she asked to call her lawyer. "It says here that the doctor reported that Teddy is most likely the victim of shaken baby syndrome, and his injuries could have only occurred from being severely shaken. It also says that when the DCW worker asked you if you shook him, you said 'I don't think so.' Did you say that?"

"No."

"Then why did he write it? Tell me what happened."

"It was all confusing," she said between sniffles. "There was the doctor and a nurse and the DCW lady and I was so tired and worried about Teddy. And everybody kept asking me questions and people were coming in and out and stretchers and emergencies. But I didn't say that. They misunderstood me or something."

"Do you remember saying anything like that?"

She shook her head.

"All right, that's enough for tonight. I'm going to find out what's going on and hopefully get you out of here. If not, you'll have a bail hearing tomorrow. Is there someone who can post a bond for you?"

"Just AJ."

Great. "What's his phone number? And what about the

restraining order? Did you have it dismissed?"

She shook her head. "I didn't know I had to."

Frustration blossomed inside of me. "Is he still married?"

AJ lived a dual life for a while, sleeping with Violet part of the week and with his wife and kids the rest. He would tell his wife he was working a double and go to Violet. Violet thought that he'd left his wife and was working extra shifts to pay child support. The prison has trailers that guards use to catch some sleep when they're doing extra shifts, and so AJ's story to the women was not implausible.

She started crying again. Officer Decker came back. Impatient this time.

"She's not talking to anyone tonight," I said. "And I'd like to take her home. There's no risk to the public."

He shook his head smugly, the bastard. Pointed a fat finger at the Complaint. "It's an Arrest Warrant, not a Summons."

"Where's Officer DiCicco?"

"I told you. Emergency."

"Call him. Or page him."

"No can do. It's a personal emergency. He's off duty."

Sure, I thought. A personal emergency with a poker game. DiCicco used to be poker buddies with Marco, but they had a falling out over I don't know what. I stared hard at Decker, but he was enjoying pissing me off, and there was nothing I could do about it.

"I'm sorry to leave you here," I said to Violet. "I'll see you in the morning. Don't talk to anyone." I left her there, crying, with Officer Decker and his bad breath, and then chatted with the desk sergeant for a few minutes, signed out, and nodded to a cute young cop who entered as I exited. Outside it was still raining.

3

It was after nine-thirty when I pulled the Jimmy into the driveway. The persistent rain and sleet matched my mood. Tommy's car wasn't there and I was irrationally disappointed. I forced myself out of the Jimmy and dashed up to the porch where Cat waited for me, then paused to inhale the briny, dangerous freedom of night on the bay.

Port Grace, like most cities, is defined by its geography. The bay, formerly a port of call and a living for much of the population, flows into the Atlantic. The river, whose headwaters are a hundred miles north, feeds into the bay and marks the northern boundary of the city. Like many rivers, it served as a dumping ground for one hundred and fifty years of active mills and factories that eventually shut down, one after the other, like bedtime lights in a house full of children. Only recently is the river clean enough to induce contemplation and recreation.

Sleet blew and Cat meowed, so I located my key and unlocked the door. "I'm home!" I called, hoping that maybe Jake, Tommy's sixteen-year-old son, was in. The house felt emptier than it was. I dumped food into Cat's bowl and then toweled off and shimmied into flannel pajamas. There was no note from Tommy and no pot of soup on the stove. I picked up Cat, not a simple task because he weighs nineteen pounds. But he was warm. I wanted a shot of scotch, to feel the slow burn followed by a softening of the edge that follows me wherever I go.

What I did was put Bonnie Raitt on the CD player and cook scrambled eggs with pepper jack cheese melted into them. I flicked in oregano and tarragon from the potted herbs on the windowsill, herbs my dad sends from his nursery every winter, and ate standing at the counter, staring out the window at sleet sliding down glass.

Tomorrow, the prosecutor would review the arrest complaint and either drop the case or set charges, probably of endangering the welfare of a child. I finished my eggs and rinsed off the plate. Child endangerment. Criminal court. A penniless client. I decided that if Violet were charged I would see her through the bail hearing and then find another lawyer for her. Call in a favor or two. I didn't need that monkey on my back.

I saw the headlights of Tommy's car as he pulled into the driveway, and walked out onto the porch where the wind from the bay blew more sleet and rain onto me. Tommy, who wore a raincoat and carried an umbrella, grabbed my hand and pulled me inside. "I'll be right back," I said. "Would you make some tea?"

I changed into dry pajamas and noted that the hamper was overflowing and that I would have to do something to reduce it. The basic division of labor is: I do laundry and vacuum, Tommy shops and cooks. When I returned to the kitchen the kettle was on the stove and teabags were in the mugs. "Where's Jake?" I asked.

"Practice. Open mike tomorrow night." He gave me a steady look.

"Right." Jake plays guitar in a garage band and they had a gig at his high school. I remembered promising him that I would go. That's what Tommy's look was about. "I'll be there," I said. "I can't wait to see them."

Tommy glowed. He couldn't believe that Jake actually wanted him there. "When I was a kid," he said, "I didn't want my parents near me and my friends. I would never have invited them to something like this."

I shrugged. "He loves you."

"He's pretty darn fond of you too." That was true; Jake and I are good buddies, but I figured that what Tommy was really saying was that I better not miss the gig tomorrow night.

"How's he getting home?" I asked.

"Big John's driving him."

I glanced involuntarily at the window, the icy rain still doing its thing. "Maybe we should pick him up?" Big John's license was barely two months old. He was a steady kid but it still made me nervous—inexperienced driver, darkness, bad weather, car full of revved-up teens.

Tommy's expression slid from yes to maybe to a reluctant no. "It's happening," he said. "He's growing up and we can't stop that. Unless we think they're drinking or acting unsafe, we've got to let him go through it."

Sometimes I am more protective of Jake than Tommy is. "Maybe you should call his cell," I said. "Check in. Maybe he wants us to pick him up."

Tommy glanced at the phone. "He'll call if he needs us."

I let it go. "Did you eat?" I asked.

"I had a sandwich at Murphy's." I guess I looked surprised because he filled in the blank by saying, "Research." He indicated a stack of books on the old oak kitchen table. There is almost always a stack of books on the kitchen table so I hadn't paid attention. Tommy spread them out with the pride of a teenage girl showing off after a shopping spree. *The Penguin Book of Irish Verse, Collected Poems of Seamus Heaney, Collected Poems of William Butler Yeats, Contemporary Irish Poetry.*

"Why all the Irish?" I asked.

"Next fall I'll be teaching a class on the influence of the Irish on twentieth century American culture, so I'm starting to prepare."

That explained Murphy's. There isn't much of an Irish population in Port Grace anymore, but Murphy's is a couple blocks from Winslow College and they get a lot of business from students with fake ID's, as well as the legitimate ones; professors, and grad students. They serve food, but it is primarily a bar, which is why I was surprised that Tommy went there.

"Does Marco's band still play there?" he asked.

"Once or twice a month, I think."

"Let's go one night when they're playing," he said. "I'd like to set up interviews with some of the band members, ask them to visit my class. Or maybe I could take the class to Murphy's."

"Like a field trip," I said.

He nodded, pleased with his idea.

Marco plays percussion in an Irish band that was started by Liam, his friend from the police academy. The lead guitar player is Liam's cousin who immigrated from Ireland, and works construction. They get a lot of mileage out of having a Portuguese member of the band. I've seen them a couple of times, but not as often as I'd like. An Irish bar, even when most of the patrons are college students, has an obligation to be a serious drinking establishment and I feel out of place sipping club soda; but more to the point it makes me miss drinking in a way that I try to avoid.

Tommy picked up one of the books and thumbed through it. "Seamus Heaney," he said. "A great man. Wrote wrenching poems about The Troubles." He said "The Troubles" in a way that annoyed me, as though anyone would know what he's talking about. Tom interprets life through the lens of culture, and for me, our marriage was a cold plunge into the ocean of the arts. I come from a town where TVs dominate living rooms and black velvet paintings aren't a joke. Faculty parties are a nightmare, because I miss most of the cultural references that academics enjoy lobbing to one another. I know who Hemingway is, and Monet, and even Emily Dickinson; which is not bad for someone who majored in basketball and alcohol; but if it's deeper than College 101 I'm over my head.

However, once an academic discovers that I am a lawyer, especially when I practiced criminal law, it didn't matter if the only book I ever read was *The Little Engine That Could.* People have a fascination with the world of crime, obviously fueled by television and movies. So when I said I'm a criminal defense attorney, they looked at me with a mixture of horror and fascination, and a desire to hear stories filled with lascivious details.

"I'm sorry I missed dinner," I said.

"I'm used to it." Four years before, we were separated for a year; our marriage crumbled under my obsession with work, inconsistent moods, insecurity, and unreliable ways. Tommy had his ways too, that were hard for me, but my flaws are more obvious and I blame myself for most of our problems. The good news is that we patched most of the rips, even though I haven't changed much and neither has he; but we expect less of each other, and that makes it easier.

He reached into the shopping bag and pulled out a hefty hardcover. "For you," he said.

"Yes!" The latest Robert B. Parker. Spenser, Hawk, Susan and Pearl. Parker's books are comfort food for me. "Thank you. I need this."

Tommy gathered books and tea. "I've got reading to do," he said. He selected a Miles Davis album from his vinyl collection, got the turntable going, and settled in on the living room couch. I opened my briefcase and pulled out a motion for increased visitation, filed by a client's ex-husband. I sat at the kitchen table and began drafting a reply, but kept staring into space, distracted by visions of Violet, alone in the holding cell, and Teddy, alone in his coma. I stole glances at my new book, but wouldn't let myself touch it until I got some work done.

At eleven-thirty I was on the Internet reading about shaken baby syndrome when the door slammed and Jake bounded in. He slowed enough to plant a kiss on the top of my head. I caught a quick whiff of a familiar musty scent on him. Pot? Incense?

"What's up?" he said as he removed a pepperoni Hot Pocket from the freezer.

"How was practice?" I was almost positive it was pot. But maybe it was incense.

"Great. Are you psyched for tomorrow?" He put the Hot Pocket in the microwave and filled a twenty-six-ounce BK souvenir cup with orange juice.

"I am. I haven't heard you guys for so long." They practice in Iggy the drummer's garage, and so I rarely get to hear them. I decided not to mention the smell.

"Yeah, well, we're gonna rock the gym." The microwave dinged. He grabbed a thick paperback from a pile of books near the toaster and stuck it in the pocket of his sweatshirt jacket, put the Hot Pocket on a paper plate, cut it in half, picked up the plate and juice. "Is Pop in bed?" I nodded. "Okay," he said. "Later." He moved toward the stairs.

"Jake? Homework?"

He flashed a big smile. "Under control."

"What're you reading?"

"Robert Jordan's *Eye of the World.* You gotta read it, it's amazing."

"Six hundred pages of epic fantasy? Maybe when I retire."

"Night, Ginger."

"Good night."

4

A sound wave, shrill, relentless, assaulted my eardrum. I groped, reached, grabbed, knocked the yellow princess phone onto the floor, and almost rolled off the bed retrieving it. "What?"

"Good morning to you too."

Marco. "Why you calling so early?" Whiney. Not my best.

"It's nine-thirty. Judge Bird is wondering why you aren't in her courtroom putting Carmine Silvano's divorce through. Not to mention what Carmine is thinking."

"Damn." I looked at my clock. It said nine-thirty too. I had read until three o'clock, and then fallen into an unhappy sleep.

"And why," Marco continued, "is Michelle Bonpietro calling here? I thought you weren't taking felonies."

"I'm not. I'll explain later." I sat up. "Damn! Make an excuse to Judge Bird for me. Please. I'll be there in forty-five minutes. Half an hour."

"Covering your butt for Judge Bird means you buy me a good lunch." He was ordering sausage and peppers as I hung up. I hurtled into the shower, yanked on clothes, dumped food into Cat's bowl, and almost fell down the porch steps on my way to the car. Tommy teaches an eight o'clock class Friday mornings. He always wakes me up before he leaves, but occasionally I drift back to sleep. Jake leaves for school at seven-thirty, and I usually hear him banging around, but on that morning I slept through it all. The one thing I'd done right was to put five copies of the judgment of divorce in my briefcase—one for the client, one for my files, one for the ex-wife who had run off with the pastor of her church, two for the court.

Running up the courthouse steps I saw Michelle Bonpietro, but I ignored her. She is a bitchy little prosecutor and former friend of mine. We parted ways when I left the D.A.'s office; even in school she went by the book and I was always looking for loopholes. Free-range lawyering is a challenge; I work within the parameters of a 2,672-page rulebook, thousands of state and federal statutes, the rules of evidence, and a century of case law. I search for new angles, fresh ways to present old stories, but it's hard to be a genuine renegade lawyer these days, with all those rules, not to mention the proliferation of malpractice suits. Michelle evolved into a gray-suit prosecutor, stern, unforgiving, narrowly focused. I'm no legal genius, but I enjoy giving the system a nudge now and then.

Michelle followed me right into Judge Bird's courtroom. Not a good idea. Her turf is Criminal Court. Mine is Family Court. I know whose courtrooms you can burst into and whose you can't. Many lawyers view family law practitioners as bottom feeders, lower on the food chain than even personal injury lawyers, the ones who advertise on billboards and cable TV, who have phone numbers like 1-800-SUETHEM. They insinuate that family law is social work, not real law. Screw them, I say. Family law is the most meaningful work in the courthouse; it's possible to help people get their lives in order, to move forward in a positive manner. That's the pep talk I give myself now and then, when working as a cocktail waitress or tollbooth collector looks appealing.

Judge Bird cast a chilly look my way. "Ms. Reddy. You have kept counsel and the parties waiting for well over an hour. I am of a mind to sanction you. And Ms. Bonpietro, why are you in my courtroom? Perhaps no one has informed you that the Family Court is a closed court."

"Please accept my apologies, Your Honor," said Michelle. "Ms. Reddy represents a defendant who will be arraigned today and I urgently need to speak with her about The People's position."

Judge Bird's demeanor turned downright frigid. "The People are going to have to wait until this divorce is finalized. And unless you, or The People, are a party or a witness to this case, I suggest that you leave immediately."

Family Court judges get testy when lawyers try to make them feel like criminal matters are more important than what they do, that their courtrooms, where there are no juries, aren't quite real courtrooms. Judge Bird is the only African-American sitting on the Family Court bench in this county, but she gave no leeway to Michelle, who is the only female African-American assistant district attorney. Instead, she nodded to the sheriff's deputy whose job it is to protect her and her courtroom. He moved from his position near the bench, in Michelle's general direction, and she rapidly exited the courtroom. I enjoyed seeing her rattled, even though she would take it out on me later.

Judge Bird folded her hands in a deceptively prim manner. "Counsel, are you ready to proceed?"

"Yes, Your Honor." Thank goodness it was the rare uncontested divorce. I put it through on autopilot. And thank goodness I've built up some credibility with Judge Bird, because sanctions were not mentioned again.

I walked Carmine downstairs to the matrimonial office where he got a fancy gold seal affixed to his copy of the judgment of divorce. We shook hands and he was out of my life, except for the eight hundred dollars he still owed me. Marco would take care of that. I made a quick stop at the courthouse coffee shop, picked up a large coffee to go, added milk for protein, then climbed the steps to the sixth floor—pausing on each landing to sip my coffee—where the prosecutor's offices are located, and looked around for Michelle. She wasn't in her office. "Harrison," I called to a fast-moving man, "where's Michelle?"

Harrison pivoted on his highly polished black wingtips, a smile slowly spreading across his face. "Well, well, look what the cat dragged in." Harrison was a year ahead of me in law school and we dated for about five minutes. It is ancient history, but he still gets as much leverage out of it as he can. He is the consummate alpha-male prosecutor, sporting the G-man look in his dark suit, white shirt, modified buzz-cut, and Ray-Bans tucked into his breast pocket. "You coming back to the sunny side of the street?"

"In your dreams. Look, I'd love to chat, but I need to find Michelle before she lynches my client."

"Arraignments."

"Thanks." I blew him a kiss and moved on.

Court rules state that arraignments must take place within twenty-four hours of an arrest, but that doesn't always happen. Cases stack up, there aren't enough judges, and lawyers must be found for the indigent when the Public Defender has a conflict. Port Grace is a small city and doesn't have night or weekend arraignments, so if you are unlucky or stupid enough to get arrested on a Friday night, you will spend the weekend in jail. Arraignments are brief but important. An arraignment is the beginning of the judicial process and the tone for everything to follow is set in that brief colloquy. Charges are read, a plea is entered, the prosecutor requests bail, the defense attorney makes an argument for lower bail, all in front of an impatient judge who is eyeballing stacks of files—yellow for misdemeanors, red for felonies—to be disposed of before he can leave the bench for the day. He can dismiss minor cases or order the defendant to community service or counseling.

I walked down six flights, entered the small windowless arraignments courtroom, and sat in the back row to scope out the situation. The young woman next to me tried to contain a squirmy toddler. She might spend her whole day there, since arraignments are not held in any particular order, and I smiled at her, overly conscious of my navy blue pantsuit and briefcase that screamed "lawyer," but she smiled back, especially when I amused the baby by making goofy faces.

Judges are assigned to arraignments on a rotating basis and Judge O'Hara was on the bench. He is forty-three years old, a former public defender who has been on the bench for two years. He sentenced a first-time minor drug offender to community service and admonished him to get treatment. "I want you to walk out of here and go straight to a Narcotics Anonymous meeting," he said sternly. He quickly dismissed a few prostitutes, pot smokers, and firework vendors, and set high bail on a rape case. He spent less than five minutes on most cases, and the stacks of yellow and red files were still too high. Police officers strode in periodically, requesting search warrants and temporary restraining orders, which the judge rubber-stamped.

I checked in with the arraignments clerk and headed for the basement bullpens to talk to Violet. I flashed my attorney ID, got scanned for metal, and stowed my briefcase in the sheriff's command center, since lawyers are only allowed to carry files and a pen when they meet with a client. I was placed in a cramped windowless room that was furnished with two chairs and a metal table, all bolted to the floor. A sheriff's deputy brought in Violet, wearing a jail-orange jumpsuit and shackles on her ankles and wrists.

"Can you take those off?" I asked the officer, knowing full well that he couldn't.

He fired a granite look my way, and then nodded toward a video camera on the wall. "Wave when you're done." He departed, locking me in the room with Violet.

"I'm sorry," I said, indicating the shackles.

She didn't even seem to notice them. "When can I see Teddy?"

"Later today, I hope. We'll be appearing before a judge and maybe we can get the charges dropped. Otherwise you will probably be charged with child endangerment and the judge will set bail." She was somewhere far away and it wasn't clear that she was processing my words. "Violet. I don't do much criminal law any more, nothing too serious. I'm not confident that I can give you the quality of representation that you'll need if the charges aren't dropped. I'll find another lawyer for you."

She heard that. "No. I want you. I can't trust anyone else. Please."

I quit working for Eduardo after acting as lead attorney on an attempted rape case. It was my fourth felony trial as lead attorney: aggravated assault, sexual assault, rape, attempted rape. One theory is that juries are less likely to convict a man accused of assaulting a woman if his lawyer is a woman. I had handled hundreds of misdemeanors, dozens of plea bargains, and second-chaired Eduardo on many felony trials, including murder and brutal assault cases; but acting as lead attorney put me over the edge. I didn't want to become Port Grace's go-to lawyer for rape cases. Eduardo was a pragmatist—after I was with him long enough he assigned routine misdemeanors to his youngest associate, and rape and domestic violence defense to me. I despised myself for not being tough enough to handle it, but I could not get psychically centered in a way that allowed me to defend violent criminals on a routine basis. I amused Eduardo and he didn't want me to leave, but he was used to it—his associates rarely lasted the four years I put in.

"Violet, your case could get complicated. You don't just have the criminal case, there's a Family Court case too, and the same lawyer can't represent you on both. DCW already has emergency custody of Teddy, and later today there will be a hearing where they'll ask the judge to grant them continued custody. If that happens, he'll go to a foster home when he gets out of the hospital."

"They can't do that."

"Yes, they can and will. You need to understand how serious this is."

"I'm his mother. He can't go to a stranger."

"What about your family? Is there anyone who might take him?"

She shook her head. Her father, who she'd lived with off and on all her life, was in prison. Her mother's whereabouts were unknown. Her paternal grandmother, who Violet moved in with when she was sixteen and her father went to prison, died several months ago. Her maternal grandmother was down in Richmond taking care of other grandchildren and great-grandchildren, and had made it clear that she wasn't taking in any more babies. Violet couldn't think of any aunts, uncles, or cousins who might be able to help.

I pressed her. "Violet, if there is any evidence indicating that you hurt Teddy, or that someone else hurt him while he was under your care, it will get very bad for you." She was looking at her hands. "Look at me, Violet. If you are convicted of child endangerment you'll go to prison. If that happens and you don't have a suitable relative for Teddy to live with, your parental rights will be terminated." I was ready to retreat within legalese, the vocabulary of statutes, legislation, case law and precedent, the language that lawyers and judges use to distance themselves from the reality of their work.

Violet shook her head hard, long braids flipping through the air. She tried to reach up to fidget with her hair, a habit of hers, but her wrist shackles were attached by chain to a wide leather belt around her waist so she couldn't reach above breast level. She finally caught a braid and worried it with her fingers. "What do you mean, terminated?"

"The judge can decide that you aren't a fit parent. They'll terminate your rights, which means you will never see or have contact with Teddy again, and they'll find someone to adopt him."

A sheriff's deputy, 6'4", 240 pounds, loaded gun and all, opened the door. "Rosado? You her counsel?" he asked.

I nodded.

"The judge is breaking for lunch. Court is recessed until two o'clock. You have to leave now."

"Thanks, Officer. Okay, Violet."

I stood up to give her a hug but the deputy shook his head. "Sit down," he said sharply. He pulled Violet's chair back and steadied her as she stood up, made awkward by the shackles.

"I'll be back to handle your arraignment," I told her. She looked young and pathetic, five feet tall, fragile as a bird, that mass of tiny braids falling to her waist. When she smiles she is as pretty as a sunflower. But she was not smiling.

5

Lunch. Food. I was suddenly, dangerously, ravenous. It was one o'clock and the only nourishment I'd had was the milk in my coffee. I needed to keep Marco happy, so I double parked at the Italian deli and ordered sausage and peppers on a long roll for him, and potatoes and eggs on a round roll for me. While I waited I eyed the candy rack and debated buying a chocolate bar to eat immediately, but settled for a pack of gum.

"You're up, Counselor," called the sandwich man. I looked up from the gum display and realized that he was speaking to me. Eight years since I passed the bar and I still get a thrill when someone calls me Counselor. It took me a long time to get here. A lawyer. A great husband and stepson. My own practice. Clean and sober, more or less.

Where am I from? I am a child of the 60s, grandchild of the Dustbowl. Raised in California's San Joaquin Valley, in a town that sprouted out of the labor of Okies, Arkies and Texans who spent the 1930s heading west on Route 66 by car, foot, truck, and bicycle, escaping drought, boll weevils and the Great Depression. Upon their backs the Central Valley flourished—a biblical abundance of lettuce, peas, lemons, potatoes, apricots, grapes, artichokes, and strawberries. That is what my father was born into; his own father got out of the fields and into the construction business, and worked his way down the spine of the Valley through Sacramento, Stockton, Modesto, Fresno, and

Bakersfield, building houses and stores, canneries and factories. After World War II he built a pretty stucco house on three acres for his wife and sons, and that is where my father has lived his whole life, except for a few years up by San Francisco. I lived in that house too, from the time I was two years old until I tore out of there for college.

By the late 1970s of my childhood, it was a hot, smoggy, cinderblock town full of bikers, migrant workers, and burnt-out Vietnam vets. Too many bars, whose jukeboxes were loaded with Merle Haggard, Dolly Parton, and Hank Williams. *Hee Haw* and the Grand Ole Opry blasted from console TV's that were the centerpiece of homely flat-top houses. Half of my classmates were pickers' kids, migrants who attended school sporadically and were put in special ed classes because they didn't speak English.

By the time I went to the big regional high school, the wealth of the 80s started to trickle down to parts of the Valley, and big new split-levels with in-ground pools were built for middle-managers of the western Valley towns, and for people who couldn't afford to live closer to San Francisco, who were willing to commute for hours every day so that their kids could have a cul de sac to ride their bikes on.

I carried the bag of sandwiches into the office, Marco pulled some sodas from the fridge, and we walked outside to the brick patio, a sanctuary, a place to escape from telephones and clients. It was chilly but sunny, and a vision of Miami crossed my mind—a cottage filled with jasmine and bird of paradise, Cuban music, Cuban men, rice and beans and beer. I zipped my jacket and Marco zipped his. He was dressed in jeans, flannel button-down over a white T-shirt, and a brown leather jacket. As he pulled the sandwiches from the bag and unwrapped them, I filled him in on Violet's plight.

"We're talking a good chance of shaken baby syndrome. Subcranial bleeding. Retinal hemorrhaging. Baby in a coma. They're going to X-ray for old fractures."

Listening to me, his expression changed from neutral to grave.

"What do you think?" I asked. I took a bite of sandwich and a long pull of root beer.

"You don't want to know what I think." He looked grim. "I hate these cases. Kid cases."

I looked away from him and watched a robin hop around beneath the oak tree that shades the yard in summer. "Tell me. I want your input."

"I think the client is buried." He crumpled his soda can. "Ginger, do you really want to take this case? Didn't you quit Eduardo to get away from this sort of thing?"

"I'm not convinced she hurt him."

"As a defense attorney that can't matter to you. You know that."

"Of course I do. But listen, I'm really thinking it was AJ, the baby's father, and she's afraid to tell."

"You think it's him?"

"He beat up Violet when she was pregnant. He could have done it. And . . ." I snapped my fingers, remembering. "When he beat her up? The first time she came to me? He was angry because he'd told her to get an abortion and she didn't."

Marco and I locked eyes, grasping the possibilities. He picked up the scenario and kept it rolling. "So he had his little arrangement going—wife and kids in the ranch house in West Windsor, Violet in the projects in Port Grace. He got to live a dual life, and he knew that if she had a kid it would screw things up for him."

I nodded. "He's a firecracker waiting to be lit. The baby could've easily set him off." I chewed one more bite of sandwich and stuffed the rest in the bag. "I have to do a more thorough interview with her. One important factor is that the shaking doesn't necessarily occur just before the coma. That may be a key to the defense: Nobody can pinpoint precisely when it happened: it can be days, weeks, even months before the baby goes into a coma."

Marco flicked some bread to a squirrel and smiled when the peppy rodent snatched it up and scurried away. "So if your guy was around the baby in the last month or so, he could have done it."

"Exactly."

"Maybe it's not shaken baby syndrome; it could be a disease or something. God forbid. Not that I'd ever wish harm on a baby." Marco has a vast extended family, living, along with many other children and grandchildren of Portuguese immigrants, in Deer Point, the northeast corner of Port Grace, where the land that juts into the bay has not been populated by deer in living memory. His immediate family is him, his mom and his sister Cecilia. His father's family was depopulated by alcoholism, low-sperm count and bad luck on the job—men of three consecutive generations killed in work-related accidents. His mother's prolific family compensates for the lack of paternal relatives; in fact it seems like Marco's relatives own most of the small businesses in the city. Bottom line? Kids are sacred to Marco.

I watched him enjoy his sandwich even though he was obviously distressed. He is a few years younger than me, thirtyish; but the lines on his face could make you think he's older. Something happened, I don't know what, and he left the police department four years ago. He spent six months in Ireland and Portugal. When he returned I was trying to get my business off the ground, and floundering. Eduardo, who is Marco's second cousin, sent him to me and he saved my ass. Tommy and I were separated, and I was depressed and losing confidence. I hated my shitty little studio apartment, so I slept in the office most nights. Marco strolled into my life—he made me coffee, he made me laugh, he got me and the business organized, and brightened my days with his kindness and good looks. He had the good sense to turn me down, ever so gently, when, lonely and lost, I hit on him. He kept to himself when it came to his personal life. "Mystery man" is the way I thought of him.

I took another look at the police report. "There's nothing in here about them securing the apartment. Maybe they did later. Or maybe they didn't bother." I finished my soda, pulled a pack of Big Red from my pocket, and held it out to Marco. He took a stick and we busied ourselves with our gum. "She wants me to defend her. I planned to refer her out. But I'm thinking about keeping it."

Marco looked skeptical. "Ginger, a case like this can take over your life."

"I know. But I feel an obligation."

"There's no obligation. Yet. But if you appear for her after the arraignment there will be. You won't be able to get off the case." That was true. Once I was in, court rules prevented me from getting out unless she fired me, or something truly heinous happened—like I discovered that she was planning to commit murder. "And," Marco continued, "you can't afford it financially or emotionally."

He was right about that too. I work constantly but am always scrambling for money. Divorce clients are terrible about paying their lawyers, because people who get divorced usually take a big hit economically. And most of my clients don't have money to spare—they are firemen, cops, bank tellers, and small-business owners, with minimal savings and major mortgages. Violet couldn't pay me and her case could get expensive. If it went to trial I would have to retain experts, file interrogatories and motions, conduct depositions, and perform other costly litigation tactics.

Emotionally? I used to get way too involved with my clients. I took them to the doctor, the welfare office, the unemployment office, and the therapist, using time I never got paid for. Now, I give them referrals to social service agencies, and stay within the legal parameters of my duty to them. Unfortunately, sometimes a case gets personal, and I can't stop my life from getting shredded by it.

My cell phone rang. Marco's pager vibrated. Lunch was over.

6

Courtrooms induce claustrophobia, especially in those of us who sit on the defense side of the room. The arraignments courtroom was carved out of a storage closet, and is particularly suffocating. The players: judge, court reporter, sheriff's deputy, arraignment clerk, prosecutor, defense attorney, and the defendant of the moment, cram into a small cordoned-off area. The rest of the room is rows of benches crammed with families, friends, children, and lovers, who, because arraignments aren't conducted in any particular order, arrive early and may wait for hours to see their loved one get his five minutes before the judge.

In the conveyor belt of cases passing before Judge O'Hara, Violet was just another sack of potatoes, albeit one charged with endangering the welfare of a child, a second-degree felony which carries a sentence of five to ten years in state prison. Michelle used her drama-queen skills when she announced that Teddy was in a coma, the doctor suspected shaken baby syndrome, and The People reserved the right to file additional charges. When the judge heard the word coma his eyebrows shot up to where his hairline would be if he had hair, and he momentarily disengaged cruise control. However, when Violet and I stood up he listened closely, and it was probably a teensy bit helpful that I had helped his sister get a child support increase; he wouldn't do anything unethical, but he treated us fairly, something you can't count on when you enter a courtroom.

Laura the florist closed up shop, came to court, and spoke on Violet's behalf. After Violet got the restraining order I had introduced her to Laura, who gave her a job. Violet only worked for her for a couple months, but Laura managed to talk her up to the court without committing perjury. Laura is big and sunny. She radiates credibility. Judge O'Hara even smiled at her—dressed in a flowered skirt and red sweater, she was a relief from lawyer gray and navy, not to mention jailhouse orange. She managed to let it slip that Violet was a victim of domestic violence, and Judge O'Hara is sympathetic on that issue, but he wasn't very sympathetic about Violet.

She pleaded not guilty. Bail was set at $5,000. The judge moved on to the next case. "Am I getting out?" she asked me as I followed her to the elevator that would take her back down to the pens.

"Stop right there, Counselor," the deputy escorting her said.

"Two minutes. Please," I said. He nodded. "Violet, you don't have any money or property, so I'm going to have to get you a bail bond. Are you sure there's nobody else who can help you?"

"No. No one."

"Okay. I'll come over to the jail as soon as I can. Then we have to go to Family Court."

The elevator opened and Violet shuffled in.

I walked from the courthouse toward the jail, passing storefront lawyers, the Juror's Luncheonette, the Hispanic Cultural Center, a methadone clinic, a day-care center, an army-navy surplus store, and a furniture store featuring seven-piece velveteen and laminate living room suites. It was a spring-fever afternoon—the temperature had momentarily spiked into the 60s and last night's bitter rain was forgotten in a fresh landscape of sunshine and spring training. I went into ABC Bail Bonds and signed away my life to get Violet out of jail.

I waited outside while Violet got processed out, trying not to think about the stack of files on my desk. She finally appeared, rumpled and exhausted, dressed in the jeans and pink T-shirt she wore the day before. We walked to the Family Court, which is in the new courthouse, an unattractive cement box that also houses the county administration offices. We didn't talk. Violet was deep inside herself, and I didn't feel like making the effort. In the park across from the courthouse a Frisbee was being tossed and the pretzel man was doing a good business.

The Lowell County Family Court obtained jurisdiction of Violet's case when DCW filed abuse and neglect charges against her after Teddy was admitted to the hospital, and a doctor, suspecting child abuse, called DCW. Judge Holmes and Judge Bird hear child welfare cases on alternate months, and unfortunately Judge Holmes was assigned to Violet's case. I much preferred Judge Bird, who listened with an open mind and made thoughtful rulings. Custody of Teddy had been transferred to DCW on an emergency basis, and this was Violet's chance to respond to the charges. My adversary was a deputy attorney general, and she got to address the court first.

"Good afternoon again, Your Honor," she said, while thumbing through the file. She spends most of her working hours standing in court defending DCW's actions and making recommendations based on caseworkers' legwork. "We are here on an Order to Show Cause involving Theodore Mulligan Rosado, a ten-month-old infant. Two nights ago he was brought to St. Joseph's Hospital by his mother and was found to be unconscious. Actually," she paused to take a closer look at the file, "he was in a coma. And is still in a coma. Dr. Maratha reports that she suspects the infant was severely shaken, and may be suffering from shaken baby syndrome." She snapped the file shut with satisfaction. "Therefore, the State recommends that legal care and custody of the infant remain with the Division and that this case be reviewed in thirty days."

Judge Holmes raised his head slowly, like an ancient turtle. "Ms. Reddy?" he said. He was ready to retire a few years ago. However, word got out that the wheels were in motion to raise judges' pensions by a considerable amount, and he was hanging on, waiting for that to happen, since the new law would affect only sitting judges. He is burnt-out and short-tempered. I knew that no matter what I said, he would rubber-stamp the State's recommendation, but I had to make an effort on Violet's behalf. I stood up and tried to catch the judge's eye, but he was retreating into his shell.

"Thank you, Your Honor. Violeta Rosada is Teddy's mother. The day before yesterday began as a normal day for them. After breakfast she took him for a walk in his stroller and took care of some errands. They went to the park and then went home for lunch and Teddy's nap. She had trouble waking him up from his nap and realized right away that something was wrong, so she called 911. Immediately. She did what a mother is supposed to. What a parent is supposed to do. And she is devastated. Worried sick about him. She has never been accused of child neglect, or of any wrongdoing whatsoever." I paused to look at her briefly, hoping the judge would follow my glance. A frail girl with long braids and a pink T-shirt. Grief-stricken and pretty. No attitude jumping off of her. Nothing mean or edgy. Not a skinny, jittery crackhead like a lot of the mothers who pass through here. I returned my gaze to the bench. "Your Honor. Violeta loves her baby. She did not hurt him. I respectfully request that the court restore full custody of Teddy to his mother, and that this case be dismissed from litigation."

He didn't even look our way. Just spoke the words that he says fifteen or twenty times a day. "The court has heard applications from both sides on this matter and orders that the Division of Child Welfare retain legal care and custody of the child. A law guardian for the infant will be appointed."

The DAG popped up from her seat. “Your Honor. Excuse me? We also request that the mother be barred from visiting the infant in the hospital.”

I jumped up and butted in. “Your Honor, that request goes against the laws and policy of this state. She has no history of hurting this child or any other child and is entitled to visitation.”

“Supervised only,” the DAG said.

“Your Honor.” It was time to plead. “The Division takes weeks to set up supervised visitation. And then it’s only for one hour a week.”

Judge Holmes exerted himself slightly. “Ms. Reddy. These charges are serious. The mother is not to be alone with the child. Even in the hospital. Visitation to be supervised by the Division.”

I spoke without thinking. “Your Honor?”

He was annoyed. “Ms. Reddy. It is almost five o’ clock. I have heard twenty-two cases today and I am finished with this one.”

I don’t grovel well, but I tried. “I’m sorry, Your Honor. I know it’s late. However I respectfully request that I be allowed to supervise visitation between Ms. Rosada and the baby while he is in the hospital.”

He glanced at the DAG who shrugged. She’d had a long day too. “All right, Counselor.” He actually wagged a finger at me. “I’ll grant your request. But you better hope that nothing happens to that baby on your watch.”

A return date was set. An order was drawn up and the judge signed it. We left the courtroom and waited in the hall while the caseworker made copies of the order. I put my arm around Violet, and felt her shoulder blades through her shirt. “Please,” she said. “Take me to see Teddy.”

Marco was alone at the office. I had dumped two client appointments on him and I had a 6:30 for a domestic violence client who I hadn't even met yet. And a brief to write for a vicious custody dispute. "Wouldn't you like to go home and shower first?" I said. "Eat something? Get some sleep?"

"No. I have to see him. Please."

I emitted a sigh strong enough to knock over all the little pigs' houses. I shouldn't have opened my big mouth; I was already way too involved. I called Marco. "I'll be there in an hour. I promise."

Teddy was in St. Joe's, a public hospital that was dingy, crowded, and reeked of bleach and disinfectant, attempts to mask illness, fear, and death. Eventually we found the Neonatal Intensive Care Unit, NICU, where six babies lay threaded with tubes and wires. Cheerful nurses, rainbow murals, and dangling Mickey Mouse mobiles did not disguise the gravity of that unit. Violet sat in a chair next to Teddy, while I stood in the hall and peered through the window. She appeared to be talking to him. Maybe singing. I pulled a law journal from my briefcase and tried to read. After twenty minutes I dragged her out. The magnitude of the situation had punctured her and she disintegrated into a disembodied state as we journeyed down crowded corridors and elevators, and navigated the streets to my car.

It was a relief to sit in the Jimmy, the familiar smell, the seat molded to me from ten years and 105,000 miles. I inserted the key and said, "I don't think it's a good idea for you to return to your apartment. I don't want you to be alone." I eased onto the road. "Do you have a friend you can stay with?" She didn't answer, so I glanced over and saw her staring out the window. "Violet?"

"I'll be fine."

"I want you to stay at the women's shelter for a couple of nights until we can find a better situation for you." I spoke firmly, and she reluctantly agreed, too exhausted and dazed to argue.

I drove to her apartment so she could pack. She lived in a housing project comprised of four-story brick buildings built around a concrete courtyard. Built as a progressive alternative to the hideous high-rise projects of the fifties, they were now, twenty-five years later, shabby and depressing. People clustered in the shadows, the air was alive with the sharp sweet smell of crack, the ground was littered with shattered glass and fast-food wrappers, a skinny dog roamed and a baby cried. Violet's apartment was a third-floor walk-up. A walk up past landings choked by apartment overflow—strollers, tricycles, stacks of newspapers, bulging garbage bags, and broken electronics. A walk up past urine and cooking smells. A walk up past the colliding sounds of television, music, and the voices of people living behind battered doors that have too many locks on them.

The apartment hadn't been secured as a crime scene. The police hadn't bothered to take prints or gather any other evidence. I guess they considered it to be *res ipsa loquitur*—the thing speaks for itself. They were certain that Violet did it. They weren't going to look for another suspect.

It was obviously a grandmother's apartment. The lace curtains, ceramic knick-knacks, large Bible, and wooden dinette set with a lazy Susan on the table were the composition of a tidy old lady. Violet's grandmother, her father's mother, was one of the original tenants. She moved in amid dreams of a new kind of housing project, one that would foster community and pride. Basketball nets were raised, picnic tables and swings installed, a common room was furnished with visions of teens doing homework and old people playing cards. There was talk of a community garden.

Now, the hoops are gone, the swings are rusted out, the picnic tables splintered and covered with graffiti. Drug dealers commandeered the common room. Police stay away unless someone gets shot, or it's election year and the mayor issues directives to sweep the criminals, vagrants, and disorderlies off the streets of Port Grace.

I walked through the apartment while Violet gathered her belongings. Teddy was everywhere—in the white crib in the room he and Violet shared, wrapped in the quilt with yellow ducks on it; in the high chair with a half-empty jar of baby applesauce still on the tray; in the Piglet music box that I absent-mindedly wound. *You Are My Sunshine* filled the room for a moment or two, until it wound down to silence.

7

I took Violet to the shelter, and then drove too fast to my office where my 6:30 was waiting. Marco left as soon as I walked in. "Tommy called," he said on his way out. I interviewed and prepped the client for her trial which was scheduled for the following day, a mini-trial before a Family Court judge, but a trial nonetheless. Right after she left, the phone rang and I ignored it. Then my cell phone rang. I took a quick look at the clock, 7:45, and grabbed my cell.

"Tommy?"

"The open-mike starts at eight o'clock and I think Jake's band plays second."

"I'm on my way, but I have to come back to work after. I'll meet you there." I changed out of my pantsuit into jeans and a sweater, and left the office lights on. I slid into the gym just as Jake's band went on. A rush of energy hit me, that crazy, invigorating, wide-open teen energy. Tommy and I hung back and watched the kids dancing to the post-punk-manic-rap songs that Jake wrote; his lyrics were clever, his voice decent, and his stage presence overwhelmed us. He seemed separate, not defined by us; it was the rare objective glimpse, as though he was someone else's child, not the boy we raised through the Winnie the Pooh years, the G.I. Joe years, the water balloon and science project years.

We left when the next band started, warmed by the glow of Jake's success. Tommy walked me to my car. "Can't you come home?" he asked. He was pumped-up from the concert and his pride and wonderment in Jake.

"I wish I could, I really do. But I took a case yesterday that's thrown me off-course and I've got to play catch-up tonight." He was so disappointed. "I'm sorry," was all I could say.

Although I'd left the lights on, it was depressing to be back in my office. I flipped on the radio and tackled the mess on my desk. Sorted piles of papers and files, arranged them into new piles, and made a priority list for the next few days. Then I tackled a brief—pulled files labeled *Custody Rules and Statutes,* and *Custody Case Law.* Scrolled through my documents until I located the last custody brief I'd written. I cut and pasted the boilerplate sections and began my statement of facts. I was inserting applicable cases and statutes when Marco walked in with a pizza box.

"I was driving back from the library," he said. "Saw the lights on."

I ate three slices. Marco ate four. I looked longingly at the last one. "I need to start running again," I said. "But when? I've got no time."

"Five-thirty in the morning," he said. "It's quiet. The air smells fresh. A good start to your day. You get to feel all healthy and virtuous."

"You know me better than that." I'm a night person; the sounds and smells of darkness focus my energy. Occasionally I consider moving to New York or L.A., cities with twenty-four hour arraignments, cities where it's normal to work deep into the night. But Port Grace is home. "I love running at night," I said, reflecting on the pleasures of late night calm, the busyness of the day evaporated, the air both open and embracing.

Marco looked stern. "Then you need to get a partner. Or a dog. You can't be running by yourself at night."

I resented the implication that I couldn't take care of myself, but he was right; weird people prowl the streets of Port Grace, just like any other city. I know that better than most; I defended many of them. Sometimes I consider getting a gun, but it's such a loaded thought that I let it slip away into the repository of things I'm not ready to deal with.

I set aside that last slice, and flattened the pizza box. "Go home, Marco," I said. "One of us has to be well-rested tomorrow." He ignored me and hunkered down on the couch with his constitutional law book and a highlighter. I drafted the analysis section of the custody brief, and signed letters left by Gloria, who types, copies, fields phone calls, and generally runs the office. "Damn."

"What?" asked Marco.

"I was supposed to drop the Jimmy off at Victor's. It's been making a weird noise and he said he'd look at it tomorrow."

"Drop it off tonight. I'll run you home."

It was 12:45. "Why bother going home?" I said. "I might as well work all night."

He patted the couch. "Come here."

It was late. I was tired. Tommy was disappointed. I should go home, not sit on a couch next to Marco. But I sat on the couch anyway, and leaned into him. He felt nice and solid. We sat quietly for a few minutes. Then, "Time to go," he said.

"Do we have to? I'm so comfortable." Our body warmth merged and I was getting drowsy.

He nudged me. "You've got court in the morning." Our warmth dissipated under his practicality and I struggled to my feet. It was that weird time on a weeknight when most people are asleep, the streets are quiet except for the occasional bar ruckus, and bad things seem more likely than good.

I parked my car at Victor's, pushed the key through the door slot and climbed into Marco's Blazer. A copy of *The Outsiders* by S. E. Hinton was on the seat. I took a look at it. "What's this?" I asked.

He flicked on Al Green. "My all-time favorite book. I must have read it twenty times when I was a kid. I was at my mom's fixing her door and I saw it on the bookshelf. Still there after all these years."

"Wasn't it a movie?"

"Yeah, but the book's better. I'll loan it to you after I read it again, but you have to give it back."

"Sure." I looked out the window. "Would you mind going by way of the bay?" He nodded and drove cop-style, confident and casual. He parked, knowing that I'd want to get out, and we walked down the dock, the sound of our footsteps on the old boards magnified in the dark. Boats rocked, the bay tossed and sprayed, the moon was half-full, hanging on in a clouded night sky.

"What are you thinking?" Marco asked.

"Teddy. Violet's baby. I can't shake the way he looked in the hospital, the needles and tubes. Not crying or moving. Almost not there at all." He took my hand and squeezed. "I keep wondering what happened."

A car door slammed. We turned and watched a group of teenagers pile out of a big old sedan, laughing, smoking, tossing beer cans into the water.

"What's she like?" he asked.

"Sweet. But unformed. A lot of kids have attitude, they think they know more than me, and it's pretty much impossible to help them. But Violet? She seems receptive. Like if she were given opportunities she'd make the most of them. She's like a shy twelve year-old." We sat on the edge of the dock, legs dangling. I gazed at the water and the reflected moon, trying to visualize the kingdom beneath the waves, the world of fish, whales, and shipwrecks, a world I don't understand, a true mystery. "I don't think she hurt him," I said. "But I'm afraid to know the truth."

"People under stress? Do things they don't mean to do," Marco said. "She's a single teen mom, no support, no money, in love with an abusive man. That's a lot of stress. Maybe the baby wouldn't stop crying and she just snapped."

"You think that happened?"

"My mom used to snap, chase us around the house, yelling, give us a good whack on the behind."

"Did she ever really hurt you?"

"No. But maybe that was just luck. She would never have intentionally hurt us, but it could have happened accidentally."

"And you think that's what happened with Violet?"

"Didn't your parents ever lose it with you?"

"No; but my situation was different."

"How do you mean different?"

Car doors slammed again and the teens sped away, much too fast. I cringed, waiting for the pitch and shatter of brakes, metal, and glass. The breeze intensified and I was overcome by the smell of night on the water, enticing and dangerous. I inhaled deeply.

"This air," I said. "I can't get enough of it."

He put his arm around me. "You're avoiding my question."

"You've met my dad. He's a stoner. But gentle as they come."

"Was he like that when you were a kid?"

"Always. I don't remember him ever raising his voice at me."

"What about your mom?"

"You know, they were divorced."

"And you lived with your Dad."

"Yup." I tensed and he felt it.

"Did you see your mom much?"

"No. Only once since I was two. She left us."

I never talk about that, people don't understand. Marco and I had been friends for four years. When I was separated from Tommy we spent a lot of time together—we ran together, ate meals together, even went to a few movies. But we rarely ventured into the past. And now, we were there. Something about Violet's plight had opened the door. I tried to move away from him, regain my space, but he turned toward me, slipped his hands under my jacket, put his arms around me and pulled me to him. Held me tightly until I relaxed into the security of his embrace. I buried my face in his shirt. He smelled like soap and Old Spice, and his T-shirt was so soft that I felt the contours of his chest and the fundamental decency that is Marco's essence.

After a while he whispered. "I'm sorry."

"It's okay."

"No. It's not okay." He kissed me and we let ourselves get lost in each other for a while. Eventually he pulled back and I looked in his eyes—melancholy, chagrined. "Let's get you home." He stood and pulled me up; we walked to the Blazer and he drove me home. Tom had left the porch light on. Cat heard the car pull up and scampered out of the shrubbery. I kept envisioning Teddy in the hospital crib. And feeling Marco's lingering warmth.

"Are you all right?" he asked.

"Of course." I slipped out of the car. "See you later." I jogged up the porch steps, almost falling over Cat on the way. It was two o'clock in the morning. Tommy and Jake would have been asleep for hours. I called my Dad; it was only eleven o'clock in California and he'd be reading. He answered on the first ring. I pictured him in his recliner, hash pipe in one hand, book in the other, Tostitos, salsa, and two-liter bottle of root beer nearby. That's my dad.

"Hey, Dad."

"Hey, Sunshine. What's up, little girl?" The soft slur and touch of inherited Texas drawl. He lives in the house he was born in, in 1948, the youngest son. Uncle Roy died in a car crash when he was seventeen. Uncle Donny escaped Vietnam because he's deaf in one ear; he took over Grandpa's construction business and lives in a split-level with an in-ground pool out by Bakersfield. Dad did Vietnam, inherited the house, runs the nursery, smokes a lot of weed, and is systematically working his way through the entire public library collection.

"Not much. Haven't talked to you for a while; thought I'd check in."

"What time is it out there? Shouldn't you be in bed?"

"I had to work late. Bed's my next stop."

"You shouldn't work so late. You need routine."

"My job makes it hard to stick to a routine."

He's never quite comprehended that I'm a lawyer, what that means. He won't fly, and has only visited four times since I left California fifteen years ago. Once when I had knee surgery junior year; once when I graduated from college, the first in our family, and he bought me the Jimmy; once when Tommy and I got married; once after September 11. That afternoon he just got in his Ford F-150 and drove all the way across the country. He stayed with us for a week and then drove back. I visit him once a year, and sometimes Tommy and Jake go with me. We eat steak dinners and play pool. Drive around in his truck listening to Waylon Jennings and visiting the people of my childhood, the ones who took care of us after my mother left and my grandparents died.

"How are Tommy and Jake?"

"Good." I told him about Jake's gig.

"You okay?" he asked.

"I'm good. Don't worry."

"Get to bed now."

Tommy was snoring. I tried to be quiet because he's a light sleeper, but he woke up when I got into bed. He didn't bother looking at the clock but rolled over to cuddle up with me, so I knew he wasn't mad that I came home late. "Make sure I get up in the morning," I whispered. I lay there trying not to think about kissing Marco, or whether Violet shook Teddy, or whether Teddy would come out of the coma, and eventually I fell asleep with Tommy's arms around me.

8

The next day I got out of bed on time, because Tommy promised pancakes. When I cruised into the kitchen feeling better than I had a right to, he was flipping silver dollars. Maple syrup, raspberry jam and cinnamon sugar brightened the table. I poured coffee for myself, then walked over to the stove and wrapped my arms around Tommy's waist. "Jake's gone?" I asked.

"You just missed him."

"Was he happy about last night?"

"I think so. He said they're playing at a party next weekend."

"Good for them." We sat down to our pancakes and all was well with the world. Tommy didn't ask why I was so late the night before, and I didn't bring it up.

I met Tommy at an AA meeting when I was in my third year of law school. I had only been sober two months at the time, whereas he had eight years under his belt. It was my first time at the Thursday night meeting in the basement of Northside Presbyterian and I was highly caffeinated and fidgety.

"Hi. My name is Tom and I'm an alcoholic." He stood before the group in his khakis, white Oxford shirt, tweed blazer, and wire rim glasses, his brown hair going gray around the edges, looking like the college professor that he is.

I, on the other hand, was depleted and disheveled, hanging on by my fingertips, barely managing to stay both sober and afloat in law school, going to a meeting every day. The following

Thursday night I saw Tom again and made it a point to go to the coffeepot at the same time he did. He appeared so completely sane that I wanted to crawl inside of him and never come out. I sipped my coffee and caught his eye. We edged away from the crowd of fellow substance abusers who were gathered around the coffeepot.

"You look like you could use a good meal," he said.

"Food's not my priority these days."

He surveyed me kindly. His eyes were very blue. "How long have you been sober?"

"Two months."

He nodded knowingly. "You need to eat, and take care of yourself. You need vitamins and protein; bananas are good for potassium."

"What are you, a nutritionist?"

"No, just someone who's been sober long enough to know how hard it is." I gave him a look. I didn't need any preaching. "Sorry," he said. "I didn't mean to sound like your seventh grade home ec teacher."

"I never took home ec."

"Well then, I didn't mean to sound like your mother."

"I don't have a mother."

He looked chagrined. "I'm really putting my foot in it, aren't I?"

I studied him. I didn't have enough energy to be nice, but I didn't want to drive him away either. "I'm sorry. I'm irritable these days."

He was happy again. "Understood. No apology needed. Do you like diner food?"

I had been living on candy bars and coffee; I spent most of my time in the law school library trying not to flunk out. "Yes."

"Do you know the Straight Street Diner?"

I shook my head.

"It's the best diner in town. Can I buy you a meal?"

I followed Tom's Cherokee to the diner, where I consumed a plate filled with scrambled eggs, home fries and rye toast, with a chocolate shake on the side. "I didn't realize how hungry I was," I said. "This is delicious."

"You feel a little better?"

"Definitely."

We chatted over coffee; me about law school, a job offer from the prosecutor's office, and whether to stay in Port Grace or move back to California; him about work as a professor of American Studies at Winslow College, divorced for two years, and custodial parent to seven-year-old Jake.

Tom paid the check. I put down a tip. We walked outside. "I want to show you something," he said. We strolled a few blocks and stopped in front of a wooden two-decker with a wide porch and small front yard. "I'm thinking about buying it. I'm tired of living in an apartment. I want Jake to have a real home, and a yard to play in."

"It looks like a nice house. Homey."

"It's got a great back yard. And the bay is a block away."

I pictured him playing catch with his son. Mowing the lawn, reading in the hammock. I felt how much he wanted that house. We moved into it together a few months later.

I demolished my pancakes. "What do you have on tap today?" Tommy asked.

"A domestic violence. I'll probably lose. And a settlement conference where my adversary is a moron. Worst of all, a child endangerment case."

Tommy looked dismayed and sympathetic. "Sounds ugly," he said.

"What about you?"

"Office hours ten to twelve. At 1:15 I teach Introduction to

American Studies. Then a faculty meeting." He made a sour face at the latter.

"Let's trade places," I suggested, thinking of the Winslow campus, with its gothic architecture, million-volume library, and atmosphere of intellectual inquiry and real-world naiveté. I checked my watch. Eight-thirty. I checked the kitchen clock. It said eight-thirty too. Late again. I didn't want to leave our warm kitchen, the comfortable domestic disarray of home. But I had to go to court. And deal with Violet and her baby in a coma. And my clients were stacked up like planes over O'Hare.

"What's going on?" Tommy asked, knowing that I rarely complain about work.

I wasn't ready to discuss Violet. "Just the usual squalor. The D.V. is a he-said, she-said harassment case. She's terrified of him; but if Judge Washington doesn't see bruises and there's no witness, he'll say it's a domestic contretemps and throw it out."

"A domestic contretemps? Do they actually say that?"

"Yes, some of them actually do. Some judges call it a marital quarrel, but domestic contretemps is used a lot."

He was amused. "Did we ever have a domestic contretemps? You and me?"

"You're kidding, right? Remember all those nights I was so wrapped up in work that I forgot to call, forgot to come home? You weren't smiling then."

"Maybe I did call you unreliable once or twice. Inconsiderate is a possibility. It's in my vocabulary."

"And irresponsible, impetuous, and insecure."

"I thought those were lovers' quarrels." He grinned. His hair flopped over his forehead in the way that always makes me want to kiss him.

"You're pretty cute," I said. "And I like your selective memory."

"You're worth it. Usually."

Oops. He wouldn't say that if he'd seen me with Marco on the dock last night. "Can you drop me off at the office?" I asked. "The Jimmy's at Victor's."

"No problem."

I nodded and punched a number into my cell phone.

"Judge Washington's chambers."

"LaTanya. It's Ginger Rae. I'm running a little late. Is he on the bench?"

"He's doing his defaults now. He won't get to you before ten o'clock." She spoke with the confidence of a woman who has managed the same judge for seven straight years.

"Thank you. You are an angel."

"No problem, Ginger Rae."

We hung up and I made a mental note to stop by chambers and ask about her kids.

9

A judge's staff is like a family—the judge, his law clerk, administrative assistant, and sheriff's deputy work together every day in the close confines of chambers and courtroom. Like all families they develop their own rituals, inside jokes, and particular ways of doing things. I enjoy courthouse culture, the interaction of the players; in a small city like Port Grace we spend a lot of time together. Entering the courthouse has the comforting sense of being where I belong.

I poked my head into Judge Washington's chambers. LaTanya's beautifully manicured fingers fluttered at the keyboard. On her desk were silver-framed photographs of her family, a neat stack of files, and a bowl of hard candy. I swiped a lemon sourball and glanced at my own ragged nails and cuticles. LaTanya smiled at me.

"How's it going?" I asked.

"Can't complain."

"How are the kids?"

She beamed and pulled a folder of photographs from the credenza. "Here we are at the amusement park last weekend. It was opening day." There they were: LaTanya, her mom, and her kids, three generations enjoying roller coasters and cotton candy.

"It looks like a blast," I said. "Do you know, I've never been to an amusement park?"

"You're kidding! Where are you from?"

"California. Not near Disneyland. But it wasn't the kind of

thing we did." I regretted my words. Explaining would reveal more than I wanted to. But LaTanya didn't comment, except to shake her head at my deprived childhood.

"Next time we go, you should come with us," she said.

"I would love that." I'm always ingratiating my way into other people's families. I imagined holding the hand of Raheem, her youngest, how warm and trusting that little hand would feel. I returned the photos and noted a copy of *Fast Food Nation.* "How's that book?"

"Let me put it this way: I'm on the lookout for a good vegetarian cookbook."

"It's that bad?"

"Worse. You can borrow it when I'm done."

"I don't think I have the stomach for it." She grinned at my pathetic humor and I said goodbye and walked to the small waiting room reserved for the (alleged) victims of domestic violence. Several women were in there. Two were with lawyers I knew and nodded to; one was talking to a counselor from the shelter. My client, Anna Trochmann, sat at the back of the room, with her head bowed. I sat down next to her. "Anna, hi." She looked at me and tried to smile, though she had obviously been crying. I pulled her file from my briefcase and reviewed the questions I would ask to elicit testimony from her. We had gone over them in my office the previous evening, but I wanted her sharp. "Remember," I said. "Your only chance of getting a restraining order is if the judge believes that you are afraid of Rick, and that what happened last week is part of a pattern of harassment."

She nodded wearily. In her hand was a substantial paperback.

"What are you reading?" I asked, hoping to divert her nervousness. She showed me the cover. *The Death of Vishnu.* "How is it?"

"Strange," she said. "Sad. I got it for a college class I was taking, but I had to drop out."

"Why?"

"Oh, you know. He doesn't want me making friends. And he's jealous. He even gets jealous of books when I read them."

"I'm so sorry. You should go back to college. And you deserve to have friends and read any damn thing you want to."

Eddie, Judge Washington's deputy, poked his head in the door. "You're up," he said to me.

Anna's husband Rick was a *pro se* litigant, he represented himself. I would have preferred it if he had a lawyer, because without one, Judge Washington would perceive him as at a disadvantage even though he wasn't supposed to. We arranged ourselves in the courtroom, plaintiff on the left, defendant on the right, and judge on the bench, court reporter and sheriff's officer at their places near the judge.

"This is number four on the calendar, Docket Number GV-7-84-05," Eddie intoned.

"Appearances, please," Judge Washington said without looking up from the file he was flipping through. We were off and running. It was a classic harassment case—controlling husband, terrorized wife, no bruises. The night he threatened to put Anna's cat in the microwave, after he found out that she'd gone to visit her sister without his permission, Anna did all the right things: called the police, took the cat to her mother's, and called the women's shelter twenty-four-hour hotline. She got a ten-day temporary restraining order against Rick and we were in court trying to get her a permanent one.

Rick wore a suit to court, managed a suburban sporting goods store, had no prior record, and exuded self-confidence and stability. Anna was a mess, disheveled, weepy, and wavering. She had no witnesses, so the testimony was he-said, she-said, and Judge Washington could only rule based on who he thought was more credible. He found Rick to be more credible. Despite the ring of authenticity in the microwave threat, he said that it did not rise to the level of harassment, that no pattern of harassment had been established, and therefore he had no basis upon which to issue a permanent restraining order.

As we left the courtroom Anna turned to me. "What do I do now?"

"Maybe stay with your mother. If you don't feel safe there, go to the shelter. He can't find you, and you'll meet other women in your situation. The counselors are excellent; they'll help you get on your feet."

Rick walked up to us. "Excuse me," he said sarcastically. "I'd like to talk to my wife."

I blocked her with my body. "Not now."

He stood too close. I felt the heat rising off of him. "She's coming home with me."

"I'm talking to her now," I said. "Why don't you go back to work?"

"I'm not leaving without my wife."

"Yes you are. She's not going with you."

He leaned around me so he could catch Anna's eye. "Annie, come home." Soft. Pleading.

She bent toward him. "Ricky?"

"Anna, please." I cut her off. "We aren't finished talking."

Eddie walked out of the courtroom. "Problem here, Ms. Reddy?"

"I think we're fine; I believe Mr. Trochmann was just leaving." I took advantage of Eddie's bulky presence and the gun on his hip, and led Anna into a small conference room, noting that Eddie remained in place until Rick slunk off. I would thank him later. I had no doubt that Rick would wait for Anna outside of the courthouse, or at the bus stop, or near her mother's house. I could escort her outside, but eventually she'd be on her own.

"See, it's no use," she said. "The judge didn't believe me. I went through that for nothing. And now Rick's really gonna be mad." She had put her finger on one of the unexpected difficulties I have encountered in domestic violence work. We encourage women to trust the system, but when the system fails they pay, big-time.

"I believe you," I said. "And if we'd had a different judge you might have gotten the restraining order. I don't usually appeal these cases, but it might be worth it. That threat about the microwave was very specific and detailed. There's a case the Appellate Division overturned, where the husband said, 'I'll bury you.' That's the one I raised to Judge Washington, but he didn't get it."

"What difference would that make." Her voice was flat. She had given up on me.

"Judges have to follow precedent, rulings that higher courts make. I'll get the tape of today's trial, and after I listen to it I'll call you and we can decide whether to appeal."

"How long will an appeal take?"

"Two or three months. At least."

Her face shadowed. "And what am I supposed to do in the meantime?"

"Stay with your mother. Or at the shelter."

"No. I'm going home."

"Please don't, Anna. Give it a try; you don't need him."

"Yes, I do need him. I don't have any money, no job, nothing. Besides, he loves me."

"Try it for a couple weeks. Come on, I'll drive you to the shelter."

"I'll think about it. I'll talk to my mother. Maybe I'll stay with her for a while."

"But he'll find you there."

"Ginger, he's my husband. With everything he's done, I still love him."

"Next time he might really hurt your cat. Or you. It's going to get worse, not better."

"I appreciate your help," she said, her voice stronger. She stood up. "I'll think about what you said."

"Please do. Call me anytime. I'll be happy to talk to you and do whatever I can for you."

And then she was gone. I let her go. I was so frustrated that I couldn't even stand to go down in the elevator with her. Restraining orders aren't magic, they are often ignored, but they do deter some people. I slumped in a chair in the waiting room, discouraged, a sense of failure pulling me down. It used to be easy to get restraining orders. Judges were fearful that if they denied one they might wake up the following morning to headlines of a domestic murder, and the victim would be the woman they denied. Now, there's a backlash; some women misused the law, made false accusations, ruined a few men's lives, and the judges are more cautious; that hurts people like Anna, who have no bruises, but live in terror.

The divorce settlement conference was a bust. They hated each other so much that it was worth it to them to pay lawyers to listen to them argue over who got the toaster. They were married for only three years and had no children. It should have been a slam-dunk uncontested divorce. My client was a twenty-eight year old nurse earning $45,000 a year. Her husband was twenty-nine, "in real estate," and claimed he earned $25,000 last year. My client said that he earned much more working at his brother's bar and getting paid under the table.

He demanded that she pay him alimony. I asked his lawyer to step out of the conference room. "Your client's request for alimony is ridiculous," I said. "It's a short-term marriage, and each of the previous two years he earned over $50,000. They both have bachelor's degrees, and their earning ability and employment history are roughly equivalent. You and I both know that no judge will grant him alimony."

My adversary, Marvin Brady, was inexperienced, pompous, and ready to set me straight. "I believe he has a valid claim," he said. "The real estate market has flattened. She has stable employment and gets a good raise every year, whereas his prospects are uncertain at best."

I felt like smacking him. "Then tell him to get another job. You're giving your client bad advice and you seem to be prolonging the litigation in order to run up your fees. I'm considering asking the judge for attorney fees based on bad faith litigation."

That ended the settlement conference. Marvin and his client left in a huff, and I couldn't get away from them fast enough.

I strode across the street to The Juror's Luncheonette for a sandwich. As I swung through the door I saw Emma Greene just ahead of me. She is a public defender who represents juveniles and who used to defend parents in child abuse cases.

"Emma! Can I buy you lunch? I need your advice."

She checked her watch. "I was going to eat at my desk, but I can spare a few minutes for you. And you don't even have to pay."

We grabbed a booth. It was a few minutes before the official 12:30 court recess, when the tables and booths would quickly fill up. The waitress knew us and poured our coffee before we had a chance to ask.

"What's up?" asked Emma. She frowned at the stack of files she had placed on the table. More files were sticking out of the battered briefcase on the floor next to her chair.

"I need a crash course in child abuse cases. I've got one that could turn nasty."

Emma gave me a thoughtful look. "Are we talking abuse-

abuse here, or neglect? A minority of cases involves physical abuse. Those heinous ones that make the news and get caseworkers fired? The kid chained to the radiator? The one starving in the dog cage? You get maybe one of those a year. Maybe two. You do have the euphemistic excessive corporal punishment cases—parents who think it's okay to beat the kid with an extension cord or make them kneel on grains of rice for hours. But most of the cases that came my way were neglect. Drug addicts who forget to feed the kids don't send them to school, and so forth."

"What's the process?"

"DCW and the Family Court step in, usually put the kids in foster care, and give the parent one year to get their act together. If they don't? DCW petitions the court to terminate the parents' rights." She paused while the waitress took our order: BLT on rye for me, minestrone and a house salad for Emma, keep pouring the coffee for both of us.

"What percentage of parents gets it together in a year?"

"Miniscule. A crack or heroin addict? Who's been using for years? It's nearly impossible to turn it around in a year. They go in and out of programs; not all the programs are good, and the good ones have long waiting lists, so you can lose months waiting. Plus, they have so many other issues. Poor health care. Substandard housing or no housing. AIDS. Minimal education and job skills. Drugs and mental health often intersect; I call crack the poor man's Prozac." She paused to sip her coffee. "I need a vacation."

"Burnt-out?"

"You bet. I went over to Juvie thinking I could do some good, catch 'em early, but there's a heavy backlash against kids. They're getting pushed into adult court younger and younger. The concept of rehabilitating kids is out, and it drives me nuts." She shook her head in despair. "What's your case?"

"Nineteen-year-old female, indigent, no family support. Got a restraining order against baby's dad when she was six months pregnant. Now baby is in a coma, and she's accused of baby-shaking."

Emma smoothed the plastic tablecloth, a vibrant tropical fruit pattern. "That's serious stuff, Ginger. I guess that's why she got a private attorney."

"I tried to refer her to the Public Defender but she thinks I'm the only one she can trust. I got her the restraining order after baby's dad beat her up. And believe me, I'm not getting paid; I'm losing money."

"Is the restraining order still in effect?"

"Technically, yes. But she's been seeing him again for a couple months."

"Do you think Dad's responsible?"

"Probably. But he hasn't been arrested. I don't think they consider him a suspect."

"Then you'll have to make sure they figure it out."

Lunch arrived and I lit into my sandwich. The bacon was crisp. So was the lettuce, and it was a nice thick stack of lettuce topped with juicy tomato slices. Emma's soup looked hearty and she didn't seem to mind that her salad was mostly iceberg lettuce. She dribbled ranch dressing from a little white paper cup onto the iceberg.

"Are there witnesses?" she asked. "Does she have a history of violence or anger problems? People who can testify on her behalf? Character witnesses who will testify that she's a great mother, dotes on the baby, and so forth. Has anybody seen him around her? Can you link him to the scene? A coma is not good. Was it an accident? What did she tell the police? Lay it out minute by minute. Get a description of the room. Did she trip and drop him? Was she half-asleep when she picked him up, and he banged his head on the crib? Consider every possible scenario."

She paused to sip her soup. I pondered her words. Was she feeding me stories for the jury or did she really think those things might have happened?

"You know what a trial is," she continued, "your version of the facts versus the State's version of the facts. Two interpretations of the same story; you have to make the jury doubt the State. And make your client sympathetic as hell, put her in a sweet dress, remove all piercings, cover all tattoos . . ."

"I'm hoping it won't go to trial."

"Of course. But even if Daddy shook the baby, they'll hold her for failure to protect her child. If they have something solid on her, plea it down, request community service, probation, treatment, you know the drill. Talk the prosecutor into dropping the charges, get it out of Criminal Court and let Family Court handle it."

"You think that could happen?"

"Yes. Maybe. They should have bigger fish to fry: rapists and drug lords and such. Who's the ADA?"

"Michelle."

Emma grimaced. "She's such a bitch."

"No kidding. Can you believe we were friends my first year of law school? We used to smoke weed together." I smiled, remembering squeezing into Michelle's battered Civic, getting high in the law school parking lot after Contracts or Torts.

"Man, what happened to her?"

"Zealousness of the converted, I guess."

"Think about this: In Criminal Court if you're found guilty you go to jail. In Family Court? You lose your children. Convince Michelle that for your client losing her child would be a worse punishment than hard time. Remind her that a plea will assist judicial efficiency. Get the case off the judge's calendar so he can go after pot smokers and vagrants." She hurriedly swallowed a final cup of coffee, put down six bucks, stood up and hefted her stack of files. "Call me. I'll give you some good case citations." She picked up her briefcase and jammed down the files that were sticking out haphazardly. I caught a glimpse of a battered paperback.

"What are you reading?" I asked.

She followed my glance, pulled the book out. *To Kill a Mockingbird.* "I brought it with me the day I interviewed for the Public Defender's office. For good luck. Seventeen years ago, and I've carried it with me ever since. Seventeen years, can you believe it? I must be some kind of fool."

"How do you keep doing it?" I asked. When I started doing defense work Emma was a beacon; she'd spent ten years defending criminals, then she went to the state capital defender's unit, where she worked on death penalty cases. A couple years ago she transferred to special units thinking it would be semi-retirement defending neglectful parents and juvenile delinquents, but she was worn out. I could tell.

"Honestly?" she said, lowering her voice. "Don't tell anyone but I'm almost ready to go to the appeals unit. Enter the cave of research and writing."

"But seventeen years! What keeps you going?"

She shrugged. "It's my job. What else would I do?"

10

When I returned to the office, around one-thirty, Gloria was typing away. "Hey!" I said. "I missed you so much last week!"

"I missed you more," she smiled.

Gloria has a day job entering data at a pharmaceutical company located in an industrial park on the outskirts of the city. She works there for three ten-hour days every week, tedious work, but she gets full benefits. She puts in another fifteen to twenty hours a week at my office, and the occasional week that she can't come in because she has to work overtime at her other job, things fall apart around here. She is a calming force, an influence I desperately need.

"Messages?" I asked.

"On your desk. And Marco's waiting for you. Oh, and Ellison wants to know if you want him to come in after school." Ellison is Gloria's seventeen-year-old son who works in the office a few hours a week, filing, copying, and running errands.

"Yes, please. Desperately. He was a big help those extra hours he put in last week."

"It's good for him to be busy."

"He's the busiest person I know. School, debate, basketball, track, work. . . . Don't worry about him."

"I always worry."

"You're a good mother. He's a lucky boy." I flicked the Hawaiian hula-guy-on-a-spring that Gloria suctioned to her desk, and picked up a slender book. *Selected Poems of Gwendolyn*

Brooks. "What's with this?" I asked.

"I'm writing a paper on her," Gloria said. She goes to college at night, one or two classes at a time and she's hoping to graduate the same year that Ellison, a high school junior, does.

"Call Tommy if you need any help," I said.

"He wouldn't mind?"

"What, are you kidding? He eats this stuff for breakfast." I put the book down and went off to look for Marco. He was sipping coffee and looking uncharacteristically somber. "Hey." I tossed my blazer over the client chair. He did not give me his usual warm smile. My mood slipped and I started whining. "I don't need this aggravation."

"So give the case away."

"How did you know what I was talking about?"

"What else would you be talking about?"

"The D.V. I lost this morning? The settlement conference where my adversary is dumb as a stone?"

"I know you pretty well. I've seen what gets to you and what doesn't."

I brightened up. "The good news is, if the baby gets better, I'll bet you twenty bucks I can get the criminal charges dropped. DCW will make her go to parenting classes, they'll monitor the case for a while and then it's over. Done. Finished. Finito. Off my plate."

"You said *if* the baby gets better." I looked at him and then looked away. "Have you called the hospital today?" he asked.

"No. I'll do it later."

"Your client called three times this morning. She wants you to take her to the hospital. And she doesn't want to stay in the shelter."

I pulled all of the pens and pencils out of the Bruins mug on Marco's desk and started replacing them one by one. "She has a name. Violet. Violeta Marguerite Rosada."

"What's your problem?"

"I'm not used to you being in a bad mood. I count on you to be cheerful and I take it personally when you're not."

He leaned back in his chair and looked at the ceiling. He wore jeans, a navy sweater and black work boots. He looked good. He always looked good. "I get in bad moods all the time," he said to the ceiling.

"Really?" I studied him. He looked tense, unhappy. There is a certain darkness to Marco, but I viewed it as being directed outward, not inward, and he always seemed in control. Like if he's angry about something it's a reasoned anger, not just flipping out the way I do. I've never had to walk on eggs around him.

He shrugged me off. "The good news is that Mrs. Abbott stopped by with the retainer check."

"Excellent! She signed the contract?"

"You bet. And told me to call her Mary."

"Did you?"

"Yup. Especially when she asked me to play tennis at the club with her."

"Marco. We don't sleep with our clients."

"Who said anything about sex? I'm excited about saying 'I'm going to the club. Sorry, I can't have a beer with you; I'm going to the club.' He looked down at his sweater and jeans. "Don't you think I'd look good in tennis whites?"

"You'd look good in anything."

"I could get used to that life."

"Then you better go into corporate law. You're not getting into any country club working for me."

"I'm just playing with you." He stood up, stretched, and swung his arm as though executing a killer backhand. "If I walk into a country club, people will think I'm a waiter. She's not my type anyway. And the closest I get to a tennis racket is watching ESPN."

"What is your type?"

He ignored my question. "Time for the bad news."

Oh crap, oh no. "What." I really did not want to hear it.

"Did you see the paper?"

"No."

"Take a look." He handed me the local news section, front page below the fold. *Teen Mom Accused of Shaking Baby into Coma.* A three-paragraph story that included my name but made no reference to Teddy's father.

"Damn that was quick. How did they find out?"

"Probably the prosecutor's office leaked it. It's to their advantage to make the news on this one."

"Because it will taint the jury pool?"

"That and the judges will see it and everyone in the courthouse will see it and even if they know it's not supposed to influence them, it will."

I tossed the newspaper into the wastebasket. "Maybe I should make a motion to forbid press contact."

Marco reached down and retrieved the paper, smoothed it out and placed it on his desk. "That only happens in really big cases."

"This is a big case to me. It's a big case to Violet. And Teddy."

"No one cares about you. Think First Amendment. Freedom of the press and all that. No judge will find that the risk of harm outweighs hassling with the ACLU."

His confidence irritated me. "You're awfully sure of yourself."

"And you are avoiding the subject. You have to face what this case is about. Face the whole friggin' thing. You can't keep ducking and weaving. It's not fair to her and it's not fair to you. You've gotta decide if you're in or out."

Boxing metaphors. Marco was wound up pretty tight.

Although we'd worked together smooth as a figure skating team for four years, I had no idea what I'd find if I unwound him.

I stopped mixing sports metaphors, went to my desk and phoned the shelter. The newspaper was on my desk and I wondered if Gloria had seen the article. If Tommy had. If Jake had.

Violet was brought to the phone.

"How are you?" I asked.

"Terrible. I've been calling you. Did he tell you?" Her anxiety and neediness radiated from the phone so that I had to pull it away from my ear.

"I was in court all morning and only just got a free minute. What's up?" I didn't really want to know and I really didn't want to be needed.

"Will you take me to see Teddy? And also, I don't want to stay here anymore."

I sighed. Kicked off my shoes and checked out my toes through the sheer knee-highs I wear with pants. Chipped coral polish on my toenails. "Listen, Violet. I can't force you to stay there, but I think you should. This is a bad time for you to be alone at that apartment."

"Have you talked to AJ?"

"No. Have you?"

"I called his cell phone, but he didn't answer."

"I don't want you calling him anymore. You can't count on him for help."

"I want to tell him about Teddy."

"I'll tell him," I said. "I'll have my investigator contact him."

"There's something else," she said. "Laura came to see me. She brought me flowers and a sweater that she doesn't wear anymore, but it's in perfect condition, it's really soft. Anyway, she said I could stay with her. She said she'd call you."

I riffled through the stack of messages on my desk; they were written on pink paper in Gloria's neat cursive. Sure enough, there was a message to call Laura.

"I'll try to reach her," I told Violet, "and I'll pick you up at 5:45 to go to the hospital, but it's going to have to be a short visit because I have plans for this evening." I didn't have actual plans, but I planned to make plans, for I sorely needed some distraction and I owed it to Tommy to get home in time for dinner. Maybe I would put fresh polish on my toenails. I hated feeling responsible for Violet. I couldn't force her to stay at the shelter, but I also couldn't let her go back to that apartment in the projects. She'd be calling AJ soon enough, or getting herself into some other kind of trouble. I punched in Laura's number.

"Flowers," she answered cheerfully. She confirmed that she had indeed invited Violet to stay with her.

"I'm not sure that's a good idea," I cautioned.

"Do you know something I don't? She only worked for me for a short time, but she didn't strike me as trouble."

"She's not; but I don't know who she's been hanging out with. And the baby's father is bad news; you don't want him coming around."

"That's ridiculous. I'm not afraid of some cowardly guy who has to hit a woman to prove he's in charge. And it's very safe here. Besides, no one will know she's here. And I thought she could do a little work for me. You know, while she's waiting."

"You're an angel," I said. "She does need something to keep her busy."

"She can make a few bucks. I can't pay much more than minimum, but it's something."

"Can you really use her help, or are you just being saintly?"

"I can definitely use her help. I'm swamped. I've got two weddings this weekend."

We agreed that I would bring Violet over after she visited

Teddy. "Take my cell number," I said. "If there are any problems I'll get her."

"We'll be fine," she replied, and we hung up.

Nobody wanted to follow my advice.

"How come nobody listens to me?" I shouted out to Marco.

"We all listen to you."

"I'm not feeling the devotion and admiration I deserve."

"Get a dog."

I walked back to his desk. "I need you to investigate Teddy's father. AJ Mulligan. He's a corrections officer at Western State. Canvass Violet's neighbors and find out if they've seen him in the past month. Or ever. If they've seen him with the baby. Whatever you can get."

I spent most of the afternoon working on a motion to constrain a client's ex-wife from having her boyfriend sleep over when the children were at her house. Then I read case law on child endangerment, which was damn depressing, and exactly what Marco meant when he said I had to face what Violet's case was about. I called Tommy and asked him to check out the movie listings, an escape movie I said. No subtitles or subtleties. Nothing too meaningful.

When I left the office I saw Mr. Ziznewski sweeping the sidewalk.

"Ginger," he called. I walked over to him. "What a beautiful day." I looked around. I had been so preoccupied I hadn't noticed weather or season. It was cool, and evening was blowing in. But purple and yellow crocuses were everywhere and puffy clouds wafted across the sky. One neighbor was installing screens and another was polishing his car. "Spring is my favorite season," Mr. Z continued. "It's a new beginning. Every year," he flung his arm in a sweeping motion, "new leaves on the trees, new flowers in the garden, a new baseball season." He slowed down on the poetry for a second and took a good look at me.

"What's wrong with you?"

"Nothing. Just a tough day at work."

"Well, tomorrow is another day."

"Yes it is. I have to get going. You have a good evening."

"You too. Do something fun, get the smile back on your face."

"I'm working on it." As I walked to Victor's to pick up my car I tried to relax into the moment, to summon up some spring energy and the attendant feelings of hope, possibility, and renewal. I stopped at Carrera's produce stand and bought California strawberries and a Costa Rican pineapple to take home to Tommy. Johnny Carrera added a bunch of champagne grapes, on the house, and for an instant I felt spring touch me, ever so lightly.

11

Mr. Ziznewski's rubber-ducky–yellow spring day turned gunmetal gray as Violet and I walked toward Teddy's room. I tensed when I saw Michelle standing outside of the Neonatal Intensive Care Unit.

"Go on in," I told Violet. "I'll be there in a minute."

"You can't let her in there alone," Michelle said. "Judge Holmes signed an order stating that she must be under the supervision of you or DCW."

Screw you, I felt like saying, but I restrained myself. "Relax. I am supervising her. I can see her through the glass, and there are two nurses in there." Through the plateglass windows I saw the nurses tending other infants. Violet sat in a chair next to Teddy, and placed her hand on him. Tubes and an IV line snaked into him. His eyes were closed and he was completely still. Michelle glared at me and turned to leave. "Wait. Michelle," I said. "Let's talk." She paused. "You should drop the charges."

She was disgusted. "Don't even try."

I stepped closer to her and spoke quietly. "Just listen for a minute. Violet is not a criminal. She's a nineteen-year-old mother and a domestic violence victim. Why don't you arrest the father?"

"He wasn't on the scene," she snapped.

"Are you sure?" She paused long enough for me to know that she was behind the ball on that one. "Your ace investigative team never secured her apartment. I bet they would have found his fingerprints there. And he has a history of domestic violence. You haven't even questioned the neighbors, have you?" I let the thought linger and then completed my pitch. "She loves her baby. She's a teen mother who's had some rough times, not some sociopath or drug addict or gang member."

She cast a cursory glance at Violet. "Wrong. What I see is a wild teenager who is not fit to be a mother. Who deliberately, maliciously hurt a ten-month-old baby. Kids shouldn't have kids."

"Deliberate! Malicious! Where did you get that? What the hell happened to you?" I said. "We used to be friends."

"Listen, Ginger Rae; you prepare your case and I'll prepare mine. You'll get no deals for that girl. And the fact that you and I went to law school together is irrelevant."

I tried again. "Let the Family Court handle this. She'll get services, parenting classes, support. DCW won't let her have him back unless he's safe."

"He might not ever leave this hospital. What if he stays in a coma for years? Forever? I want her to pay for that."

"Look at her. What could you do that would make her feel worse than she already feels?"

"It doesn't matter. I'm going to make an example out of her. I'm sick and tired of all these kids having babies they can't take care of. No baby deserves that. Maybe if she goes to jail some other girl will stop and think before she puts her kid in a coma. Or in the morgue." She picked up her briefcase and uttered a parting shot. "I don't know how you can live with yourself."

I watched her walk toward the exit sign in her conservative gray skirt suit, low-heeled pumps, and black Coach briefcase that was a law school graduation gift from her parents. Ten years ago she was a bright light who loved techno-music, Cheese

Doodles and Seinfeld. Now she was just another humorless prosecutor.

I simmered for fifteen minutes and then walked into the NICU and touched Violet on the shoulder. "We have to go."

"Just another minute. Let me say goodbye to Teddy."

We drove to Laura's without talking. Violet looked absolutely spent and I was weary. I flicked on college radio and we listened to Phish as we rolled down the road. Laura lives and works in an old textile factory converted to live-in artist lofts, the result of unusually generous action on the part of city government, as part of their plan for Port Grace to become a renaissance city. On the way we drove past decrepit row houses that mill owners built as housing for the workers—crowded tenements that were abandoned for years and currently comprise one of Port Grace's two worst neighborhoods. Crime, drugs, and poverty, the usual litany of sadness and despair, permeate those streets.

I pulled into the parking lot, but left the engine running. "We need to talk."

"What about?"

I turned to face her. "About what happened to Teddy. Tell me exactly what happened that day."

She fidgeted with the fringe on her cotton purse. "I told you already. He was a little fussy. He spit up, but not much, and babies do that. He had an ear infection. I put him down for his nap and then I fell asleep too, just like I told you. I woke up and when I went to check on him he didn't look right. I tried to wake him up. Then I called 911."

"Did you shake him?"

"No!"

The Jimmy vibrated with tension. I bowed my head to the steering wheel and closed my eyes, trying to find my way. Then I took a deep breath and slowly exhaled. "You must have been very lonely taking care of Teddy by yourself." I spoke carefully. She was silent, so I continued. "I'm sorry I didn't help you more after you got the restraining order. I thought you were doing okay."

"I was."

"You mentioned you were seeing AJ again. When did that start?"

"A few months after Teddy was born. When my grandmother died I was so lonely." Tears slid down her cheeks. "Then around Thanksgiving he stopped coming. I knew it was because of his wife. She said he'd never see his kids again. Then he came back again. On Valentine's Day he came to me. He brought flowers and a teddy bear. You know, for Teddy. I wanted to leave that bear at the hospital but they wouldn't let me."

"And what happened on Valentine's Day?"

"Nothing. He played with Teddy. We went for a walk. Ate pizza. Like a family."

"Did he stay overnight?"

"No, he had to work the graveyard shift so he left about ten. He was doing a lot of overtime. Some of the guards quit and he didn't have a choice."

"How many times have you seen him since then?"

She paused, thinking. "Four. No, three."

"Was he nice to Teddy?"

"Yes! One time we went out and he bought him Pampers and a little Celtics T-shirt, then we got Burger King."

"Did he hurt you?"

"No. I told you he's changed. It's just when he's been drinking a lot he gets mean."

"Was he ever drunk around you?"

"No. Except for the last time."

"The last time you saw him. When was that?" She hesitated before answering. Did she think it was a trick question?

"Two days before, you know. The hospital."

"That was the time he came in late? When Teddy was sleeping?"

She nodded.

"Before that, what was the most recent time you saw him?"

"About a week ago. No, two weeks ago. I'm confused with all that's happened." She paused. "About a week before the other time."

"What happened that time? The one before last?"

"Nothing. He had trouble with his truck, so he was in a bad mood about that. But not at me."

"Did you do anything? Go anywhere?"

"I went to the corner for pizza and sodas. He gave me money."

"Did you take Teddy with you?"

"No, he was sleeping."

"What happened when you came back?"

"We ate and watched basketball. March Madness. AJ, he loves basketball. He had a bet on Syracuse."

"Did they win?"

"No, and boy was he mad."

"How was he with Teddy that night?"

"Fine. I mean, when I got back with the pizza Teddy was crying. AJ said he didn't know what to do, whether he needed his Pamper changed or what, so he left him crying in his crib. But not to be mean. He doesn't know about taking care of babies."

"You said he was in a bad mood when he got there. Did he stay in a bad mood? Did he get angry at you?"

She didn't want to tell me.

"What is it?" I said impatiently.

"We got in an argument. About his wife."

"What happened?"

"He said he couldn't see me anymore. That he had to try for his kids."

"Do you think he shook Teddy?"

"He wouldn't do that."

"But you don't actually know what happened when you went for pizza, do you?"

She shook her head.

"I'm sorry," I said. "This is hard for you. But I don't want any surprises."

"What do you mean, surprises?"

"Suppose the prosecutor gets AJ to testify that he saw you shake Teddy."

"He wouldn't do that."

"People lie all the time. Even under oath. And it's my job to think of every possible scenario, so we're prepared. Maybe a neighbor heard him yelling at Teddy when you were out. I have to think like a detective, and I have to be able to count on you being honest with me." I tried to catch her eye. She was staring out the window. "That's enough for now. Let's go in."

We entered the old brick factory, faded letters still painted on the walls. *Textiles, Weavers, Warpers, Quillers.* The words of another generation. The air was fragrant with linseed oil and turpentine. We took the steps to the second floor and I knocked on Laura's door. The door across the hall opened and a Coltrane lament drifted down the hall, followed by a lanky young man maneuvering a large canvas. A joint was tucked between his lips and he nodded to us. Laura's door opened and she saw us looking at him. "Need a hand?" she asked him. He shook his head and leaned the canvas against the wall, took a hit off the joint, then held it out to us. Laura, Violet and I glanced at each other and shook our heads. He was not as young as his boyish body led me to believe. Around my age, early to mid-thirties.

I squatted by the canvas. "Where is this?" I said, reaching out, wanting to touch the rough blue rectangle painted thickly in the center. Within the rectangle was a lake edged with pine trees that were reflected in the water. Outside of the rectangle was a painted grid and within each square was something relating to the lake: trout, loons, rowboat, fishing rod, a child wading, a dog with a stick in its mouth, a picnic basket. It was a gentle painting. I wanted to be there.

"In my head," he replied. I took a closer look at him. He was very tall with short dreadlocks and kind brown eyes over which he wore hip, rectangular black glasses that were taped together on one side, which kind of detracted from the hipness.

"Where's it going?" Laura asked.

"I'm hanging a show at Mama Jo's on Little River." He took another hit off the joint.

"When does it open?"

"Hold on," he said. "I've got some invitations to the opening."

He ducked inside the door and returned with postcards in his hand, and no joint.

"Are you an artist?" he asked me.

I smiled at that. "No."

"She's a lawyer," Laura said.

"No kidding." He looked me up and down thoughtfully, in a sort of detached way. "You're tall," he said. Who was this guy? He held his hand out to me. "I'm Miles Stephano."

I shook his hand. "Ginger Rae Reddy. And this is Violeta Rosada." Violet was standing in Laura's doorway, somber as a Renaissance Madonna.

"Nice to meet you," he said to Violet. I watched them exchange a flicker of recognition, which I took to be acknowledgment of their mutual mixed-race heritage. Maybe that sounds racist, but I was a sociology major, and take a clinical view of such things. Plus my mother was a Native American, so I know that look; when I see someone who obviously has Native blood we acknowledge it with a nod or a hint of a smile. Like,

"It's good to know you're out there . . ."

Miles returned to moving his paintings and we went into Laura's loft.

"You like him, don't you?" Laura asked me.

"I like his painting."

"Come to the opening with me. Next Friday."

"Maybe. Will you guys be okay?" I wanted to go home.

"Sure. I'm going to fix us a nice dinner and Violet will be settled in in no time."

I gave a nod to her optimism. "Good. We'll talk tomorrow." I took a quick look back before I closed the door and saw Laura walking to the kitchen, and Violet, looking lost.

12

"I don't know how she can live with herself." I sat at the kitchen table with Tommy, simmering over Michelle's attitude toward Violet and stuffing my face with an overflowing taco shell. A beer would have hit the spot. Even better? A Margarita. I could taste the salt and the grainy melt mixed with sour, the icy jolt. I made do with seltzer and a twist of lime, which was crisp and refreshing, but I miss real drinking—the edginess, the rituals, the camaraderie.

"You *are* adversaries, right?" Tom said.

"Of course, but she's acting unprofessional. Most prosecutors are at least cordial. A lot of them become defense attorneys eventually. And we all understand the game. She seems to be taking this case way too personally. She's bitter." I mashed guacamole with my fork, feeling a wisp of nostalgia for the taco wagon that rolled through my hometown daily on its way to the fields for the pickers' lunches, later returning to park under a shade tree, the aroma of fresh tortillas luring customers, three fillings for a dollar. "Remember? That's why I left the prosecutor's office, that *go for blood* mentality. Everything in black and white. No maybes."

"What's a maybe?"

"Doubt whether the right person was identified. Doubt whether an act was accidental or intentional. Premeditated or spontaneous. Heat of passion. Criminal law is shades of gray." A blob of salsa and sour cream fell onto my blouse. I rubbed at it ineffectively. Tommy got the seltzer from the fridge and handed it to me.

"So you see shades of gray where Michelle sees black and white."

"Do you understand what I'm saying?" I dabbed seltzer onto my blouse.

"Sure. Michelle's an objectivist and you are a relativist."

"In English, please?"

"Objectivists believe that reality exists outside the mind; that how someone feels about something does not affect its identity. Relativists see everything in context. For example, this client you just told me about? You see her in relation to her childhood, the domestic abuse, the fact that she's poor, and so forth. Michelle doesn't care about any of that. I'm no philosophy professor, but you get the gist?"

"I can't imagine not seeing things in context. You might as well be a robot. Anyway I don't believe it."

"What?"

"That Michelle's a whatever-you-said. She's projecting her own stuff onto the client, plain as day. She's fixating on Violet as a monster who deliberately hurt her child. She's become the prototypical zealous, myopic prosecutor. And you know what else ticks me off? Do you think for one minute that if Violet was white and lived on the hill she'd have been arrested?"

"You believe that?"

"Absolutely. There's an undercurrent of racism and classism in this case, just like most criminal cases."

"I thought Michelle was black."

"She is. And I think that makes her hate the client even more."

"The client's black?"

"And Latino. And Michelle's decided to make an example of her. To lynch her."

"Isn't that a little harsh?"

I slapped the table. "No. It's real life. Not some academic exercise or philosophical debate. Not some jerk-off's Ph.D. thesis on the effects of popular culture on today's youth." I stood up and paced. "Violet didn't play video games and decide it would be cool to throw her baby out the window. Worst-case scenario? She's a young, exhausted, single mother who got momentarily frustrated. More likely the baby's father did it and she won't give him up." I stopped. Tom didn't dignify my outburst with a reply, just started clearing the table. "Sit down," I said. "I'll clean up. Why don't you read to me?" He was hurt; but he turned off the 1961 recording of Bill Evans at the Village Vanguard playing in the background, picked up the *New Yorker,* and started reading out loud: a story about an American woman living in Japan, cooking Thanksgiving dinner, and playing a Lou Rawls recording of *One for the Road* thirty-two times in a row while the turkey roasted.

The summer after we moved into our house, Tommy knocked out the wall between the dining room and the kitchen. The house almost collapsed, but fortunately we have the kinds of neighbors who know how to keep a house upright, and who were willing to help us do it. Tommy got what he wanted—a couch and a big bookcase in the newly expanded kitchen. The first couple years we often sat there in the evening. He could tell when I wanted a drink, and he'd make tea and read to me. I put my head in his lap or curled up next to him. Jake often joined us, and Tommy read to both of us. *Charlotte's Web. A Wrinkle in Time. Charlie and the Chocolate Factory.* Books that I never read as a kid, and I enjoyed them as much as Jake did.

Later, we walked to the bay. "Let's just take one of those boats and go," I said.

Tommy took my hand. "Sure. Where shall we go?"

"Maybe South. Louisiana. Or Montana."

"Take some time off this summer. Let's take a trip."

I took a good look at him. "You're serious."

"Why not? We've never gone anywhere for more than three days." (Subtext: I was always working.)

"What about Jake?"

"We'll take him with us. Or he can stay with his mother. Or a friend."

When I was a kid vacations consisted of short trips with my Dad. We'd toss a change of clothes in the pickup and drive, Willie Nelson and Tanya Tucker on the tape deck, usually winding up on the coast or at a lake. Half Moon Bay, Big Sur, Lake Berryessa, Mendocino. One time, all the way to the Oregon coast where we were mesmerized by the soft, thick, green Northwest. "Where would we go?"

"Paris. Hawaii. Prague. New Zealand. Kenya. Anywhere."

I shook my head at those words. "I've never been out of this country."

"We could take a road trip. Discover American culture first hand. Get me away from my books and into real life, like you've always wanted me to."

I flinched at his reference to past quarrels. "You don't need to change, Tommy. You're perfect the way you are."

He looked me over for signs of sarcasm, and saw none.

"Maybe a road trip," I said. "I'm not ready to get a passport."

He grinned. "I'll get some travel books." He was happy at the thought of us traveling together, and I was sad because it took so little to make him happy, and I didn't try often enough.

Jake was at the kitchen table when we got home, eating a peanut butter and jelly sandwich and drinking milk. "Hey!" His smile lit up the kitchen. "What have you two been up to?"

Tommy swiped a bite of his sandwich and I watched the two

of them with pleasure.

Once during our separation I stayed with Jake for a week while Tom attended a conference. One day I came home from work at the hour when dusk settles, and went outside to the patio. Jake was there with his guitar, playing scales. I remember brushing my hand across the potted herbs my father sends us every year, and the scent of basil, lemon thyme, and rosemary mingled and lingered, as Jake slipped into a minor key improvisation. Something that I can only describe as grace filled the air—the convergence of rosemary, music, twilight sliding through leaves, and a gentle fourteen-year-old boy, deep in his guitar. That was the night I called Tommy and begged him to give our marriage another try.

13

A week passed. I put on a short skirt and sweet-talked Judge Holmes into signing an order allowing Laura to supervise Violet's visits with Teddy. She and I agreed to take turns. I couldn't leave Violet at the mercy of the DCW worker, who made it clear that she would only take her once a week.

"That's all the law requires," Mrs. Evans, the caseworker, announced.

"That's the minimum the law requires," I responded.

"Any more than that has to be approved by my supervisor and ordered by the judge." Which I knew would take more time and aggravation than it was worth.

At the hospital Violet sat next to Teddy and prayed. He was still on a respirator and I couldn't get used to it. Sometimes I tried to read or work, but mostly I sat with my eyes closed. Sometimes I prayed in my own little agnostic way. Sometimes I just stared at Violet and Teddy.

Marco's investigation of Violet's neighbors didn't yield any useful information, but AJ finally called me. "What the hell are you calling my job for?" he said.

"Because you didn't return the three messages I left on your cell phone?"

"That voice mail doesn't work. And you can't be calling my job saying you're a lawyer and it's urgent. People talk."

"Be glad I didn't call your wife."

"You're the bitch who got that restraining order against me, aren't you?"

"You bet. Do you have a lawyer?"

"Do I need a lawyer?"

"I'm not saying that you do; but if you have a lawyer I have to talk to them and not you."

"I don't have a lawyer, I don't need a lawyer, and why are you bothering me?"

"Because Teddy is in the hospital."

A long silence ensued. He finally said, "Violet's kid?"

"Your kid too."

"Who says he's mine? I never took any paternity test."

"Has the D.A. called you yet?"

"What about?"

"Never mind. But if they do you should probably return their call quicker than you did mine. Let's make an appointment so we can talk in person." Before I finished the sentence he had hung up on me. So much for dispensing free legal advice.

I called Laura. "Did Violet find her cell phone?"

"I don't think so," she said. "Why?"

"I just talked to AJ and he's probably going to try and get in touch with her. Don't let her go out without you."

Since he couldn't call Violet, I wondered if he would go to her apartment. Probably. He would want to know what was happening. It would be eating him up. Was it worth staking the place out? I decided to drop in on him at the prison. It would be easy enough to find out when he was working.

Laura called me back. "No sign of a cell phone," she said. "And she's not going anywhere. She spends most of her time watching TV."

"Nobody knows she's staying with you, right?"

"No. Just you. Some of my neighbors have seen her with me, but they don't know the details. It's extremely unlikely that any of them would know AJ. He's not even from here, is he?"

"No," I replied. "He has a cousin or brother-in-law or something in town, but I don't think he's ever spent much time here."

"Then I can't think of how he could connect her with me. The restraining order was in effect when she worked for me so she probably never even mentioned me to him."

"I wouldn't count on that." I walked through the degrees of separation between AJ and Laura, and concluded that they were far enough apart that there wasn't an imminent risk. "I think everything's cool," I said. "Unless you want her out of there?"

"Of course not," she said dismissively. "By the way, Miles's opening is tomorrow night. Want to go?"

I had forgotten about it. I was busy. I was always busy. "I'm swamped. And I'll feel out of place there." I flipped through my calendar and felt the threat of panic when I saw all of the appointments and court dates written in.

"We'll leave if we're not having a good time. Remember how much you liked his painting." Her voice was warm and sincere, burnt orange and sage. When I think of Laura I think of colors. "Bring your husband," she added.

"He's going to New York to visit his mother," I said. And Jake would be busy with his friends. I reflected on my attraction to Miles and his painting. The possibility of filling myself with light and form was tempting. "Okay."

"Come by my place around six o'clock. We'll have an early dinner before we go."

It was close to six-thirty when I arrived at Laura's on Friday. I had intended to pick up dessert, but it slipped my mind. Oh well. Laura opened the door looking splendid in a long, full, turquoise skirt and a pink cashmere cardigan buttoned up just enough to reveal a bit of black camisole. She radiated kindness, generosity, creativity, and sadness. Sadness was the background, the other qualities foreground. "You look beautiful," I said, bored with my black pants, white blouse and black blazer.

She pulled me in and shut the door. "Would you like a glass of wine?"

"No thanks. I'm fine." I looked around. The loft was a massive rectangle, workspace at one end, then kitchen, dining, and sitting area. At the other end were two small bedrooms and a bathroom. Books piled everywhere. Shades of copper, chocolate, and cream warming the industrial bones. "Where's Violet?"

"In her room. Watching TV."

"I'll go say hi."

"It's the door on the left."

She was sitting on the bed, riveted to a small TV, watching a show cast with healthy white teens dressed in Gap and Abercrombie. I sat on a chair next to the bed. "How's it going?"

"Okay."

"Are you coming with us tonight?"

"No."

"Did you see Teddy today?"

"Yes."

I surveyed the room. Sunny yellow walls. Simple pine furniture. Tidy. A photo of Teddy on the dresser next to a teddy bear with a red bow around his neck. I picked up a paperback lying open on the bed. *Hot Six*. "How's this book?"

She looked at me for the first time since I entered the room. "Cool. It's about this girl bounty hunter."

"It's good?"

She nodded. "Laura took me to the bookstore. See?" She pointed to the bedside table, which held a lamp, a vase of daisies, and a stack of paperbacks.

"I didn't know you like to read. I'll look through my books. I'm sure I've got some that you'd like." I have my own bookcase because Tommy is neurotic about keeping his books in order. Mine is filled with crime and espionage books blocking out most of the good-for-me books that Tommy bought before he knew better.

"Dinner's ready," Laura called.

Violet took one last look at the J. Crew teens lounging on the lawn outside of their suburban high school, and pulled herself from the TV. Before sitting down to dinner I took a look out of one of the picture windows that line the back wall of the loft. The building rises above the river; for more than a hundred years that river was polluted by the unrestrained dumping of chemicals, dyes, and waste products from the factories that used to feed and clothe Port Grace and surrounding towns. Now, the river is clean, but the unemployment rate is high.

Dinner was penne tossed with pink sauce and baby peas, garlic bread and salad. Laura and I tried to draw Violet into conversation. "The A's are my team," I said. "That's who I grew up with. I can't change just because I live here."

Laura rose to the challenge. "Do you think the A's engender the loyalty that the Red Sox and Yankees do?"

"Of course not. They don't have the history. And it's hard to be a fan these days. Just when you fall in love with a team, they trade them all away."

"What do you think?" Laura asked Violet.

"I don't watch baseball," she said.

"Tell Ginger your idea about flower containers."

She ducked her head and spoke shyly. "I was thinking you could go to flea markets and yard sales."

Laura interjected. "She was looking through my magazines and picked up on the rustic look that's so popular now, flowers in rusty buckets, old coffee cans."

Violet fiddled with her braids. "My Grandma and I used to go to the Deer Point Flea Market every Sunday." She gazed into the middle distance, thinking, I assumed, about her grandmother. I took a bite of garlic bread and looked at Laura, who shrugged. Flowers got us through the meal. Laura used to own a small shop on River Street, but she couldn't manage both street traffic and events such as weddings and parties. She preferred the latter, and so when the loft became available, she moved her business in and converted to an events-only florist.

When the dishes were washed and the table wiped clean Laura said, "Violet and I have something to discuss with you." I looked up from the bowl of freesias I had my nose in, and took in the two of them, Laura, curvy, warm, and luminous, and Violet, both translucent and opaque. She continued. "I've invited Violet to live with me while things get sorted out."

I was surprised. My take on Laura was that she cherishes her privacy. It was a big jump from taking Violet in for a couple weeks to an offer of indefinitely. I didn't think she understood the implications of her offer. "That's very generous," I said. "But let's take it one day at a time for now. Not make any big decisions."

"She's a good helper. I'm up to my ears in proms and weddings, and graduation season is right around the corner."

But she can work for you without living with you, I wanted to say. Not that I was going to take Violet home. I can't fix everything in my clients' lives. Sometimes I can't fix anything. One of my dirty little secrets? Sometime I get tired of clients. I take them on with gusto and they are thrilled to have me run interference for them. Eventually the honeymoon ends and they become just another case. Why? The tedium of litigation sets in. I can't work magic for them. Their gratefulness turns to annoyance at the judicial system. They don't want to pay me. They call me too often, are too needy, new clients come along with fresh and interesting problems. I get overwhelmed. Sometimes though, I am stunned by the uniqueness of each client's story.

All the tiny particulars that make them who they are—the flick of a cigarette, licking the cake batter, the smell of a fresh-cut lawn, an angry voice, a half-heard song. That's what keeps me going. And so, when Violet came to me a year ago, delicate, bruised, and pregnant, I tackled her case wholeheartedly. Hers was a dismal history and one I had heard too many times. I helped her get the restraining order against AJ, enrolled her in a prenatal clinic, escorted her through the public benefits maze, and introduced her to Laura, who she worked for until Teddy was born. Then, I closed out her file and she dropped off my radar screen.

"Good for you," I said to Violet. "You're learning some job skills. And Laura, that's a very kind offer. But it would be best if we consider this a short-term situation."

Images floated through the room: Teddy on a respirator, prison bars, an exhausted and desperate Violet alone with a baby who would not stop crying. We did not speak of these apparitions, but I am certain that we all saw them.

14

Mama Jo's is located on Little River Road, within a three-block area that is Port Grace's nod to all that is hip, counterculture, cutting edge, and avant-garde—a coffee bar, head shop, used-book store, vegetarian restaurant, galleries, burrito stand, and a record store stocked with plenty of vinyl.

The gallery was thick with black clothes and self-confidence. "I don't know about this," I said to Laura. My knowledge of art is limited to a college survey class, where the professor dimmed the lights and showed slides, most of which I slept through; plus some forays into museums with Tommy, for whom art is part of the American culture curriculum, as in *From Rockwell to Rothko, the Nexus of 20th Century Culture, Politics, and Society.*

"Just for a few minutes," Laura replied. "We'll say hi to Miles, check out the paintings, and then go for a drink."

All of the paintings incorporated grids into the composition. I was bewitched by a six-foot canvas with an aggressive black rectangle brushed into the center of the canvas. Within that black rectangle was a men's basketball game on a ragged city court. The outer grid boxes framed urban vignettes: a graffiti-covered wall, children in the park, a man ascending the steps of a city bus, laundry pegged on a line that stretched from an apartment window. As I studied it, I heard a big voice blow over the rest of the chatter.

"Ginger Rae!" It was Eduardo Fortunato with his fiancée clinging to him.

"Eduardo. I didn't know you were an art lover."

"I'm not. But Giselle wants to collect."

"Nice to see you," I said to Giselle. And it was, even though she is one of those awe-inspiring women—good-looking, smart, and successful. To top it off, she's a pediatrician.

"This time I'm marrying a professional," Eduardo told me when I drew up their prenuptial agreement. Despite her excessive qualifications she is friendly and unpretentious, with a wicked sense of humor.

"What do you think?" Giselle asked me about the painting.

"I can't decide if it's Norman Rockwellish or something grittier; it's teetering, I think." Damn! I sounded like an art critic! Where did that come from?

"Which would you like it to be?" She sounded genuinely interested.

"Gritty, hands down. I'm not a Rockwell fan."

"Did somebody say Rockwell?" Miles edged his way into our little group with a bemused look on his face.

"Basketball," I said, hoping to cover my stupid critique as I watched him and Eduardo knuckle bump. Eduardo introduced him to Giselle and then turned to me. "We've met," I said.

Miles looked at me. "Laura's friend. The lawyer. And I know you said Rockwell. You think I'm a black Norman Rockwell?" He tossed a challenging glance my way.

"Not necessarily," I replied.

Just then Mama Jo walked up to us. "Miles, come with me," she said, grasping him firmly by the arm. "There's a photographer from the *Herald.*"

She led him away and I exhaled. "That was close."

"I'm going for wine," Giselle said. "Can I get you some?"

"No thanks." Eduardo and I watched her gracefully maneuver her way through the crowd. Her dress was a glorious shade of periwinkle and her shoes were lavender, mocking the black uniform the rest of us wore. "How do you know Miles?" I asked Eduardo.

"Oh, you know. Around," he answered. Around could mean a lot of things with Eduardo; in addition to being a top criminal defense attorney, he owns blocks of city real estate, and is partner in several businesses, including a restaurant/nightclub and a minor league baseball team. He didn't seem inclined to offer a more detailed explanation and I knew better than to pry. "How's business?" he asked.

"Busy."

"Is Marco staying with you after he graduates?"

"I hope so." I felt a twinge of nerves at the thought of losing Marco.

"It's too noisy to talk," he said as he waved to someone across the room. "Call me; I'll buy you lunch."

I wanted to leave, so I looked for Laura. I would return another day for a closer look at the paintings, which disturbed me.

Laura suggested a drink.

"How about coffee?" I said.

"Good idea. I don't need alcohol. I've got a major wedding tomorrow."

We ambled down Little River Street toward the coffee shop. "How do you manage by yourself?" I asked. "Flowers for a wedding must be labor-intensive."

"I get grunt help. But the arrangements I do myself."

"How's it going with Violet?"

"Fine. She's a quick study. I've got her making corsages and boutonnieres, and she's doing nicely."

The Fresh Roast had tables outside, grasping the breath of spring that swirled around us, but they were occupied, as were the inside tables. "I'll make coffee at my place," Laura said.

As we drove I told her, "I appreciate what you're doing for

Violet, but it's way beyond the call of duty. Say the word if you want her out."

"I will. Don't worry. I won't let her mess up my life. It's just that I feel responsible."

"Responsible for what?"

"For her. For what happened. She worked for me almost until the baby was born. She was a good worker and didn't talk about her personal life. I respected that and never inquired."

Drop the guilt, I thought. "She worked for you for two months. You don't owe her anything."

"I visited her once after the baby was born. Her grandmother was sick, and Violet was taking care of both her and her baby. I saw how burdened she was, and I didn't do anything about it. I meant to, but I got caught up in my own stuff. You know? And forgot about her. And there's something." She paused and picked at her sweater, buttoning and unbuttoning one of the mother-of pearl-buttons. I was driving but I felt her nervousness. "There's something about her that makes me feel complete," she finally said.

"What do you mean, complete?"

"Like something was missing and now it's there."

I had no idea how to respond, so I didn't. Just kept driving. Thinking about Tommy. Maybe I should have gone to New York with him. Jake was planning to sleep over at a friend's house and it would just be Cat and me. I don't like to be alone. Laura said something that I missed. "I'm sorry, what did you say?"

"I used to be a social worker. In fact I was a caseworker for DCW for several years."

"No kidding." I took a moment to process that, to integrate Laura the Social Worker with Laura the Florist. Well into her forties, she could have easily had another career or two, but she seemed so thoroughly Laura the Florist that it was difficult to picture her as anything else. "What happened?"

"The usual story. I burnt out. I wanted to change the world and thought I could do it by helping kids. But it was too much. Too many cases, not enough time or resources. This was in the 80s. The crack epidemic was a cataclysm; Port Grace was devastated. Foster care placements doubled, everything bad doubled."

"That's an unusual leap," I said. "From social work to flowers."

"Is it?" She paused. "A baby died. Because I thought it was safe to send her home."

I steered into the warehouse parking lot and cut the engine. We sat in silence. The moon was full; it was the beginning or the end of the lunar cycle, I'm never sure which; and the transparent moonlight clashed with the offensively bright security lights.

"I'm sorry," I said. "I'm sure it wasn't your fault."

She ran her fingers through her hair. "It was my fault. Obviously I wasn't the ultimate decision-maker, the judge was. But I was the front line, the one who went into the home and got services for the family. I had the hands-on knowledge of the situation, and I made the recommendation to the judge. To send the baby home." She leaned against the window. "After that I quit. They probably would have fired me; somebody had to be held accountable. It didn't matter; I couldn't work there anymore, I couldn't be responsible for anyone or anything."

"Why flowers?"

"My apartment was near the old Bay Road Florist. Remember them?"

I shook my head.

"Before your time. Anyway, after I left DCW I crashed for a few months; I was utterly depressed. Eventually I crawled out and started taking walks. There was a help-wanted sign in the florist window. I've been in the business ever since."

Earlier that evening I had stepped into Laura's massive stainless steel refrigerator that is filled with buckets of sunflowers, lilacs, narcissus, roses, bluebells, more flowers than I could name. "Flowers make people happy," I said.

"Yes. They do. Want to come up for coffee?"

"No thanks, I've gotta get going. Back to work, I'm afraid." I looked out of the car window. Floodlights revealed scrubby grass and not much else. "You could use some landscaping. This place is pretty bare, considering a bunch of artists live here."

"Don't blame me. I only deal with plants that don't have roots." She opened the car door. "I had a good time tonight."

"Me too."

She ran to her building. She ran like a child does, both awkward and light.

15

I woke up missing Tommy. His side of the bed was unrumpled, his pillow too smooth. I clutched the pillow and inhaled the Tommy scent of books and cinnamon. My loneliness abated slightly when I remembered that Jake was home; sixteen-year-old Jake who tiptoed in well past his midnight curfew. He made an effort to silence his tread until I called to him, and then he poked his head into my room looking sheepish and slightly intoxicated.

"Hey," I said. "I thought you were sleeping at Jeremy's."

"I wanted to sleep in my own bed," he said. "J's floor doesn't cut it."

"How did you get home?"

"Some girl gave me a ride."

Some girl. "I would have picked you up. You know that no matter where you are or how late it is, we'll pick you up."

"I know. Sorry I'm a little late. I knew this girl could give me a ride but it took a while, she had to talk to people and stuff. And anyway I thought you'd be asleep."

"Nope. I got into my book."

"What is it?"

I held it up. "*A Lesson Before Dying.* It's about a man on death row, and another man who's sort of lost and becomes his friend. Your father gave it to me."

"Sounds depressing."

"Actually, it's not. But it's not a movie of the week either. It's got some grit."

"Cool." He shifted, ready to leave but too polite to just go.

"I'm glad you're home. Did you have a good time?"

"It was fun. Well, I'm gonna get a snack," he said. "Growing boy and all that."

"Good night, Jake."

"Night, Ginger."

I released Tommy's pillow and forced myself out of bed, and into sweats and running shoes. I fed Cat, and then jogged to the river path where I managed a few token stretches, and then took off. The river path is the result of one of the periodic attempts that are made to gentrify Port Grace. It winds along the river, past residential neighborhoods, the courthouse complex, the three high-rises that signal downtown, past waterfront restaurants, fishing piers, factories and mills, some boarded up and others converted to office space, artist studios, and subsidized housing.

My thoughts drifted as my body became increasingly focused and defined, slicing through air, space, and time. I started running in seventh grade, the year I first made the long trek to the regional middle/high school. That was the early 80s, when Keds and Converse were shelved and Adidas and Nike became the thing. I ran right through high school and into scholarship offers from state schools, but by then I wanted to be as far from the Central Valley as possible, preferably near a large body of water. I signed up with an East Coast university trying to improve their women's basketball team and increase their diversity percentage. I gave them both—I had learned that checking the Native-American box unlocked doors. "San Diego has water," Dad said. "So does Santa Barbara." That was his effort to convince me to stay close; but I couldn't and he knew why; he left the same town when he was eighteen, blowing off basketball scholarship offers and signing on the dotted line for Vietnam, which was a lot farther from the Valley than the East Coast was.

After my run, feeling sweaty and virtuous, I showered, dressed, and knocked on Jake's door. "Want to go to breakfast?"

"Sure," he mumbled from the depth of sleep and dreams. "Give me a few minutes."

I knew that a few minutes meant at least half an hour, so I capitalized on my sense of well being, stuffed a load of whites into the washing machine, and called Tommy. "How's your mom?"

"So-so." He didn't want to talk about her. She was sliding into dementia, to the point where Tommy wanted her to move into an assisted-care home, but of course she didn't want to. His father is dead and his sister has three kids, a full-time job, and lives in Chicago, so Tommy makes the decisions. "I'm trying to talk her into coming to live near us," he said, "but every time I mention it she gets upset." He sounded miserable.

"I'm sorry." It was all I could say. "What time will you be home?"

"Between four and five, I hope."

"I'll cook dinner. And then let's go to a movie."

"That sounds great," he said. "How's Jake?"

"Fine. We're going out to breakfast soon."

"I wish I was going with you."

"I wish you were too." When I hung up I heard the shower running and Jake singing. I made the bed, watered the plants, and sorted through mail that had accumulated into a tower of catalogs, sweepstakes offers, and no-annual-fee credit card solicitations. I tossed most of it into the recycling bin and sat on the porch to wait for Jake. Mrs. McCarthy next door was fussing with her daffodils. In May precise rows of red and yellow tulips fill her flowerbeds, and in June she pulls them out and plants marigolds and snapdragons, which last until late September when the chrysanthemums go in. "Your flowers are beautiful," I called to her.

She looked up. "Ginger Rae! I haven't seen you in a dog's age."

"Winter and work," I replied.

She cupped her hand to her ear. "What's that?"

I raised my voice. "I've been working a lot." I stood up and walked over to the small picket fence between our yards.

She came to her side of the fence, trowel in hand. "Dandelions!" she said. "They'll be the death of me."

"I think they're kind of pretty."

"Oh no! They're weeds. Pests. Did you have dandelions in California?"

"We had mustard flowers. They cover the hills. I think they're pretty, but even my dad calls them weeds."

"How is your father?"

"He's doing well, thank you."

"He's a nice man. And he was so helpful, turning over my beds when he visited you. Those were dreadful days, that week after September 11. It was early to put my mums in, but I found that gardening eased my mind a bit. I think your father felt the same way."

The front door slammed and Jake bounded down the steps. "I'm ready, Ginger. Hi, Mrs. McCarthy."

She waved to him and said, "He's such a nice boy. He helped me take my recycling to the curb last week." We watched him pick up a basketball and dribble along the driveway.

"Nice to see you," I said to Mrs. McCarthy.

"You too, dear. And say hello to that cute husband of yours."

I walked toward Jake. "One on one?" he challenged.

"Maybe after breakfast," I said. "I'm starving. I've been up for hours, unlike some people."

"He tossed the ball back to its resting place under the porch steps. "Let's rock."

"The Boat?" I asked, and he nodded.

"How's your knee?" He indicated my left knee, the thick scars a reminder of how life can be shattered in an instant. My left knee blown out on a foul by a nasty player, the termination of my college playing days, the genesis of my civil war. Surgeries and painkillers. Yellow-page doctors who, for the price of an office visit, wrote scrips for more painkillers. Rituals of vodka and orange juice. Flunking classes. The summer after my junior year spent in summer school and waitressing at the Anchor House, where I hooked up with a bartender who sold cocaine and always knew where the party was. But Jake didn't need to know all that.

"My knee is fine."

Jake had his learner's permit, so I let him drive to the Drunken Boat, our favorite breakfast place, even though I was totally nervous with him behind the wheel. "When you gonna get a real car?" he asked, as he carefully backed out of the driveway.

"What's a real car?"

"You're a lawyer. Shouldn't you be driving a Beamer or a Benz?"

"I'm not that kind of lawyer. And even if I had the bucks I wouldn't put them on the road."

"Why not?" He waited patiently for an old lady to figure out that the light had turned green.

"It's not something I care about. It's a car. Gets me from one place to the next."

"I'm gonna have a nice car."

"When did you become so materialistic?"

"I'm not. I've got a few gearhead friends; it's easy to get into that stuff. Besides, you're the one who's always so paranoid about car wrecks. I bet this thing doesn't even have air bags." He angled for a parking spot next to a Trans Am.

"Is that a real car?" I asked.

"It's awesome. But it's old."

"Sometimes old is good."

"Yeah, but no air bags."

My observations of Tommy and Jake and my years with Jake have made me aware that the relationship between parent and child is not static, but is cumulative, organic, constantly in process. Parenthood is a subject Tommy and I discuss too often, because he wants us to have a child and I don't. The conversations are all alike.

"Do you think I don't want kids because my mother left me?"

"What do you think?"

I try to imagine the desire for a child, to picture myself feeding a baby applesauce, and playing peek-a-boo, and I can't. "Maybe it's because I have no image of a mother, so I don't know how to be one. Do you think there's a genetic component, like she and I don't have the mothering gene?"

"Probably not."

"Like alcoholism. Some people are born with a genetic predisposition. Maybe I'm not predisposed to have children."

"Maybe you're scared."

"Of what?

"You tell me."

"You think I'm afraid I'll do what my mother did?"

"Ginger, you'd be a great mother. Don't be so hard on yourself. You've got a lot of baggage; you should see someone to help you sort it out."

The conversation generally ended there, because I refuse to

see a shrink.

My mother? She was young, she hated the Valley, my father wasn't who she thought he was, it was 1972 in California, a time and place of alternative lifestyles, and she knew Dad's family would take care of me. Or, maybe she just hated me. Hated the burden I was. Hated the endless cycle of sterilizing bottles and rinsing diapers, of a baby who wouldn't sleep, who morphed into a pesky toddler. Hated having a depressed Vietnam vet husband anesthetized by marijuana, a father-in-law dying of cancer, and a home in the hot, smoggy Central Valley surrounded by white trash and Mexicans, Merle Haggard and Bob Wills and his Texas Playboys. No wonder she took off and never looked back.

After breakfast I took Jake home, picked up the dry-cleaning and stopped at the market to buy the ingredients for spaghetti, one of the few things I know how to cook. Pink tulips for the table. This, I thought, is what Saturday is like for people who don't work all the time. Breakfast with the kid, chores, errands, being kind to the people you love. I decided to make brownies too. Jake would be eating with us and I was looking forward to it. We—Jake, Tommy, and I, are, in our own peculiar way, a family.

16

Laura called at eight o'clock on Sunday morning. I was asleep, but Tommy woke me. "Sorry to call so early," she said.

"No problem. What's up?"

"I have a major wedding out in Jackson. I tried to talk Violet into coming along to help, but she refuses. I'll be gone from about nine to three, and I was wondering if you would call her, or drop by. I'm a little worried."

"Of course," I said. "Tell her I'll call later." After we disconnected I rolled over and tried to go back to sleep. No luck. My plan had been to take the whole weekend off, to focus on home, Tommy and Jake. But Laura was right; Violet shouldn't be left alone for too long. And for some reason it was my responsibility. So I got of bed, drank a couple mugs of coffee, and read the Sunday comics. Tommy and I took a walk through the neighborhood, bought doughnuts from Marco's uncle, and before I knew it, it was eleven o'clock. I dialed Laura's number but Violet didn't pick up, so I drove to the loft.

She didn't answer the door either, and I banged on it until I was plenty pissed off and planning to leave. Miles heard me, and came out into the hall. "What are you doing?" he asked.

"Laura's out for the day and . . ." I stopped, uncertain about how to explain Violet. "I promised to stop in and see someone who's staying with her."

"That girl?"

"Yeah. That girl."

"Hold on. I have a key." He disappeared, and reappeared holding a key with a long red ribbon attached.

"Thank you so much." I was cooling down and starting to worry that Violet had gone out, or that there was some other, worse reason that she didn't come to the door. But first I wanted to talk to Miles. "I enjoyed your show," I said.

"I went looking for you, but you were gone."

"It was too crowded. I'm planning to go back though."

"Why don't I meet you there? I'd like to hear what you think."

"Okay. Sure. I'm just not sure when. I'm super-busy at work."

"I'll call you," he said. "I'll get your number from Laura."

"Sounds good." I put the key in the door. Hopefully Laura would also tell him I'm married.

Violet was in her room, in bed with the TV on. "Didn't you hear me banging on the door?" I asked, annoyed that my Sunday was interrupted for this.

She curled up small. "I was asleep," she said, "and when I heard the banging I got scared."

"Scared of what?"

"Loud noises, I guess."

"Get dressed and we'll go out to lunch."

"I'm not hungry."

"Get dressed anyway."

"Will you take me to see Teddy?"

That was not what I wanted to do on a stunning spring Sunday afternoon. "Yes, I'll take you to see Teddy. But not until you eat something." Thin to start with, Violet looked like she'd lost weight over the last ten days. "Go take a shower. I'll fix you some food."

She ate about one-third of the scrambled eggs and toast I prepared for her and then we left for the hospital. Just for the hell of it I took a roundabout route, crossing the river and driving through potholed streets lined with light industry and junkyards, then across the river again, past decrepit row houses and desolate apartment buildings, out to Deer Point where Marco lives and well-maintained two-family houses nestle up to each other. I followed the Old Bay Road for a while, and looked longingly at the water, but turned west on Bay Avenue and drove to the hospital. I was quiet, hoping Violet might talk. She didn't, so I flipped on the CD player and we listened to the Cold Play until I pulled into the hospital parking lot.

"What a beautiful day," I said as we got out of the car.

Violet didn't answer. As we crossed the avenue to the main entrance she asked, "When do you think Teddy will get better?"

"I don't know. Have you talked to the doctor recently?"

She shook her head.

"I'll try to find someone we can talk to." I stepped back to allow a wheelchair and a group of seniors to pass. A man stood up from a bench and walked toward us. I had the quick impression of a young man wearing a navy windbreaker and a baseball cap pulled down tight; he held a paperback with one of his fingers marking his place. He stopped next to us, close.

"Can I help you?" I said, assuming he wanted a light or directions. Violet looked up from her misery at the same time I realized who he was, and for an instant we were a paralyzed triangle.

"Hi Violet," AJ said.

I was stunned. My impression of him as he walked toward us was cute guy, and as I looked at him up close, in his Red Sox hat, marking his place in Elmore Leonard's *Tishomingo Blues,* I couldn't quite make the emotional transition to my memory of the bulky, sweaty man who stood across the courtroom a year ago. He was bulky still, spent a lot of time with the weights, but wearing a T-shirt for Vinnie's Vipers, a softball team sponsored by a pizzeria, he just looked like a guy on his way to Sunday practice with his buddies. "Why are you here?" I asked, feeling Violet swaying next to me, drawn to him, repelled by him.

"I need to talk to Violet."

"You can't."

"Why not? There's no restraining order."

Those words reminded me that I am a lawyer and taller than him, so I said, "Technically, there still is a restraining order, she never had it dismissed. Come to my office tomorrow and we'll address whether you can talk to Violet."

"Jesus," he said. "After you told me, I called all the hospitals to find out where Teddy is. I got visiting hours and drove all the way down here. I've been waiting two hours to see her and I'm not coming back to go to your office."

I pulled out my business card and handed it to him. "Call me," I said.

He took the card but ignored me. "Violet, why is Teddy in the hospital?"

"I don't know," she said, and started crying.

"Leave her alone," I said.

"Let me talk to her for two minutes. Please."

"It's okay," Violet said.

It was not okay, but I said, "Two minutes. And I'm standing right here." I wanted to watch his actions and reactions.

"What's wrong with Teddy?" he asked her.

"He's in a coma."

"What happened?"

"I don't know. They arrested me, they think I hurt him." He was visibly startled when she said that. "I tried to call you," she continued, "but you never called back."

"You can't be calling me," he said. He lowered his voice. "It's over between us. It's been over for a long time."

Violet grabbed his arm, tried to pull him to her. We were attracting attention.

"That's it," I said, pulling her off of him. "Time's up. You have to go."

He dropped my card on the ground and walked away. I tried to calm Violet.

"Maybe we shouldn't go in today," I said. "You can come tomorrow."

"No. I have to go. I have to see Teddy."

When we exited the hospital I looked around for AJ. I hadn't gotten stalker vibes off of him, but it was certainly possible. I wasn't certain that he fit the classic batterer profile, the one on the brochures at the women's shelter, the controlling manipulative charmer. He seemed like a mean drunk with a wandering eye who was normal, (using a loose definition of normal), when he was sober. "What kind of car does AJ drive?" I asked Violet.

"A truck."

"What kind of truck?"

"I don't know. It's green, I think."

"Like a pickup truck? Or an SUV?"

"Pickup."

"Ford? Chevy? A regular big pickup or one of those small ones?"

"Big, I think. I only was in it one time."

I scanned the street and parking lot. As we drove, I checked my mirrors for a green truck. "Violet. Are you sure you don't have any friends or family who could help you?" To drive you to the hospital, I thought. To watch you cry. To worry about whether AJ is a psycho. "You went to high school here for a couple years, right? Didn't you have any friends then?"

"A few. My grandmother didn't let me go out much."

"Well, who did you hang out with when you did go out? And where are they now?" She counted on her fingers. Jalisa joined the army. Andrea had two babies. Inez worked at a bakery and went to night school. "So these were good kids, your friends. You weren't ever into drugs or anything." I hated hearing myself stereotype her. Like just because she was black and Puerto Rican and went to the city school, she'd be selling crack to little kids. Although her parents were both users, so I wasn't being totally racist.

"No, I stayed away from that stuff."

"What were you going to do? Before you got pregnant?"

"I don't know. Get a job, I guess. Maybe." Maybe what. Her father was a small-time dealer, in prison for a long stretch under the three strikes law, and her mother was a crackhead. Her grandmother was a religious, hardworking woman, but she was dead. What did I expect her to say? What kind of plans could she have?

"Your friend Inez? She works here in Port Grace?" Violet nodded. "Do you want to go see her? It would be good for you to have a friend to talk to."

"No. I don't want to tell anybody."

"I need the names and addresses of some relatives. I have to contact somebody."

"That stuff is at the apartment. But nobody's going to help."

I didn't want to go back to that apartment. I'd get the information some other time. "You want something to eat?" I asked her.

She shook her head.

I drove her back to Laura's, slowly, pulling over now and then, watching for a green pickup truck.

17

Monday morning Marco and I bludgeoned our way through our weekly case conference. Violet topped my list of hot cases. "I want you to talk to her neighbors again," I said. "Go at a different time of day so the ones you missed before might be home. Push them. Did anyone see or hear anything unusual in the last month? Did they see AJ coming or going? Alone, with Violet, with the baby? Did they notice anyone or anything unusual? How well did they know Violet? Just let them talk, and maybe you'll pick up something helpful. Also, when you have a chance, see what you can get on AJ—friends, family, juvenile record, gossip, whatever. I'm filing for a paternity hearing. I want a DNA test done to establish that he is Teddy's father."

"Is that relevant?"

"Could go to motive—if Teddy's his baby and he didn't want his wife to find out. Or he was angry with Violet because she didn't have an abortion. It ties him more tightly to the case."

"The best defense is a good offense?"

"Exactly. And remember, the best way to establish reasonable doubt is to establish a plausible case that someone else did it." The trial date was set for September. I hoped that Teddy would come out of his coma long before then, and the criminal charges would be dropped. Unfortunately I had to think and act as though there would be a trial, which meant developing theories, locating witnesses, and conducting investigations. The maxim is:

Prepare for trial and there won't be one; don't prepare, and there will.

Marco sprawled comfortably in my client chair. "Five weeks," he said.

"Five weeks what?"

He looked mildly disappointed.

"You're graduating! I can't believe it slipped my mind." I thumped myself on the head.

"That's it. No more school for me." He smiled like a kitty with cream in the bowl. "Got some job offers too." He ticked them off. "The Public Defender and the D.A.; Lenrow and Shapiro; Severino, Esposito and White. And the department brass might have something good for me. I thought I'd burned my bridges, but it seems I've got some pull there."

I sat back in my chair. "That's quite a list. Congratulations. But." I paused.

"What?"

"I can't believe we haven't talked about it."

"You want to talk? Let's talk."

"You never told me if you want to stay on here."

"You never asked." He sat up straight, looked me in the eye. "I assumed there wasn't enough room for both of us. Two lawyers."

"Want something to drink?" I asked, grasping a minute to collect my thoughts.

"Just water, thanks."

I pulled a Coke and bottled water from the fridge and sat back down. "We should have discussed this long ago. I can't believe I haven't asked you about your plans."

"It's okay. I'm so busy that I haven't been focusing on it. But the jobs want answers, like yesterday. So if I don't take it they can offer the spot to someone else."

I felt the zap of jealousy. "Those are great offers. They'd be lucky to have you." I stood up and walked to the window. Mr. Ziznewski was sweeping the front walk, and the forsythia shrubs had developed buds overnight. I turned back to Marco and was overcome with the feeling that I was shrinking and he was growing. My office was cramped, the work tedious; I saw myself for what I am: a grunt of the legal world. "I can't imagine this office without you."

"Is that an offer?"

"I don't want to lose you. I don't want to work with anybody else. But you could do better. A lot better." I stared at my soda can, then pressed it against my forehead. It was cold and damp, and more than anything I wanted to dive into a deep, cool lake, the lake in Miles's painting. "I want you to stay. And not as an associate. Partner. But I don't think it's the right thing for you."

He flexed his fingers, pondered his knuckles. "I don't want to go to the D.A.'s office with all the young kids. I hate criminal defense. I'd go nuts working for a big firm. I want to be my own boss. And you and I? We work well together. You need a little fine-tuning, but I can live with that."

I knew that I should be punching out calculations and analyzing risk-benefits before I offered partner. But if Marco left my life would be duller, I would miss him terribly, and the office might fall apart. Besides, he would be a great lawyer. I raised my Coke can. "All right then. A toast to Reddy and Tavares."

"Not Tavares and Reddy?"

I tapped the can against his Poland Spring bottle. "Nope." I felt suddenly, immoderately, happy.

"I might want to take on some other kinds of cases," Marco said.

"Now you tell me. Like what?"

"Maybe environmental law. Or police brutality."

"Go for it. I trust your judgment. I only have one question."

"What's that?"

"Will you still make the coffee?"

"Absolutely."

"Good. Now get to work." He started to leave my office, and still feeling happy I said, "Hey, Marco." He turned. "How about I take you out to dinner tonight? To celebrate."

"Cool."

Only then did I think of Tommy. I left a message on his office voice mail telling him about Marco and dinner and to call me. I started writing a motion for Mary Abbott, whose husband was monkeying with their bank accounts and had cut off Mary's credit cards. He was an ass for doing that, but Mary was making me feel foolish—I had to persuasively argue that she was entitled to $500 every month for hair care, massages, and manicures. She also insisted on a monthly $2,000 for clothes, $65 for dog grooming, and a one-time $300 consultation fee for a feng shui expert to clear the house of the bad vibes that lingered from a sour marriage. I had given her a budget form to fill out that usually serves as a reality check for clients who think that two households can be maintained on the income that supported one. But her budget was unrealistic. I tried to explain to her. "At the hearing, the judge will make a temporary order of support and any other pending issues. It will probably set the tone for how he will rule at the divorce trial, if we go to trial, which we shouldn't."

"Why not?"

"It's too expensive, financially and emotionally. It's always better to settle."

"I want him to pay for what he did."

"What happened to the spiritual divorce?"

"Maybe later. Right now I want to hurt him like he hurt me."

"I understand that. But I don't think your budget is realistic. Even with his income, you won't be able to maintain the lifestyle you are used to. And if the judge thinks you're acting frivolously or for revenge, he'll get irritated."

"So what am I supposed to do?"

I tried to be gentle, I really did. "It's a matter of spending less or earning more. You might have to get a job." This was an annoying part of having a high-income client. Not truly wealthy, but rich enough that she had no perspective on the way most of the world lives. Hello? I wanted to say. Most women work. And your kid is in college, so what are you doing all day? But I didn't. I said, "You might have to shop at Macy's instead of Nordstrom. Maybe the dog can go to the groomer every two months." I tapped the budget sheet. "Realistically, the house will probably have to be sold. If you continue to live there, he's going to be living in a basement apartment."

"So, let him."

Deep breath. "The law says your property has to be equitably distributed. That means fairly divided. Do you think an objective person would consider it fair if you keep the five-bedroom house and he's in a studio?"

"Whose lawyer are you?"

Tommy hadn't called by the time I finished drafting the motion, so I decided to drive to the college for lunch and surprise him. I was preparing to leave, when the phone rang. It was Miles Stephano. "Hey," he said. "Want to set a date to meet at the gallery?"

I looked at my calendar. "I'm kind of overwhelmed right now. Let me call you back when I figure out how to free up some time."

"Sure. Anytime."

I hung up and stared at the phone for a minute. Then I left for Winslow College, a small liberal arts haven, an 80-acre oasis in the middle of Port Grace. While driving, I called the English Department and was informed that Tommy was teaching a seminar that ended at twelve-thirty. I noted the classroom number and decided to wait outside and surprise him. I never do things like that, and I knew it would please him.

It was the perfect day to be a college student—seventy degrees and sunny. The quad was filled with exuberant youth, and for an instant I felt tired and old. Then I hurried toward Hamilton Hall; I was late as always, and if I missed Tommy I didn't want to have to search the campus for him. He's the only person I know who doesn't carry a cell phone. I followed the brick path that winds around the oldest buildings on campus, looking with envy at the students in their spring attitudes, and almost bumped into Tommy. And the young woman he was with.

"Ginger!" he said. "What are you doing here?"

"I came to have lunch with you."

He looked at the young woman next to him and I did too. She was perfect: 5'3″, slender, shiny brown hair, calm and poised. Lissome. Lithe. Blithe. Someone who knew the difference between Socrates and Sophocles. A short, pretty intellectual, in a Winslow Lacrosse T-shirt. "This is Stephanie; she's in my senior seminar," Tommy said. "And this is my wife, Ginger."

I didn't feel like being gracious but I tried. I stuck out my hand. "Nice to meet you."

"You too," she said, smiling. Then, to Tommy, "Thanks, Professor Burns. Have a good lunch." She waved and walked in some other direction.

"What is she thanking you for?" I asked Tommy.

He answered automatically. "Helping her with her senior thesis." Then my tone caught up with him. "You can't possibly be jealous." I didn't answer. "Ginger, that's ridiculous, I would never, ever take up with one of my students. Even if I wasn't married."

"I know you wouldn't. I'm not jealous of her." I looked around. "It's more the idea of her. Of this whole place." I gestured in a semicircle, taking in the gothic chapel, a group of girls in shorts and crop tops, athletic guys playing Frisbee, the sound of Dave Matthews undulating from an open dorm window. "It's just so darn wholesome. I crawl out of the slime pit of humanity to see you, and find you walking through Eden with this girl who doesn't have a care in the world."

He took my hand. "Let's walk," he said. "This place is far from perfect, and these kids have plenty of problems. Maybe those problems aren't as complex as what you see every day, but they're real. The bulimic girls, the kids who cheat because they're worried about getting into med school, and then get expelled when they get caught cheating, the ones who graduated high school without learning how to write a research paper and are flunking their classes, the injured athletes, the unplanned pregnancies, kids who go to frat parties and drink themselves into alcohol poisoning . . ."

I don't know if he did it intentionally, but he jogged me into the scars on my left knee, and the life-altering injury that caused them. When I was in college. "You're right," I said. "I don't know why I'm being such a jerk. I was just walking along, thinking what an incredible place this is, and how my college education was a waste; I'd like to start over, so I could learn something. And besides, she was so damn cute."

He stopped walking and pulled me to him. "I love you," he said. "Don't ever doubt that." I didn't doubt it. But I also clearly saw his happiness as he strolled along with her.

I met Marco at the restaurant at seven o'clock. I told him to choose and he picked the Bay House, a big, dependable steak and seafood restaurant owned by his cousin Gino, and commonly called Gino's. I urged him to try something new. "There's a barbeque place in one of the old warehouses that's supposed to be great."

"Isn't the owner one of those rap producers?"

"Maybe. But so what?"

"Those people are thugs. I'm not giving them my money."

"First of all, dinner is my treat, so it's not your money. Second, you should be more open-minded; rap can be extremely clever and creative."

"Ginger. I used to be on the job. Those guys hate cops. They'll make me in a New York minute, and let's just say it'll be an uncomfortable evening."

"How about Marie's Garden?"

"The portions are too small. Order a steak and they bring this tiny thing that's gone in two bites. And it's surrounded by vegetables that nobody ever heard of. Anyway, didn't you say this was my choice? A celebration of my partnership?"

"You're right. I'll meet you at Gino's."

Gino's was a good choice—spacious, crowded, noisy, and cheerful. The food was excellent and the portions were large. Marco and I were celebrities; as news of his upcoming graduation and our partnership blew through the restaurant, a steady stream of people stopped by our table to buy him a beer and make sure I knew how fortunate I was. The whole place was suffused with celebratory energy: the swordfish mounted on the wall, the fishing net draped from the ceiling, the beer that I couldn't drink, the men slapping Marco on the back, the women who kissed him, the fish chowder, the bay breeze that drifted through the windows evoking journeys taken, journeys missed, and journeys only dreamed of.

After dinner we carried our coffee and zabaglione onto the deck, and stood at the rail admiring night on the water. The temperature had dropped considerably through the course of the evening, and we were alone. Marco put his arm around me, and I felt such a longing. But I pulled away. "Coffee's getting cold," I said, and sat down. "This is exciting." He was still looking out across the bay, lost in some other place. I attended to my zabaglione and berries.

Finally he joined me. "Did you say something?"

"I said, this is exciting. Us being partners. We'll do great things. I'm so stuck in the family law groove that I never thought about trying something else. Like environmental law? Where did you get that idea?"

He shrugged. "I took a class in law school. But it's really because of the river. When I was a little kid? It was nasty. My mom wouldn't let me near it. And over the years I've watched it get cleaner and cleaner, fish live in there now, it's vital again. And that's all because of environmental regulations. But I was also thinking about land use, about this city. This is my city; I've lived here my whole life. I hardly ever left. But over thirty years the city's changed too, mostly for the better, but not all. And it's going to keep changing. And I'd like to have a hand in that, because I know this city as well as anybody could."

"Sounds like you might become a politician," I said lightly, although I was moved by his little speech.

"Maybe. Who knows? I just want to try to do positive work. Some of the cases you worked on? I don't know how you did it; you've seen some horrible stuff."

"You were a city cop. You've seen your share of the show."

"True."

"What was the worst thing you ever saw?"

He answered promptly. "Guy tried to cut off ex-girlfriend's head. Hands down the worst. Worse than homicides, worse than anything. Because she was still alive, you know? When we found her? Somehow that made it worse. I mean it's good she was alive, but she had to live the rest of her life with personal knowledge of evil. Does that make any sense?"

"Sure. I'm with you."

"What about you? What case gave you the most trouble?"

"When I was with the D.A. Baby girl. Eighteen months old. Beaten and sodomized. Her mother lived with two men, and all three of them were arrested. She was in a coma when we caught the case. And then she died." I pushed my remaining zabaglione around the bowl with my fork. "If any case could have kept me a prosecutor, it would have been that one."

"Jesus," Marco said.

"Oh and you know what? Her name was Precious. Can you beat that? Her mother names her Precious and then lets her boyfriends rape her."

"She was in a coma? And she died?"

"Well, yeah," I said. "But that doesn't always happen. People often come out of comas."

We both stared into space, momentarily trapped in our glimpses of hell. It's difficult to articulate those cases—the truly brutal ones—to make them a narrative, to give them a beginning, middle, and end, because framing them turns them into a story and detracts from the reality of terror and evil.

"This isn't a good game," Marco said.

"No, it's not. But this is what I don't get. Why, when the reality is nothing anybody would ever want to confront, are people so hooked on crime shows? Think about it. All those *Law and Order*s. *CSI, The Wire, The Shield.* There's tons of them."

"Some of them are good."

"And movies. And books. Crime and mystery have their own huge sections in bookstores."

"I like them too."

"Even when you were in uniform?"

"Yeah. I found it validating. I think I became a cop because of Jimmy Smits on *NYPD Blue.* He always looked good. And he got to marry Kim Delaney. She looked good too."

"But the reality wasn't like that, was it?"

"Of course not, it was real. It was full of tragedies. Ordinary tragedies, that don't cause headlines, but they ruin people's lives."

"The Kim Delaney character was an alcoholic."

"So was the big guy. Sipowicz."

"And Furillo on *Hill Street Blues.* My Dad watched that when I was a kid. And you know what else? The characters in those crime books are always smoking. So anyway, why did you really quit the force? No Kim Delaney?"

He pulled over a chair from the next table and put his feet up on it. He was dressed in his usual jeans and a black crewneck sweater. It took him a while to answer. "I needed to figure out some stuff. I tried to take a leave but the department wouldn't give it to me. So I quit. Fuck 'em." He gestured moodily. "I've worked my whole life, at the docks, the doughnut shop, delivering papers, bagging groceries, you name it. In high school I bussed tables here, and then waitered. I joined the force after high school. Went to night school for six years and got my B.S. in criminal justice. Bartended a couple shifts a week too. I didn't know anything but work. I couldn't get enough."

"Enough what?"

"Money. Credentials. Respect." He moved his feet off of the chair and used one of them to shove it across the deck. We watched it smash into another chair. "My old man died in a car crash when I was seven. He was a drunk. I've spent my whole life trying not to be him."

"So what did you have to figure out?"

"I didn't like being a cop, or at least the cop I was becoming. And then I fell in love. With a woman who knew all about having fun, who kept work in its proper perspective. I discovered that I knew very little about having fun, except for playing music. And sports. She got tired of me and left. I was crushed. First time in my life I didn't know what I wanted to do." He stood up. "Let's get out of here. Go down to the beach?"

"Sure." I paid the bill. Marco said goodbye to everyone in the restaurant, and stopped at the bar for a quick shot of scotch. We exited, crossed the parking lot, and climbed down the dirt path that leads to a small stone-covered patch of beach. The bay was knocking around, tossing whitecaps.

"I thought you liked being a cop," I said.

"I did. I put on that uniform and I became someone. Just like that. I liked it all—the uniform, the gun, the car. The way people reacted when they saw me." He pulled off his boots and socks, rolled up his jeans, let the waves slosh around his feet. I did the same. He continued. "I even liked the structure and the rules. Intimidating people. I discovered that I liked to intimidate people." He zipped his jacket. Black leather. The wind was blowing hard and I smelled spring thunder coming our way. I put my hands in my pockets. The two of us in bare feet and leather jackets; I was suddenly certain that ours would be a good partnership.

"I've seen the way you can intimidate people," I said. "But you rarely do it, and when you do, it's for a good reason."

"But I started to enjoy it. Now I don't. It's a tool I use when I need to."

"What was it about the girl?"

His voice was frayed. "I was nuts about her. The first time I let somebody get that close to me. She got bored with me and went to study in Ireland. I followed her there, but it was too late. I'd lost her. So I hooked up with Liam's family and stayed with them for a few months, drinking pints, playing music, and helping his old man in the shop. Then I went over to Portugal, did a family roots thing. When I came home it was time to start law school."

"Why law school?"

"One more option. Another credential. Maybe I could have

power without being corrupt." He turned to me, moved close. My hair blew around us. "Was I right?" I heard a hairline fracture in his words. "Can there be power without corruption?" He pulled me to him, held me tight for a long, long minute. Our bodies fit together like a change in the weather. A storm was blowing in and we kissed our way deep into it. "Come with me," he whispered. "Let's go to my apartment."

"I can't."

He put his hands under my shirt and his fingers traced a map on my back. I couldn't read the map. "Why not?"

"You know why. And you've had too much to drink."

"It's not about the beer."

"I know." We'd crossed a line and if I went any farther I might never come back.

So I pushed him away.

He picked up his boots and left me on the cold wet sand, missing him. Four years working together and this was the first time I'd seen him vulnerable. Why had I never noticed the darkness that was so obviously a part of him? I stood there for what seemed like a long time, but was probably a few minutes. It was very dark, a sliver of moon lost in that terrifying, endless night sky. When I finally turned around I thought I saw Marco at the top of the path. I waved. Whoever it was disappeared from my sight, and when I reached the top, no one was there.

18

Marco skipped work on Tuesday; he advised the office answering machine that he was taking a personal day. This was good, because I needed a day away from him to shake off the previous night. Wednesday morning he bounced in looking rested and carefree. "How was your day off?" I asked.

"Great. I slept, read, ate, and played softball. I did no work whatsoever."

"Good for you."

"What do you have for me today?"

"Talk to AJ. You'll have to call Western State to find out when he's on."

"Sneak attack or appointment?"

"I assume sneak, so he won't have time to prepare."

"I might get more out of him if I politely request an appointment. He'll like being treated like a professional. Maybe it's just a cheap psychological theory, but I suspect I'll be able to get inside his head faster if he thinks the playing field is level."

"Do whatever you think is right. While you're there you can slap him with this." I handed him a court notice for the paternity hearing. "Tell him that the judge will order him to give saliva. But if he does it on his own, we can dismiss the hearing. I've included the name of a lab up there that will send his swab to the lab here to get worked up with Teddy's."

He stopped by later and reported. "His shift ends at three o'clock. I'm meeting him at a coffee shop up there."

I was impressed. "How did you manage that?"

"He's easy; I've handled a thousand guys like him."

At five-thirty I met up with Tommy to go see Miles's paintings. As we walked along Little River Street I told him about the opening. "I liked the paintings, but they disturbed me and I can't put my finger on why."

The gallery stayed open until seven o'clock to entice the after-work crowd, but Tommy and I were alone except for a young assistant with a pierced eyebrow who sat at a desk reading and ensuring that we didn't deface the art. Red dots were stuck on the wall next to four of the paintings, indicating that they were sold.

"They're nice," Tommy said as we slowly circled the room. "But they aren't disturbing to me." They all followed the same format: large inner square or rectangle with a scene painted inside, surrounded by a grid, with something related to the inner scene painted inside each grid box. There was the lake painting, the basketball one, one that referenced rap music and musicians, another that did the same thing for jazz. There were several, including the basketball one, that were obviously Port Grace: a church, a community garden, the PBA boxing club, and some streetscapes.

"Do you think they're good?" I asked him.

"Well-painted, obviously. They're pleasing. I don't know if they say anything new, but yes, they're good paintings."

"I like them too," I said. "I'd love to have one hanging in our living room, the city ones especially; you can see that they're Port Grace. Maybe what bothers me is they're too pleasing. There's no darkness in them, there's nothing below the surface. There are no unanswered questions."

At that moment Miles entered the gallery. I introduced him to Tommy, who started chatting away, inviting Miles to speak to one of his classes. Tommy's always doing that; he says it make the classes more meaningful if the students meet real people involved in American culture.

I wandered away from them and peered out the front window of the gallery. Across the street was a small art-house movie theatre. A panhandler was hitting up the crowd for the BuÑuel retrospective. Amazing. There are enough people in Port Grace interested in BuÑuel to support a retrospective. I've never seen a BuÑuel and probably never will, but I suppose that the world is a more interesting place because of the people who do.

My focus returned to the gallery. Tommy and Miles appeared to be exchanging phone numbers. The assistant looked up from her book and smiled at me. "What are you reading?" I asked.

"*Motherless Brooklyn.* It's a novel."

"How is it?"

"Good. Funny. Funny and sad."

I noted her backpack and an unopened philosophy textbook. "Are you a student?"

She nodded. "I'm doing an internship here. I'm a double major at Winslow: literature and art."

"Nice job," I said.

"I usually study when I'm here. But I can't put this book down; it's so bleak. That man you came in with? I took a class from him. I don't think he remembers me."

"I'm sure he does," I said. "He's just focused on the paintings." My cell phone rang. "Excuse me." It was Marco. "Hey." I walked toward the door and out of earshot of the intern. "How did it go?"

"Great. I'm on my way home now."

"Tell me everything." I pushed open the door and stepped outside. The gentle scent of spring mingled with the slightly metallic smell of the river. The BuÑuel crowd was inside enjoying *Los Olvidados,* and the panhandler was seated on the curb and engrossed in the pavement.

"He's repenting," Marco said. "He says the whole thing with Violet was a mistake, and he's trying to work it out with his wife. He joined the army when he was eighteen, got married when he was nineteen, and had three kids, bing bang boom. He's twenty-seven, and he's been a corrections officer since he was twenty."

"Are we supposed to feel sorry for him?"

"No, I'm just giving you his perspective. His father's a C.O. too. His wife's brother's a cop, both their families live in the same town. He'll never leave there. Violet was a toy for him, something exotic."

"Exotic?"

"Compared to where he's from? Yeah. Anyway, his story is that the time he hit Violet, he was in an alcoholic blackout."

"Not another fucking alcoholic," I said. "Is there anybody who isn't an alcoholic?"

"Me," said Marco. "Anyway, he says he's a reformed man, hasn't had a drink for three weeks. Says he was upset when Violet had the baby, and he's not even sure if it's his, but he categorically denies hurting him."

"What about the paternity test?"

"He'll do it. I told him that judges always sign off on them and it would be a waste of his time to go to court."

"What else?"

"He says there's no way she would have hurt the baby."

"When was the last time he saw her?"

"Late March. A few weeks before that he broke up with her, and she kept calling his cell phone. She threatened to tell his wife about Teddy. He says at first he went ballistic but then he calmed down and he went down to talk to her in person. He says she got hysterical and he couldn't do anything about it, so he just left. He says he didn't even see the baby that night."

"That's pretty close to Violet's story. What do you think?"

"I think he's a smooth talker. He probably is a drunk and I bet he's reformed plenty of times before this. He might have been a nice kid, but he's infected by his job. Hardened. Cynical. Self-centered. He's remorseful right now, but that won't last."

"Do you think he hurt Teddy?"

"It's possible. He came off superficially credible, he wears his uniform well, but I smelled something off. The blackout mention bothers me. Maybe he's setting up a defense?"

"He'd have a hard row to hoe with that one."

"He seemed a little shaken. And I'd say he's getting scared. Like maybe he's in over his head and he knows it. Maybe he was in a blackout and doesn't know if he did it. Something scared him sober three weeks ago."

"See if you can get any info on his drinking habits and how he acts when he's drunk. Do you have any contacts in the department up there? Has the D.A. questioned him?"

"No. I'm surprised they aren't onto him."

"We'll have to decide if he's a useful witness for us, or if we'll go hostile with him. I think we can use him to establish reasonable doubt. And maybe you should tip off DiCicco. He was Violet's arresting officer. He's the idiot who didn't secure the crime scene. Michelle's already convicted Violet. We've got to point them in AJ's direction."

"Let's sleep on it. We'll talk tomorrow."

We disconnected and I wandered up to the corner, where a pair of musicians, a guitarist and a conga drummer, were entertaining a small crowd. They finished an upbeat Afro-Caribbean number, and moved into a slow blues that showcased the guitarist. He looked to be about twenty, with a long brown ponytail and pensive expression that reminded me of Jake. I tuned into his words: "From Little River to the Bay, all that I can say, I got the Port Grace blues." Not the best lyrics, but they were well-executed, and the open guitar case was receiving many coins and dollar bills. I threw in a buck and felt someone come up behind me. Close. I turned and saw Tommy.

"Here you are," he said.

"I was thinking that Jake would enjoy this."

"Definitely. I hope you don't mind, I've invited Miles to have dinner with us tonight."

"Really?" I was surprised because I knew Tommy was looking forward to the two of us having an evening together.

"He's a good guy. I have an idea for a project we might work on together. So let's call Jake and ask him to join us."

And that's what we did. Jake took a taxi to Mama Jo's, and we ate at an Asian fusion restaurant, pleasuring ourselves with a rhapsodic blend of flavors: curry, basil, lime, coriander, and spicy peanut sauce. I gazed around the table—at Jake sporting shaggy brown hair, baggy jeans and a *Support the Right to Arm Bears* T-shirt; Miles with his short dreadlocks, rectangular black glasses, sage brushed-cotton shirt, and gray slacks; Tommy's earnest expression, L.L.Bean khakis, and white Oxford cotton button-down; me in a black pantsuit and red heels; a typically eclectic Little River crowd.

I told Jake about the guitar player and his Port Grace blues. "I was thinking how many songs could be written about Port Grace," I said. "It's not just one thing, a city. It's all these different communities and types of people, and history—there's Deer Point, the Oaks, Pig Hollow, the old factories and mills, the Heights. Even though they're separate, they're connected too. They affect each other, so that the whole is more than the parts. Depicting that could be a life's work for a writer, or songwriter, or even an artist."

Jake smiled tolerantly. "That's a good idea," he said, but I could see that his inspirations lay elsewhere.

Tommy, who had been listening, said, "It's positively Whitmanesque."

★ ★ ★ ★ ★

Part Two

★ ★ ★ ★ ★

19

Teddy remained in a coma for a month past that raw March night when Violet called me from jail. A full lunar cycle, time enough for forsythia and iris to spark our yards with color. Violet remained depressed. Local reporters grew bored with her and lasered in on pedophile priests. Even so, despite comas, depressions, and pedophiles, spring continued to illuminate. Birds gathered softness for their nests, never stopping to consider—should I build a nest this year? Do I really want to lay eggs and spend my summer looking for worms and bugs for the babies? On the bay, sailboats skimmed like dragonflies. The river path welcomed a rare and notable mix of generation, race, and class. We were in the heart of spring, a seasonal interlude, when optimism bloomed like the flowering cherry trees that spattered Port Grace with their blossoms.

Another Friday rolled around. It had been a difficult week at work, and my head, neck, and shoulders ached from accumulated tension. I had missed the deadline to respond to a motion to compel my client to pay spousal support, been chewed out by Judge Bird for being late, started a custody trial, and a client's ex-husband had disappeared with their daughter. I was scheduled to attend the Women's Shelter Annual Awards Dinner, but what I wanted to do was go home and shoot baskets until I was as exhausted physically as I was mentally, and then drink a bucket of lemonade and go to a movie. I am frequently invited to rubber-chicken functions sponsored by bar associations and non-profit organizations. I could create an excuse to miss the dinner, but I was being presented with an award, and even I am not rude enough to blow off such an honor and the people bestowing it upon me. Besides, I genuinely like the staff of the women's shelter; I just wished they would put together something more original than an evening of tedious, gentle speeches and mediocre food in the Marriott ballroom.

I decided to compromise. Go home and shoot baskets, an inning or two of the Red Sox game, and arrive at the awards dinner after the cocktail hour. That settled, I shut off my computer and started closing up. Marco and Gloria had both left early, citing elaborate excuses of onerous tasks to be dealt with, but I knew they wanted to take advantage of the glorious weather and start their weekend early. The phone rang. It was late enough on a Friday that I didn't want to talk to clients or potential clients, so I let the answering machine pick it up, half-listening as I reached into the closet for my jacket.

"Ms. Reddy, this is Harriet Borden from the Division of Child Welfare. I am calling from St. Joseph's Hospital in regards to your client Violeta Rosado. I regret to inform you that the child Theodore Rosado passed away a short while ago."

I grabbed the phone. "Hello, hello," I said, yanking it so hard that it tumbled to the floor.

"Oh. I thought that you were not in your office." Her accent was melodic. Jamaican maybe. Some island. A vague mental map of the Caribbean zipped through my mind, and then mango-lime was replaced with darkness in the split of a second that it took for me to process not only her accent, but her words and their meaning.

"Teddy." It was all I could say.

"He passed away an hour ago." Her professional tone was at odds with the words that she uttered. "We have also contacted

Ms. Bonpietro from the prosecutor's office. I thought that you might want to be the one who informs the child's mother."

I don't remember hanging up the phone, only tearing out of my office. My heel caught on one of the porch steps and I tripped and fell, a hard fall, my pants ripped, baring my left knee, my bad knee. I hobbled to the Jimmy and gunned the engine. *Nirvana Unplugged* shot out of the speakers like a fist to my belly as Kurt Cobain covered Leadbelly's *Where Did You Sleep Last Night,* stripped down, pure, and mournful. I was seized with a longing to drive straight out of town, steer the Jimmy south and go. Go. Go. Abandon Violet and Mary Abbott and all the other needy clients who were sucking the life out of me. I was momentarily possessed with the possibility of escape. Memphis, Austin, places where I could enjoy a drink, relax in the pleasure of a mahogany bar lined with delicious alcoholic beverages: Margarita, Martini, Gin & Tonic, Vodka Tonic, Sam Adams, Johnny Walker, Jim Beam, Rolling Rock, Scotch on the Rocks, jukebox loaded with Patsy Cline and B. B. King. I found myself turning hard into the crowded parking lot of Tony's Mexican Cha Cha House. Happy hour was winding down and Tony's was busting out with a pleasant mix of young professionals and college students. I elbowed my way to the bar, caught the bartender's eye. "Nachos and a Margarita, please." My cell phone vibrated. Damn. I should have turned it off. Reflexively I checked the caller ID. Marco's cell phone. I couldn't ignore Marco. "What?" I raised my forefinger to the bartender, indicating that I would be right back, and edged away from the bar and noise. "Hold on, I can't hear you." It wasn't until I was near the bathrooms that I heard him clearly.

"Where the hell are you?" Angry. Staccato.

"Getting food. Why? What's up?"

"I'm at the station. I was picking up Spagz to play ball, and he told me they're going to arrest Violet. The baby's dead."

"I know."

"And you're eating?"

"Marco, don't yell at me."

"They let me call you first as a courtesy. They'll be on their way to pick her up soon."

"They as in the police?"

"No, Santa and his merry elves."

"Tell them I'll bring her down. Ask. Please."

"Hold on." Minutes passed. I held the cell phone to my ear and slowly walked back to the bar. Pulled a cigarette from my purse and looked around for a light. The bartender arranged my Margarita on a beverage napkin at the same time that Marco came back on. "You've got a half hour to get her here."

"I'm on my way, tell them forty-five."

"Don't push it, Reddy."

I put a ten on the bar, looked wistfully at the untouched Margarita. I wasn't hungry anymore but I would have loved to down that sucker. However, it seemed that I wasn't going to drink a Margarita; nor would I burn onto the highway with Kurt Cobain, drive past midnight, and sleep in a motel that smelled of cheap disinfectant and pine needles.

I drove too fast with Nirvana turned up too loud, braked in front of the warehouse, noted Laura's van parked outside and lights on in her second floor loft, forced myself out of the car, walked down by the riverbank, shook a cigarette from the pack, lit it, and inhaled deeply. It was coming on twilight, mosquitoes were biting, and along the river path a young woman pushed a double stroller loaded with a baby and a toddler, grocery bags hanging off the handles. In the distance I heard the thunk-thunk of a basketball being dribbled. Beneath the weeping willow tree a couple was entwined. The Red Sox game drifted from an open window. I've performed many grim tasks, but never this. I should have asked Marco how police do it; do they receive special training? Is there a script to follow when you have to tell a mother that her child died? I stomped on the cigarette and slowly walked up the stairs to Laura's loft.

We didn't talk on the way to the police station. Violet was suffering. It was Friday, so I knew she would spend the weekend in jail. I swerved into the police station lot and she looked out the window, bewildered. "Is Teddy here?"

"No, Violet. They're arresting you." I had already explained but she obviously hadn't heard a thing past the fact that Teddy died.

"Why?"

"I don't know, honey." I had a pretty good idea, but wasn't ready to tell her what I was thinking, and she wasn't ready to hear it. "I'll talk to you as soon as I know what's going on." She scrunched into the seat. I touched her foot. She wore orange flip-flops. Her feet were small and clean. "Come on, Violet. We have to go in."

"I need Teddy. I need AJ. Where's AJ?"

"You don't need AJ." I got out of the car, walked around it, opened the passenger door. At the edge of my field of vision I saw a couple of cops watching. I looked over, caught the amused looks on their faces and gave them the finger, down behind the door so they wouldn't see.

Violet pulled away from me. "You don't know what I need. You are wrong about everything," she said. We struggled briefly.

"Goddammit, Violet, get out of the car. If you don't, those police officers over there will be glad to get you out, and trust me, you don't want that."

I turned her in for booking and fingerprinting, and left her there with orders not to talk to the cops. Alone in a holding cell. She would be transferred to county jail in the morning and charged with manslaughter, maybe even murder, and if convicted, go to prison. Teddy was dead, a possibility that I had not allowed myself to imagine.

The desk sergeant reported that Marco had left the station for his softball game. I was piqued that he didn't wait for me to bring Violet in. It was my case, and I knew that comfort from Marco was not something I should seek. However, going home alone seemed unbearable. Tom was at a poetry reading at the college, which I could crash, but no way could I sit quietly and listen to poetry. There was no one else within easy reach who knew me so deeply that I could call them and voice my despair. I couldn't possibly deal with the awards dinner, so I left a quick message with my regrets, and drove around, finally stopping at my usual place, the docks, where boats rocked and the ropes that tied them strained, emitting a plaintive sound like summer crickets, or birds, lost at night.

Eventually I returned to my office, because, since I stopped drinking, work is my default setting. The seductive Margarita at Tony's seemed like part of a dream. Did I really go there? I hung up my jacket and sat at my desk, gazing at stacks of files, notes, law journals, bills, and other detritus of my occupation. Accomplishing something wasn't a possibility, so I just stayed there and tried to calm down.

I saw my mother once after she left my father and me when I was two. I was seven by then, and one night after dinner, Dad said, "Your mother wants to see you." Maybe he hoped I'd say no. But I said, when? He didn't want to see her, so he arranged for Aunt Marilyn to take me to meet her at a Denny's in Modesto.

I had two weeks to get wrought up. For the first time I allowed the image of mother into my life. I had no internalized mother, no memories of a mother baking brownies or admiring my drawings, putting on lipstick, or holding my hand to cross the street. No memory of her smell, no imprint of her voice. Because I didn't remember her, I didn't walk around feeling abandoned. My town, where my father grew up, where his father was one of the original settlers, was my family; it was an insular world where everyone knew me and I was always busy—feeding chickens, riding ponies, hanging out at my dad's nursery, swimming in our pool, and playing tag on the dusty streets. My life was full, and at seven, I wasn't aware of missing anything.

I hadn't spent much time wishing for a mother, but now that I was going to have lunch with one, I became consumed with mothers; they were everywhere: mothers selecting grapes at the market, mothers choosing books at the library, mothers packed in a booth with their kids at the diner, mothers buying popcorn at the movies, mothers in flowered dresses and short shorts, pony tails and pixie cuts, dancing at the grange hall, buying plants at the nursery, gently flirting with my father. I was intoxicated with the idea of having a mother. I was certain in the way that only a child can be, that when I walked into Denny's I would have a mother, I would be filled with mother, that thing that most everyone else had, that I hadn't realized that I was missing.

Of course none of that happened. I had lunch with a stranger and I have only the vaguest memory of what transpired, which is not surprising, since I was seven years old. What I remember: I didn't recognize her, and I had thought that I would. She let me order soda, which my father didn't. She asked me a lot of questions and I answered them politely. Some years later Aunt Marilyn told me that my mother had explained that she planned to become a nurse and return to the reservation where she had spent her early years until some do-good missionaries sent her away to boarding school and she ran away and became a hippie and met my father and I was born when she was eighteen. Aunt

Marilyn gave me the chronology, because my father couldn't talk about her and I couldn't ask. My mother told Aunt Marilyn that she wanted me to visit her, but when my aunt asked me if I wanted to I said no; because I didn't want to or because I knew Dad wouldn't want me to, I'm not certain. Now, with hindsight and the perspective I've gained over several years of working with splintered families, I realize that she was only about twenty-five at that time, and her ambition to become a nurse and return to the reservation was admirable, and that with some effort, she and I might have developed a relationship. But then? The five years since she left us were an eternity to my father, I didn't remember her, and everyone had given up on her.

20

I was still at my desk, staring into my past, when the phone rang, startling me into the present. I listened as the machine picked up and Laura's voice came on. I'd forgotten that before I took Violet to the police station I told Laura that I would call her later.

"You sound awful," she said.

"So do you."

"Come over. You aren't going to get any work done tonight."

She was standing outside when I arrived. We embraced. "Let's go up," she said. When we entered the loft she offered me some wine.

"No thanks. Just water, please."

"Oh comc on. It's a California Chardonnay. Bonnic Doon. Aren't you from California?"

"Yes, but no thanks. I don't drink. Alcohol." I pushed away the dream-like memory of my close call at Tony's.

"Oh, I'm sorry." She got that look that people get when they're trying to decide if it's because I'm an alcoholic, or for reasons of health or religion, but they're embarrassed to ask.

"Please. Don't worry about it. Go ahead and have some; it won't bother me." I didn't explain. I was too close to the edge. Of the wagon. And everything else.

She paced the length of the loft, adjusting lights, tidying, nervous.

"Laura, sit down."

"I can't. I have to do something."

"There's nothing you can do right now." I poured a glass of wine and handed it to her. I wanted a smoke but knew she wouldn't want me smoking in there, so I just collapsed into a chair.

"What will happen to her?" Laura asked.

"She might be charged with murder, but it'll probably be manslaughter. If she's convicted of aggravated manslaughter she'll get ten to twenty years in prison."

"Murder? That's impossible."

"Oh it's possible." It was so possible that I was dizzy. I went to the kitchen for a bottle of seltzer and a lime.

"I don't believe that she hurt that baby. Do you?"

"What I believe doesn't matter." I grasped a sharp knife and sliced a wedge of lime. Filled a wine glass with seltzer and squeezed the lime into it, watching the juice drip into the glass.

"Of course it matters."

I turned to Laura, the knife clutched in my hand. "What I think has no bearing on the case, or on how I represent Violet. The prosecution will build their case, brick by brick, and my job is to knock down a couple of those bricks."

Laura continued pacing. "I'm having trouble comprehending this. I absolutely don't believe that she hurt Teddy, but if she did, it must have been an accident. How can she be convicted of manslaughter for an accident? If she didn't mean to hurt him?"

I sighed. First year criminal law was burned into my brain. "For manslaughter they don't have to prove intent to harm, only that she acted recklessly. For regular manslaughter that means she knew that there was a possibility that Teddy would die. For aggravated manslaughter, it would have to be proven that the risk of death was a probability and that she was indifferent as to whether he lived or died."

She stopped in her tracks. "Well there you go," she said. "Let's say, hypothetically, that she did shake Teddy. How would she have known that it was possible that he might die?"

I shrugged. I was tired and distraught and not in the mood to parse statutes. "I have to do research," I said. "But I know there've been plenty of major convictions on these types of cases."

"What about Teddy's father? Why aren't they arresting him?"

"They probably will. They've been working sloppy."

"Come here," she said, "I want to show you something." I put down the knife and picked up my glass. She led me to Violet's room. Indicated the neatly made bed, with its white chenille bedspread, the vase of daisies on the nightstand. "She loved this room. She couldn't believe that I cooked her dinner every night. She was becoming a little bit happy."

"She's had a rough life. I'm sure that what you did meant a lot to her."

"She was starting to talk to me. I think there's hope for her."

I studied the photograph of Teddy that was on the dresser, and tried to grasp the fact of his death. A laughing, squirmy baby. All gone: his life, his life force, his energy, his very being, evaporated. Hope for Violet? "There might be. If she wasn't in jail and her baby wasn't getting autopsied while you and I . . ." I couldn't finish. Turned away from Teddy's picture, Violet's bedroom, and walked to the window. I wanted to punch my fist right through it. "I should go. I'm not good company tonight."

"Don't go. Please. Are you hungry?"

Was I hungry? I tried, without success, to recall my last meal. "Probably." I stared out of the window at the river while she grilled cheddar cheese on rye.

"There's something so comforting about grilled cheese," she said as she pressed the sandwiches with a spatula so that the cheese oozed out of the sides of the bread. We ate in silence, satiating our grief with protein and carbohydrates. Finally she spoke. "When did you stop drinking?"

"Summer after my second year of law school." She looked at me carefully. I knew what questions she wanted to ask me, and answered one or two of them. "I was a binge drinker. I could easily go weeks without a drink. But then I'd drink all weekend. One night I drove my boyfriend's car into a tree." I stopped there. Left out the part that he almost died. "I went into rehab after that." It wasn't that simple; it never is; but that was all that I could give to her. Laura's expression—concerned, questioning, horrified, sympathetic. All the right things. I couldn't stand it. "I'll do the dishes," I said.

Laura poured herself another glass of wine and I filled the dishpan with warm soapy water. "There is a possibility that Violet will come out of this all right," I said. "She's not as damaged as a lot of kids I've seen. The fact that she's nineteen helps. A lot of girls have babies when they're fifteen, sixteen, even fourteen." I shook my head at the image of a pregnant eleven-year-old girl I was once the law guardian for. "She didn't get pregnant until she was eighteen, she isn't a substance abuser, she finished high school, and those are all positives." I washed and rinsed the plates, glasses, and skillet; arranged them in the drainer. Dried my hands on a soft white dishtowel. "Unfortunately, she doesn't have family support, and she's vulnerable to abusive men."

"So. What's next?" Laura asked. Still stunned.

"Hopefully she'll be out on bail next week. The D.A. will charge her. The autopsy results will be released. We're going to have to arrange a funeral, because I don't think anyone else will. I'll try to contact her mother and AJ. But they're both worthless."

"Do you really believe that? Isn't her mother just a victim?"

"Victim of what?"

"Poverty. Lack of education. The illness of drug abuse. She probably really loves Violet."

"That and a buck will get Violet a bus ride across town."

"That's harsh."

"Look. I hope to keep Violet out of prison. But I gave up rescue fantasies a long time ago. And I thought you did too." I walked over to her worktable. Looked at shelves neatly filled with tools of the florist's trade. Fingered a roll of gauzy red ribbon shot through with threads of gold. "I admire your work."

She struggled to smile, gave up. "Really? It's frivolous."

"No. It's positive work. It makes people feel good; you create beauty. Giving people pleasure is a gift."

"That's nice of you to say. But flowers don't keep people out of jail."

I shrugged, grabbed my jacket. "I'm gonna head out. Thanks for the company. And the grilled cheese."

"Take some flowers with you."

I started to say no, but I wanted flowers.

Laura stepped into the stainless-steel walk-in refrigerator and came out holding lilac branches. She trimmed and arranged them in a slender glass vase. "Violet was getting good," she said. "I think she has a flair for this kind of work."

"If she gets out on bail, do you want her to come back? You're under no obligation. I can find her somewhere else to go."

"I enjoyed having her here. She was becoming like a daughter . . ." Her voice thinned out. "I have a daughter."

"You do?"

"Nobody knows. I gave her up for adoption right after she was born. That was thirty years ago."

"I'm sorry."

"I still remember exactly what she felt like when I held her. The weight of her in my arms." She looked past me, a thousand-yard stare. "I don't know why I told you that."

"We're both feeling pretty raw." I slipped into my jacket. Zipped it up. "After all, Teddy died today."

21

When I finally got home that night, Tommy was in bed reading. He took in my wretched expression. "What's wrong?"

I sat on the bed next to him and kicked my shoes across the room. "That baby in a coma? He died."

"I'm sorry," was all he said. But it was enough. I didn't want to talk or answer questions and he knew it. I lay next to him, feeling the wound spread throughout me. Then I took a long hot bath and got into bed. "Do you want me to stay home tomorrow?" Tommy asked. "I can take Jake on Sunday." He was going to drive Jake to Brooklyn to spend spring vacation with his mother, and then visit his own mother in Manhattan, where he planned to lavish attention on her, and butter her up for a serious conversation about moving out of the apartment she had lived in for forty years.

"No, don't mess up your schedule. And you don't want to rattle your mother." I held onto him until he went to sleep, and then I held him some more, soothed by his breathing. Later, unable to sleep, I got up and watched Nick at Night, and eventually succumbed to troubled dreams. A couple hours later I awoke, heavy with sadness, and light with an emptiness that terrified me.

I pushed myself into a short run and shower, and then drove to my office, stopping on the way to pick up a large go-cup of coffee and a bagel. I was at my desk by seven o'clock, sipping coffee and scrawling a list:

—Find Violet's family
—Tell AJ
—Outline trial strategy
—Theory of case
—Eye witnesses: AJ violent? AJ w/ Teddy?
—Talk to A.D.A.
—Plea???

A rush of energy sweeps though me in the early stages of trial preparation, and it kicked in that morning, moving me forward, displacing Teddy's body and Violet's plight, pushing me deep into the chess game phase, where I dream up the prosecution's case and plan how to destroy it. I opened a 3″ binder and filled it with dividers, then labeled sections for case law, statutes, witnesses, experts, evidence, cross-examination, contacts, notes, and strategy. That would be my trial bible, the book that held the answers to everything I needed to win Violet's trial. I added to my list:

—Criminal Complaint
—Medical Examiner's report
—Psychological evaluation of Violet?
—Research battered women's syndrome defense
—Experts: neurologist, pediatrician, medical examiner
—Character witnesses
—AJ as hostile witness?
—AJ as perpetrator!

I telephoned the police station and was informed that Violet was being transported to County Jail, so I dialed the jail and said I'd be there at nine o'clock. My next call was to Western State Prison where I left a message for AJ to call me, urgent. I swallowed coffee and made progress on my bagel. Marco walked in at 8:30. He looked as tired as I felt. "How are you?" he asked.

"Hanging in there." I held up half of my bagel. "Want this?"

"No thanks. I'm not hungry. But I'm going to make coffee."

I followed him into the kitchen. "Would you do me a favor?"

"Depends." He poured coffee beans into the grinder.

"We've got to talk to AJ. I left a message for him but I don't think he'll call me back." I practically shouted to be heard over the blade of the electric grinder crushing coffee beans into powder. "Will you contact him?"

"What are you trying to accomplish?" He filled the coffee pot with water.

"He needs to know that Teddy died. Take it from there depending on how he reacts. And we need to get a message to Violet's father. He's an inmate at Western."

Marco got the coffee situation assembled and dripping. "No problem." His voice was tight and he didn't look me in the eye. He hadn't shaved.

"What's wrong?"

Now he faced me dead-on. "I don't like this case."

"Meaning what? You want nothing to do with it?"

"I won't put you in that position."

"Come on, Marco. Don't get all self-righteous with me."

"I'm not. I'll work with you. But I can't believe the baby's dead. It's sticking me in the gut."

"You don't think I'm upset?"

He rubbed the stubble on his face. "What I think is that you've connected with the baby's mother, and I haven't. I'm a hired gun on this one."

"You can stay out. You know, if that'll help you look in the mirror."

He snorted. "Don't worry about that. I've looked worse. I'm just trying to . . ." He paused to collect the words. "Act decent. This case is a tragedy."

"It is a tragedy. And you have to do what you think is right."

I returned to my office, ran a Westlaw search on shaken baby syndrome, and discovered a shocking amount of case law on the subject. Conviction after conviction, all over the United States people were shaking their babies to death. Violet's case was distinguished from the majority in two ways: most of the convictions were of men, and there was usually a documented history of child abuse. The men were the mother's boyfriend or the baby's stepfather, occasionally the biological father. They were usually convicted of second-degree murder or aggravated manslaughter, and the mothers were convicted of child endangerment, for failure to protect their child. That bolstered the theory that AJ shook Teddy. And Violet had no history of child abuse. If we could convince the jury that AJ shook Teddy, and Violet was present when it happened, I was reasonably certain that a charge of aggravated manslaughter against her would be dropped to manslaughter or child endangerment, shaving off five to fifteen years of hard time. And leaving another five to fifteen to be served. It would be better to prove that AJ did it and Violet was not present; that she was out getting pizza when it happened. We didn't even have to prove it; just imbed reasonable doubt in one juror's mind.

The most recent on-point case in this state was a twenty-year-old woman who shook her eighteen-month-old son after he broke a vase; he went into a coma and died two weeks later. But they had a ten-year-old who witnessed the act. The mother pled guilty to aggravated manslaughter and was sentenced to seventeen years in prison. Most of the cases never went to trial—plea bargains were arranged. The victims were usually crying infants. Their parents were exhausted, high, drunk, frustrated, or just plain mean, and the baby cried one minute too long, and something snapped and the world stopped spinning. The details of the abuse some of the children suffered before their deaths were relentless. Toddlers who wouldn't use the potty, dunked in scalding water. Ribs crushed, skulls battered, spiral fractures in legs and arms, broken fingers, cigarette burns, iron burns, babies put in the freezer, tied in cribs, imprisoned in dog cages.

Sickened and frustrated I stopped, closed my eyes, conjured up my dad's nursery—musky eucalyptus, pink geraniums, olive trees, sunflowers, poppies, scarlet lupines. I laid plants upon the images of tortured babies, trying to heal them. It didn't work, so I spent a few minutes shooting the Nerf basketball that Jake gave me for Christmas. Then I grabbed my briefcase and stormed out. My lack of sleep was catching up with me and I felt over-caffeinated and irritable. I paused by Marco's desk. "I'm going to the jail to see Violet. Can you do some quick research on a visitation case? I'm meeting the client Tuesday and I completely forgot about it."

"Sure. What's the story?"

"It's a State case; Judge Bird referred it to me. Our client is mentally ill, schizophrenic I think, she lives in a group home. She sees her children once a week for an hour, supervised. According to her case manager she's doing well; she's taking her meds, working part-time in a pet store, her illness is under control. Her kids are eight and twelve, and she wants more time with them. Unsupervised. She wants to be able to take them for a walk, get a slice of pizza, that type of thing. Do a search for relevant case law."

"No problem. Sounds interesting." He looked me over, reached out and took my hand. "Are you okay?"

"Not really. But I'll keep it together for now. I'm on a mission here. I'll fall apart later."

He squeezed my hand. "I'll help you. I want to."

I touched his unshaven face. "Thank you." At the door I paused to pick up the mail and rip through it. The paternity test results were in and there was a 99.9% chance that AJ was Teddy's father. I tossed the letter onto Gloria's desk and banged my fist against the doorframe on my way out.

I shambled through the cool mid-morning light. A baby was dead. Teddy was dead. Yet traffic continued to flow, dogs strained at their leashes, babies bounced in their strollers. Daffodils, daffodils, daffodils. It was like walking outside after a matinee and being shocked by the bright light of day. Even though Teddy was dead, the citizens of Port Grace were going about their business.

Violet was wrecked as a storm-tossed ship, smashed at the hull, taking on water. After spending the night in a holding cell, she was transported to the county jail, which is only a few blocks from the police station, but involved being shackled, searched, and enduring various forms of harassment from law enforcement officers. I thought briefly of Marco, about what he told me that night at Gino's—the uniform, the weight of the duty belt, the gravity of the gun, the custom cop Crown Vic, the power that comes from objects. It was obvious that Violet hadn't slept, and I didn't have the energy to carry her emotionally, so I kept it businesslike. I told her that we would contact her father, and she reluctantly divulged where I might locate her mother.

"There's no point," she said, "you'll be wasting your time."

"Don't you want to see her?"

"Doesn't matter to me. She never came to see me for two years. I took Teddy to see her when he was two months old. She was selling herself for crack, living on the streets. She got all mushy over him, crying and shit about how much she loved me. Until it was time to get high. Then she asked me for money."

22

I lit up as soon as I exited the jail. Once in a while I need a smoke, and that was one of those times. There were a lot of those times that spring. I opened the Jimmy's glove compartment and rummaged though my maps. Violet was from Old Bridge, a small city fifty miles northwest, another old mill town that rusted away after the mills shut down, except Old Bridge never got the money kick that hit Port Grace in the 80s. Port Grace has advantages—its location on the bay is the big one, and with a college in city limits and the flagship campus of the state university twelve miles west, stagnation is prevented. Local politicians dream of turning it into the next Providence or Baltimore. They want high-priced waterfront townhouses. The old docks loaded with seafood restaurants and T-shirt stores, outdoor concerts on summer nights.

I flipped through my CD wallet and reloaded the player. Van Morrison, Etta James, Pearl Jam, Springsteen, Dispatch, Led Zeppelin, Cry Cry Cry, Black 47, Otis Redding, and Johnny Cash. Speeding down the highway put me in a better mood than I'd been in for weeks. On the road, a car full of good music, and a Visa card in my wallet.

Eventually I slowed for the exit ramp, and crossed the bridge that separates Old Bridge from the rest of the world, a bridge beneath which runs a river that hasn't been clean for a hundred and fifty years. I cruised past block after block of shuttered businesses and shabby houses, finally locating one of the few blocks of Main Street that remains alive, and pulled over to the curb in front of Frank's Barbershop. There wasn't any competition for parking spaces. A clump of young teens hung out on the corner, next to a no-name bar. They checked me out as I eased from my car and stretched out the driving kinks. Next door to the barbershop, three older men were gathered beneath the awning of a bodega. Other than that, the block was quiet. Old Bridge was just waking up. I sensed the bystanders watching me as I tried to decide whether or not to lock my car. I was overly conscious of the fact that I was the only person in the vicinity who was not male or black. I decided not to lock, and stepped up to the barbershop door. As I pulled it open, one of the older men said, "Can I help you, young lady?"

I held the shop door open while I turned to look at him. Average height, slender, short gray hair, pressed navy slacks, and a beige, short-sleeve, button-down shirt. The look he sent my way was not friendly, but not unfriendly either. "I'm trying to find someone," I said.

He walked toward me and I stepped back out, letting the door close. "You a social worker?" he asked. "Private investigator?"

"What makes you think that?" Though I knew. If I were an undercover cop I would have exited my vehicle with authority, not hesitating the way I had. A lawyer was expected to wear a suit and carry a briefcase. I was in jeans, T-shirt, and leather jacket even though it was warm. I indicated the Jimmy. "Social workers drive state cars."

"Not all of them." He was ready to play. "DCW, yes. Plenty of other kinds of social workers though." He was right. Many clinics and non-profits employ social workers and caseworkers who drive their own cars when they make home visits.

"Why would I make a home visit to a barber shop?"

He smiled. "That's why my second guess was investigator.

Social workers drive Neons and Geo's. Old vans. Wear long skirts and cardigans." He enunciated cardigan in a way that showed me, and everyone who was listening, that he was enjoying himself.

I offered up a smile. "Sounds like you're the investigator."

He wasn't finished analyzing me. "White woman in black neighborhood. Jeans and leather jacket. Don't you know it's spring? Or maybe you've got a gun under your leather." The audience chuckled. His face lit up. "Maybe you're looking for drugs."

Enough. "Actually, I'm looking for a person. Her name is Monique Grey. Or you might know her as Monique Rosada."

He stopped smiling. "If I did know someone by that name, why would you be asking about her?"

"It's a personal matter."

"What about?"

Game over. "I'm a lawyer." He looked disappointed. "Defense attorney. I need to see Monique about a personal matter. A family matter. I'm not getting into her business. I just need to give her some information about a member of her family."

"Why you looking here?" He indicated the barbershop.

"The last time her daughter saw her, she was here."

He took this in. "Which daughter?"

"Violet."

"You know Violet?"

I nodded.

"Come on in." He tipped his head toward the barbershop.

His name was Frank. The barbershop was his. The story he told me was that he and Monique's uncle, her mother's brother, had been best friends. Monique's father took off when she was a baby and her mother had a heart attack when she was a young teen. Frank and his wife took her in. "My wife and I though, we had five between us, younger then Monique, and I was working all the time to keep my business going and food on the table. So we didn't give her the attention she needed."

I took a minute to sort through the various relationships among the people he had mentioned.

"You want some lemonade?" he asked.

"I'd love some lemonade. I can't remember the last time I had lemonade. But I was craving it just the other night."

"My wife makes it fresh." He opened a mini fridge and pulled out a blue plastic pitcher. "We live right upstairs from here. I like to have something on hand to offer my customers. Lemonade or iced tea usually." He filled a paper cup and handed it to me.

"What happened to Monique's uncle? Your friend."

"Vietnam. He got taken over there. I came back and he didn't. So I felt an obligation. There weren't any family members stepping up."

I drained my lemonade. It was just the right blend of tart over sweet. "This is delicious. I'm gonna have to try to make some myself." I thought about telling him that my father was in Vietnam. Maybe that would move him toward trusting me. More than that, I wanted to tell him because knowing that he'd been there made me feel connected to him. But this wasn't about me. "I'm sorry," I said. "About your friend. About Vietnam."

"Yeah, well, I lost more than one friend to that place between one thing and another."

I waited a respectful beat. "If you have any idea where Monique is, I really need to find her. Violet told me that last time she saw her was here."

"That's right. I was here. Violet came with that baby of hers, a good-looking little boy. Her boyfriend sat in the truck. He looked like a cop."

"Prison guard," I said.

"That might be worse." He palmed his hair. "Monique's been on drugs for years. Sometimes she goes into a program. A few times she's stayed in long enough that I think maybe she'll make it. But she slips back down every time."

"Do you know where she is?"

"Soon after Violet came by we had to ask Monique to leave. We have a little apartment in the basement. Sometimes we rent it out. Sometimes one of our own kids stays there. Between times, we've let Monique have it a couple times. We let her stay upstairs with us once, when Violet was a girl, but she started stealing from us. That was the beginning of the crack years—destroyed what was left of this town. I had to call DCW on her." He gazed wistfully out the picture window with the barbershop pole painted on it. "This last time she was in a bad way, and I told her she couldn't stay anymore. I offered to help her find another program. My church would help her. But she just took off. I really don't know where she is. I could direct you to the parts of town where she might be. But you shouldn't go there by yourself."

"You think there's any chance she's in a program?"

"Well, maybe." I could see that he didn't think that was probable. "More likely the hospital. She's got the virus."

"I'm sorry."

"What's this about anyway?" he asked. "Is Violet in trouble?"

"Yes. I'm sorry to have to tell you, but her baby died. She's been arrested."

"They don't think she killed her baby?"

"Not exactly. They think she shook him and that caused his brain to bleed. He died yesterday and I thought her mother should know."

Frank looked down at the floor. "I'm real sorry to hear that. That was a beautiful baby. I thought Violet might come out all right." He shook his head, settling this new, unwelcome information into place. "You could try calling DCW. Monique has young kids in foster care. One's been adopted. But DCW might have a lead on her whereabouts. Call the hospital too. She's in and out of them when the virus gets to her. And I can ask around some." He hesitated. "Better try the jail too. She gets picked up now and again."

I pulled my business card out and wrote my cell phone number on the back. "I appreciate it. Here's my card. You can reach me by cell phone almost anytime."

"Cell phones," he said, shaking his head.

A bell jangled and a man accompanied by two little boys walked into the shop. Customers. I crumpled my paper cup, dropped it into the wastebasket and held out my hand. "Thank you for your help," I said. "I'm sorry I brought bad news."

He shook my hand. "I'm real sorry about Violet. I wish I could help."

"Sounds like you've done more than your share for her family."

The men outside the bodega and the boys on the corner were positioned pretty much the way they'd been when I got out of the car. For me, something had changed, and it seemed wrong that they were the same. I waved to them before I slid back into the Jimmy. My good mood was over. I would call the area hospitals and jails. I'd call the rehab centers too. Confidentiality rules would prevent them from telling me if she was there, but I could leave a message that if she was, to call me about her daughter Violet. I was pretty sure it was futile.

When I returned to my office Mr. Ziznewski was sweeping the sidewalk. "It's Saturday," he said, "too nice a day for you to be working. Look!" His arm swept the vista of spring—children chalking hopscotch squares, vigorous window-washing, upbeat pedestrians; all of Port Grace appeared to be enjoying a spot of sunshine and conversation.

"You're right. But I've got stuff that has to get done."

"Make sure you come out for air."

"Will do." I waved and stepped toward the porch.

Once inside, I grabbed a soda and looked around. Marco was gone. Softball probably. Where to start? I flicked on the answering machine. A hysterical woman wanted me to make her husband move out of the house. A smooth-talking man offered me free high-speed Internet service (if I changed phone companies). In the week ahead I had an appellate brief due, three court appearances, a motion to write, and several client appointments. I decided to focus on Violet for the next few days and jam out the brief and motion mid-week. My office was quiet, dark, and oppressive, even after I pulled up the blinds and opened the back door. Unable to stand the thought of sitting at my computer, I yanked a large tablet of newsprint from the supply closet, scooped up a couple of markers, and went to the patio. I flipped the pad open and began constructing charts that would become the blueprint for Violet's defense. On the first sheet I wrote:

MANSLAUGHTER

1. Criminal homicide
2. Committed recklessly.

On the second sheet I wrote:

AGGRAVATED MANSLAUGHTER

1. Criminal homicide
2. When the actor recklessly causes death
3. Under circumstances manifesting extreme indifference to human life.

Those were the elements of the crimes—what the state would

have to prove beyond a reasonable doubt. Was it a criminal homicide or an accidental death? If it was homicide did the perpetrator act recklessly? If so, did the recklessness cause the death? And if the recklessness caused the death did the perpetrator act under circumstances manifesting extreme indifference to human life?

I ripped out two more sheets, drew three columns on each and labeled them:

DEFENSE			PROSECUTION		
witnesses	evidence	other	witnesses	evidence	other

I wrote defense notes in black, prosecution notes in blue, and taped all four sheets to my office wall. As the case developed, I would fill in the columns with ideas and inspiration, fragments that could prove useful. I paced and stared at them for a while and then tore off another page and wrote "AJ" in big red letters and taped it up there too. MOTIVE, I wrote beneath his name. OPPORTUNITY. Then I wandered outside and leaned back in my chair, the sun warming my face, my eyes closed.

I woke up two hours later with a stiff neck and a bad mood brewing. I checked the answering machine at home for messages. One from Tommy, reporting that he'd dropped off Jake and was taking his mother out to dinner, and one from Miles, inviting us to a party, something he thought that Tommy would find interesting. I closed up the office, drove to the ice cream parlor, devoured a double scoop of vanilla with hot fudge on top, and then pulled out my cell phone and punched in Miles's number.

The summer after my freshman year in college I worked in my dad's nursery, as I had every summer since I was ten. It is mainly a wholesale nursery, supplier of foundation plantings to the builders of housing tracts and strip malls. The business was founded in a rudimentary form by my grandfather, and expanded when my uncle's housing development business took off in the early 70s. Dad eased his way in and has run the whole thing for twenty-five years, gradually augmenting the wholesale business with a small retail venture. He was an advocate of using native plants before it became fashionable, but he also filled the shop with species you don't normally find in the Valley—swamp orchids, ginseng, fairy roses, lemon thyme, fiddler ferns, and blue-eyed grass—his contribution to cultural diversity; and he has cultivated a devoted group of customers, some of whom travel far to purchase whatever he unearths on his quarterly road trips.

That summer I processed orders, checked inventory, loaded and unloaded trucks, rotated sprinklers, pruned, trimmed, and deadheaded. One morning Dad called me over. I distinctly remember that I was unloading a flat of oriental poppies. We walked among the rows of trees and shrubs that filled the back lot—eucalyptus, oleander, juniper, maple, birch, and dogwood; natives and intruders mingled, creating a small forest.

"I got a call," he said. "About your mother." He appeared to be inspecting a hemlock. "She died."

"What happened?" I asked reflexively.

"She crashed. Drunk, I guess."

His matter-of-fact tone, the carelessness of his words, guided me. "Okay," I said. Nothing else. Everything I thought of was too much or too little. Like, who called? Or, what did "drunk, I guess" mean? I hadn't talked about her for my whole life and had no idea how to begin. So I didn't.

He picked it up again that night. We took a swim almost every evening, but that night I was worn out from heavy lifting, and floated on a raft, *American Beauty* on the tape deck, the air scented with star jasmine and lemon. Dad sat on the edge smoking a joint. When he was in his bathing suit I could see all the tattoos. Every couple of years he added a new one. He took a hit off the joint and in his chokey smoke-in-the-lungs voice said, "Maybe I was wrong." More to himself than me, so I didn't respond. I was thinking about going to bed. I wanted to get up by six and run before work.

"Ginger Rae," he said. Louder.

"Yeah."

"Maybe I was wrong not to let her see you all these years."

"It's OK," I said. "Don't worry about it." I slid off the raft into the deep end, flipped over and swam to the bottom, like when I was a kid looking for pennies. Then I climbed out, toweled off. "Goodnight Dad."

23

Pounding awakened me. Well, maybe it was knocking, but at eight o'clock on Sunday morning, after a night of drinking and smoking, it sounded like pounding; especially because I heard it all the way upstairs. "Go away," I yelled. The pounding continued and I was pretty sure I heard Marco's voice, so I crawled out of bed. I seemed to have fallen asleep in my underwear, so I pulled a pair of sweatpants and a Mets T-shirt from the heap of clothes on the floor, got my aching body into them and stumbled downstairs, swearing all the way. It was Marco. I pulled open the door and gave him a sour look. "I'm tired, Marco. I had a bad night." He held out the Sunday paper, folded back to reveal a front-page article headlined, *Teen Mother Arrested for Shaking Baby to Death.* "Damn." I turned around and walked toward the coffeepot, leaving the door open. Marco came in and watched as I banged around piecing together a pot of coffee.

"You look like hell," he said.

"Tell me something I don't know." I threw the newspaper across the room and slammed a couple of mugs onto the counter.

He opened the refrigerator, pulled out a carton of orange juice, filled a large glass and placed it on the table. He poured another glass of juice and took a sip. "Where's Tom?"

"New York."

He nodded and left the room. I heard him go upstairs, and a

minute later the shower was running. He returned and pointed to the juice. "Drink it." He held out three aspirins. "Take them." I drank the juice and swallowed the aspirins. Then he grasped my arm and pulled me up, walked me upstairs and into the bathroom. "Take a nice long shower," he said. "Then you can have your coffee."

I took a look at him—showered, groomed, hair combed straight back, smelling of soap and mint, body nicely tucked into faded jeans and black T-shirt. Me? Grimy, rusted-out, sweaty, unraveled, punctured. "I'm going back to bed."

"No you're not. Get in the shower. I'll wait for you."

"Get the fuck out of here," I yelled, and slammed the door behind him.

I stayed in the shower for a long time. I couldn't get clean enough.

The previous night? Miles came over. We got high and ate Thai takeout. He talked me into checking out a party being thrown in honor of Equan Wilder, a rap artist who had just released his first CD, and was being played up in the local press. Port Grace is desperate for anything that can be construed as positive coming out of its streets. "I thought you didn't like rap," I said to Miles, as I demolished a bowl of Tom Kra Ghai. We covered that ground the night we all had dinner on Little River; not only is he an artist, he also plays a little jazz sax. His father plays trumpet in a local band that's on the wedding and anniversary party circuit, with the occasional lounge gig thrown in. His mother is a third-grade teacher, and he grew up in the Oaks, a neighborhood kind of like the one Tommy and I live in, but farther from the bay and with a mostly black population. He studied art at NYU, did the New York thing for a while, and then came back with a grant in one pocket and the lease to the loft in the other.

"I went to school with Equan's sister," he explained. "And I try to support anything positive coming out of the local black community. So we'll pay our respects. Besides, I might not enjoy listening to rap, but I believe in hip hop culture; it's the freshest thing around. That's why I thought Tommy would be interested."

"I'm sure he would. He loves cutting edge stuff, or at least the idea of it. Not that rap is cutting edge anymore, except in academic circles. Bring it up to Tommy and he'll be teaching a class—From Compton to Harlem: the evolution of hip hop."

"I wouldn't exactly call rap cutting edge," Miles said. "It's been around long enough that all the white kids listen to it. Even so, I doubt Winslow is ready. The department heads would be calling emergency meetings about whether rap deserves a spot in academia. They prefer the voice of black people on their campus to be confined to the basketball team and Toni Morrison. Maybe a touch of Malcolm X if they want to put an edge on their classes. Coeds in tennis skirts reading *Soul on Ice.* So progressive."

I found myself in the unusual position of defending academia. "The American Studies Department has a survey class on African-American music; blues, soul, jazz, they probably cover a little rap; but I guess that's safe because it's presented in a historic context."

"From a historic perspective rap is relatively new. Academics are suspicious of new. And rap is angry. What scares white people more than an angry black man? And Winslow is a white college; I mean they have their token 5% or whatever, but it's strictly token."

"Was NYU any better?"

"Percentage-wise, not much. Maybe two points."

"So why don't you like rap?"

"I'm too old, I guess. I love the heartache of the blues. And jazz? It's endlessly complex, it's the poetry of music. But if I were ten years younger I'd probably be all over rap. You get my drift?"

We drifted right into the party, which was in the converted textile factory that houses the studios and offices of Blackon-Black, a hip hop label. I was desperate for distraction from the ache of Teddy's death, and that was the place for it—the music was loud, the dancing was hot, drugs and liquor flowed, and the people-watching was spectacular. Shortly after we arrived somebody pressed a glass of punch into my hand and I didn't ask if there was alcohol in it. I drank it, I drank another, and then I drank some more.

I stepped out of the shower feeling ill. Marco was gone. Tommy was gone. Jake was gone. I picked up the newspaper and smoothed it out, looking at the picture of Teddy some low-life reporter had dug up. I filled a mug with coffee, called my AA sponsor, unplugged the landline, turned off the cell phone, and spent the day recovering—sleeping, swallowing aspirins, drinking orange juice and hot tea. I wanted to call Miles to find out if I had done anything to humiliate myself, but I was too embarrassed.

By six o'clock I was able to face a bowl of tomato soup. I re-plugged the phone, hoping Tommy would call. The phone rang, but it was Miles. "Just checking in to see if you're feeling better," he said.

"Thanks," I answered cautiously.

"Can you believe I stayed till four o'clock, and I've gotta be a decade older than most of the people there."

"Me too."

"It looked like you were having a good time dancing and all. Too bad you felt sick."

"Thanks." Did I really tell him I was sick? Or is he covering for me?

"Good thing we found a taxi for you; neither of us was in shape to drive."

I exhaled slowly. It didn't sound so bad. Maybe I hadn't done anything too stupid. "How did you get home?" I asked.

"A bunch of us walked to an all-night diner; then I walked home. Felt like I was back in college."

At dusk I took a slow walk around our neighborhood, admiring the old wooden houses painted soft shades of white, yellow, blue, and gray; the children playing outside after dinner in the joy of evening light. On my way home I stopped by the bodega and bought milk, eggs, butter, and chocolate chips. I was baking cookies and listening to Marvin Gaye when Tommy came home. I told him everything. I thought he wouldn't have much to say, because he knew I'd be hard enough on myself. That's his usual reaction to my bad behavior. But I was wrong.

"What the hell were you thinking about? A party to promote a rap album?"

"That's racist. You wouldn't say that if I'd gone to a party for a string quartet."

"Racist or not, it's realistic."

"Miles wanted you to go. He thought you would be interested. You weren't here, so I went. I thought I'd report back to you."

"And?"

"And what?"

"You can't report back to me, can you? Because you got drunk and can't remember anything."

"Tommy. I shouldn't have had that first drink. I know that better than anyone. So ease up."

"No. I'm not going to ease up. You're my wife. A grown woman, but sometimes you act less mature than Jake. And I don't need that. One teenager is plenty. I spent my whole goddamned weekend driving and dealing with Jake's mother and my mother. I don't want to come home and find you hungover."

We were in the kitchen. Cookies burned. Tommy paced. He wasn't even happy that I was baking. "It's that case, isn't it?" he said. "The baby your client killed."

"Excuse me? Who said that?" I pulled the last batch of cookies from the oven.

"It was even in the *New York Times,* Ginger. I read it this morning at my mother's. All the problems New York has? And they still find room for a dead baby from Port Grace. It's eating you up, and you don't even know it."

One by one I scooped the cookies with a spatula and arranged them on a paper towel to cool. I picked one up from an earlier, less-burnt batch and held it out to Tommy. "Come on, take it," I said.

"Can't you even answer me?"

"It's only a cookie."

He deflated. Took the cookie and hugged me tight. "Don't fall apart, Ginger. I can't go through that again."

That night I slept as though velcroed to him. I wished he were a kangaroo so I could crawl into his pouch and stay there until I was ready to come out.

24

Monday morning I placed a Ziploc bag filled with chocolate chip cookies on Mr. Ziznewski's doormat. The door opened. Mr. Z in his faded flannel robe and slippers. "What's this?" he asked. He slowly bent down to retrieve the bag; arthritis made him stiff in the morning.

"Cookies."

He opened the bag and selected one. Took a bite. "I can't remember the last time I had home baked cookies. Want to come in? Have some coffee?" he asked.

"No thanks. I've got work to do."

"It's six-thirty in the morning."

"Things are kind of hectic now."

"I saw it in the paper yesterday," he said. "About the baby."

I had no idea how to respond. I wasn't up to defensive explanations or philosophical discussions. Besides, Mr. Z's position was probably clear, narrow, and in conflict with my own. I knew that he liked me too much to give me a hard time. Still, awkwardness hung in the air, so I threw up my hands and attempted a smile. "Enjoy the cookies," I said, and turned toward the stairs.

"Thanks, Ginger," he said. "You know I have a sweet tooth."

I put cookies on Gloria's desk, I put cookies on Marco's desk, and then I flicked on the answering machine. The room filled with anonymous nasty messages from people who thought I was a friend of the Devil. Who thought I loved baby-killers.

Who thought I deserved to die the way Teddy died. I stopped listening after the third one, erased the tape and prepared for two morning court appearances—a child support hearing and a motion for increased visitation. It was nice to open those files, like friends I hadn't seen for a while. Their problems, that used to seem so thorny, were now as simple as a summer dress.

I entered the courthouse without my usual swagger; the specter of Teddy on my shoulders rendered me slightly disoriented, like a Somalian refugee dropped off in Wal-mart. Not that it was such a big deal. Some of the lawyers I passed in the halls dealt me a smidgen of extra attention, but as serious as it was, Violet's case actually fell within the mid-range of icky defense cases. The general population of Port Grace and surrounding areas would forget it sooner than other crimes of the past month—the gas station attendant who was shot, the University freshman who was raped, the car-jacking of a young suburban mother. They would be in the news longer than Violet and Teddy. Why? Because those victims could have been them/us/me; Violet and Teddy were Other. No news editor could imagine himself as Violet. Sure they'd feel bad, like you feel bad about babies in Sierra Leone getting their arms chopped off, it evokes a frisson of horror, but what can you do?

I met Eduardo for lunch. We ordered our food, exchanged pleasantries and gossip, and then he said, "I heard about the baby in your case. I'm sorry."

"Thanks."

"You're taking this hard," he observed. "That's not healthy."

I contemplated my egg salad sandwich. Messy. "Don't you ever have cases that get to you?"

"Of course. We all have weak spots. But you are a defense attorney and you have to act like one. So let me ask you this: will you give her the best defense you can?"

He wore a charcoal gray suit with a barely discernable ivory stripe in the weave, an ivory shirt with French cuffs, a silver tie and silver cufflinks; his glossy black hair revealing silver wingtips that weren't there when I first met him almost a decade ago. The best-dressed lawyer in Port Grace.

"You look good," I said.

"Answer my question."

"Look, I can't imagine representing someone if I can't do my best," I said. "You taught me that. Like the Harris case; even though I knew I was leaving, I gave it my all."

My last big case for Eduardo. The day the verdict came in I emptied my desk. An attempted rape. He was convicted, but I was on top of my game throughout the trial.

"And what did you do?" His voice was gentle as he coaxed it from me.

I mentally reviewed the case. "I stayed detached. And focused." I spoke slowly, having too much respect for Eduardo to give him a glib answer.

He gave me time, ate his club sandwich, and no mayonnaise fell on his tie.

"I developed my theory of the case and it was strong."

"And what was it?" He signaled the waitress for coffee and then turned his full attention to me.

"Identity. That's what it was all about. It was a tainted show-up." The police grabbed Harris five blocks from the scene, a tall black guy in baggy jeans and dark hooded sweatshirt, a description that fits about eight thousand men in Port Grace. They drove the victim to Harris, who was cuffed and caged in a squad car. "Is this the guy?" they asked. Of course she said yes; she was wounded, terrified, traumatized, surrounded by police officers who wanted an answer, who wanted a collar, who wanted a closed case; and he was a tall black guy in baggy jeans and dark hooded sweatshirt, like eight thousand other men in Port Grace, like the man who attacked her. "That case should have been thrown out at the identity hearing," I said. "The cops fed him to her. What's she gonna say? No?"

"Did you ever ask him if he did it?"

"Of course not."

"When you were preparing his case did you think he did it?"

"I didn't let myself think that way. I stayed focused on the strategy."

"And that's what you did for every case you handled in my office. Why is this one with the baby different?"

I sipped my coffee. Absentmindedly pulled a smoke from my purse and tapped it on the table. "I've been away from it. I haven't done a felony for almost four years. Only a few misdemeanors and municipal court cases. I've lost my edge."

"That's it?"

"For me it is. Tommy thinks it's all about my childhood experiences. And then there's Marco. He has such a conscience, I feel guilty around him." I looked at the cigarette in disgust and broke it in half.

Eduardo snorted. "Marco? He was a cop. He's got a history. Don't worry about his conscience."

"But he quit. He's trying to do right, he wants to dedicate himself to positive work. Not that being a cop can't be positive, but apparently it wasn't for him."

"Does she have an alibi?" he asked.

I shook my head. "None."

"Let me give you some advice." He adjusted his cuffs. "Plead it out. You won't win. Especially if the autopsy report is conclusive, because you will never persuade a jury with that in evidence."

"What if someone else shook the baby?"

"Baby's father? Your client's boyfriend?"

I nodded.

"Can you prove it?"

"Probably not. But I might have enough for reasonable doubt."

"Only if you can get her off the scene. If she was present when the baby was shaken she'll be convicted for not protecting her child. If there was someone else involved, and she feeds him to the D.A., you might work a decent deal. Offer to plead to child endangerment. I predict that if the autopsy report concludes that the baby died of shaken baby syndrome, and you have a jury trial, your client will be convicted of manslaughter no matter what you do." He bunched up his napkin, tossed it on the table and adjusted his tie. "I'm sending some referrals to you," he said. "A couple of pre-nups. And a doctor friend of Giselle's who wants a divorce."

"You're the best." Paying clients. Hallelujah.

"Plenty of doctors get divorced. Do well on this one and I'm sure he'll send his friends to you."

"Bad news for them is good news for me."

"More or less. So. When will you get the autopsy report?"

"Maybe this afternoon."

"Plead out. You'll save yourself a lot of trouble." He was right. Plea bargains are the most important tactic in criminal law. The vast majority of cases are disposed of via plea bargains, because trials are too labor-intensive and time-consuming for any but the strongest cases or the wealthiest clients. He put a twenty on the table for a twelve-dollar lunch, prepared to stand and then stopped. "Ginger? We appealed the Harris case."

"You did?"

He nodded.

"What happened?"

"The Appellate Division reversed and remanded. A new trial was held, the show-up identification was suppressed, and he walked."

"No kidding." Defendants win fewer than 10% of appeals.

"Congratulations. But wasn't he indigent?" Appeals are very time-consuming, which means expensive.

"Yes, but remember we took it because the Public Defender had a conflict, so they couldn't do the appeal either. I did it because it was a strong case. It was the right thing to do. The trial judge needed a slap."

"It's great that you appealed, but is there a reason that you're telling me now? Did I do a bad job at the trial?"

"No. You did well at the trial. And you made all the proper objections for us to use on appeal. Something about this baby case reminded me. I think you'll plead out on it. And you should. But if you don't? Make sure you follow through. Don't take off in another direction to avoid a bitter ending. It'll catch up with you. And remember, the end isn't always the end." He checked his watch and stood up. "Anyway, Harris?" He caught my eye. "He was picked up again two years ago on a rape and kidnapping. Convicted. Lost that appeal. We didn't do the case, but I heard it was a clean trial. He pulled hard time."

Eduardo knows how to end a story. He punctuated it with a friendly kiss, and exited with panache. Even in that diner heads turned when he walked by, like he was moving down the carpet toward his Oscar.

Marco brought me the autopsy report, and the Medical Examiner confirmed that Teddy died from the effects of shaken baby syndrome. "You know what this means?" he said. "Somebody shook the little guy so hard that his brains ricocheted off the inside of his skull."

"Jesus, Marco, there's no point in being so graphic."

"What exactly is the point? And don't you think the D.A. will be at least that graphic in front of a jury?"

I didn't even try to answer. Get off it, Marco, I wanted to say, but he deserved better than that. I'd hardly seen him all day and we hadn't discussed the Sunday morning scene at my house. "Not that I'm trying to change the subject, but I'm sorry about yesterday."

"Forget it. We're friends. You're gonna screw up sometimes. So am I. You should call me next time you're ready to fall off."

"It's hard to ask you for help," I said. "You know. Real help."

"Why?"

I looked him over. Thick forearms. Dark eyes. Jeans, white T-shirt, Nikes. Angry about the autopsy report. "I don't know."

We stayed quiet for a while, looking at each other, breathing, avoiding the autopsy report that lay on my desk like a loaded gun. Finally Marco spoke. "The cookies are good," he said. "I already ate three."

25

The D.A. charged Violet with aggravated manslaughter, with lesser-included offenses of reckless manslaughter and child endangerment, which meant that even if the jury decided not to convict her of aggravated manslaughter, they could convict her of the other offenses. It gave the jury choices. And a conviction on any of them would result in Violet doing time in state prison. Her bail was set at $100,000, way too high, and I was not immediately able to come up with the bond, so she had to stay in county jail for a few days while I figured that out. Marco, Gloria, and I kept the office running while coping with the fallout from Teddy's death. Court dates, client appointments, and deadlines couldn't be ignored. We got no adjournments, no mental health days. I had to advocate for all of my clients, not just Violet. Gloria telephoned every jail, hospital, and rehab center in a fifty-mile radius of Old Bridge but was unable to locate Violet's mother. I considered driving through the wreckage of Old Bridge's south ward looking for her, but Violet didn't want me to, and therefore there was no point in burning my time on that. I clung to the possibility that AJ was the criminal, the guilty one. Even if I couldn't prove it, I could use him as a red herring to plant reasonable doubt in the jury's mind about whether or not Violet shook Teddy.

Marco drove to Western State to squeeze something out of AJ and to visit Violet's father, for whom he hoped to obtain funeral leave. I had no desire to go; I saw too many prisons when I worked for Eduardo. The first couple of times it was interesting, even exciting, because prison is so extreme. I got over that fast, and dreaded the bitterness and oppression that fills prisons like humidity, seeping into my pores as I walked the corridors past cells stacked like dog kennels, through numerous security checkpoints, trying to chat up the guards and not show my nervousness. And the clients? For a lot of them, Eduardo and I were their only line to the outside, and we were most definitely their only hope. I would think, My God, the only chance this guy has of getting out of prison is me! Sometimes I was so overwhelmed by the responsibility that on the drive home I pulled over and vomited.

Marco returned to the office at six o'clock. "How'd it go?" I asked.

"I got nothing. He's wound up tight and he's not talking."

"Nothing?"

"His line is that Violet's been out of his life for months, he only saw her a couple times to calm her down because she threatened to call his wifc."

"He isn't upset about Teddy?"

"I think he is—but there's nobody he can say that to. He can't talk to his wife or his family or his friends about it. It's messing him up big-time though."

"Do you think he's upset because Teddy's dead or because he did it?"

"I don't know. Maybe both."

"How did he react to the paternity test results?"

"He said it doesn't connect him to this mess. That's what he called it—this mess."

"We have to find witnesses, people who saw him at Violet's, who saw them together. We don't have to prove that he did it, just make a jury believe that he could have. And we've got the domestic violence case showing a history of violence."

"He's livid about that. Apparently he was on the list for the police department, but with the restraining order he couldn't carry a firearm, so they took him off the list."

"Will he testify for Violet?"

"No way. He's one of those people who are deceitful by nature. He'll shift positions if he believes it's to his advantage."

"He'll lie."

"Right. But on the plus side, he lacks credibility. A jury will see how slippery he is. They won't trust him."

"Even if there are no first-hand witnesses," I said, "and all the evidence is circumstantial, then we'll subpoena him as a hostile witness. I'll make him lose his temper on the stand." I saw it clearly. Bulky blond AJ, insecure about being a prison guard instead of a cop, history of drinking and domestic violence, I knew exactly how to push his buttons. He's from the poor and rural quadrant of the state that pleaded to have the prison built there to create jobs, steady jobs that don't require a college education and pay well enough to edge a person into the middle class, especially with overtime. I could find plenty to probe with to make him lash out at me and scare the jury into reasonable doubt. I pushed away my fleeting impression of him walking across the hospital lawn in his Red Sox cap, clutching his place in the Elmore Leonard book, just a guy, not a monster.

Marco looked sapped; the lines in his face were deeper than they were a week before, and he lacked the crisp, cocky, comic attitude that makes my office a happier place. "That might work," he said. "He certainly looks more like he could shake a kid to death than she does. Can you get her to give him up?"

"Not yet. I'll work on her. What happened with her father?" Frank Rosada was a sympathetic figure, but there was little he could do to help Violet. Picked up a few years ago for selling twenty bucks' worth of crack cocaine, he's doing fifteen to twenty on his third conviction for sale of small quantities of crack, plus another ten for parole violation. He's forty-two years old and in poor health; even with good behavior he must serve two-thirds of his sentence; and so by the time he's released he'll be an old man both physically and psychologically.

"A guard got shanked and they're on lockdown for a week." He pulled a folded piece of paper from his pocket. "He gave me this letter for Violet. He's a nice guy; just got a raw deal." That letter would be the extent of Violet's family support throughout the funeral of her child, and her impending trial.

Tuesday night I was having a quiet dinner with Tommy, trying to gain my equilibrium, when the phone rang. Tommy picked it up and after a short conversation, hung up. "That was Jake," he said. "He's on a Greyhound. He'll be at the station in an hour."

"What station?"

"Here. Port Grace."

"I thought he was coming home Saturday."

"So did I."

"He didn't call and tell you? Vanessa didn't call?"

"Nobody called."

"What did he say?"

"He wants to come home."

"I can't believe Vanessa didn't call you."

"She thinks he's an adult, that he can make his own decisions."

I sighed in exasperation. I'm in no position to tell someone how to raise a kid, but even I know that a sixteen-year-old needs guidance. Vanessa is a poet. When Jake was four she left Tommy for a guy who had just published his first novel. She took Jake with her, but brought him back a few months later. For years Tommy kept the note she sent along with him:

Why does the mother always get stuck with the kid? You take

him; you scare away the nightmares and cut the crusts off of his sandwich. You get up at six in the morning to pour his cereal. You read *Mike Mulligan and his Steam Shovel* four times in a row every night. You cook plain spaghetti for every dinner. You do the endless cycles of laundry and food shopping. You do it.

Eventually he tore it up, because he didn't want Jake to ever find it. The funny thing was Tommy already did most of that stuff. The way I hear it Vanessa was always busy being creative, out looking for new experiences and inspiration. "I think it's sweet that he wants to come home," I said. "Don't you think he's old enough to decide how much he wants to see her?"

"Maybe. It doesn't seem like it should be that simple, but maybe it is. He's at an age where it's normal to want to be with his friends. I'm sure that's what this is about. Plus Vanessa . . ." His voice trailed into the sunset. "I don't want him to ever think I kept him from his mother."

"That's ridiculous. You bend over backward to accommodate her. This must happen all the time with teenagers."

We went to the bus station together. Jake wrapped me up in a big hug. "Four days and you've grown," I said. "It's been way too quiet without you." Tommy got a hug too. We stopped for ice cream cones and then dropped Jake off at Tony's house where his crew was gathering.

"Be home by midnight," Tommy said. "And call us if you need a ride. No questions asked."

"You worry about him, don't you?" I said as we drove home.

"Of course. I'm an alcoholic, his mother is a head-case, I watch him all the time."

"He seems fine."

"I know he's had some beers. He's probably smoked pot a few times. But so far he seems in control. I was much worse at his age. He's more into playing music than getting wasted. But I still have to keep watching. And you too. Tell me if you see anything you think I should know about."

"Of course." I used to smoke quite a bit of pot myself, even after I stopped drinking, although that's a direct violation of AA rules. It calmed me down. But years ago Tommy made it clear that I can't smoke it at home because of Jake, so when I'm wound up as tight as a fastball I go for a run. Or throw things.

As we pulled into the driveway my cell phone vibrated. Marco. "Hey, what's up?"

"You'll never believe this," he said. "I just got a call from Severino; he's on the night shift and they're working with Walden County cops. They picked up AJ for questioning."

"Seriously? Did you get any details?"

"Not much. They didn't arrest him, but something's up."

"That's great news. Call me if you hear anything else."

We hung up and I gave Tommy a big kiss. I slept well that night.

26

Marco, Laura, and Gloria made a heroic effort and organized Teddy's funeral. Marco's family priest agreed to say Mass. Laura donated flowers. Gloria got on the phone and collected donations to pay for the burial. I called Mr. Frank, who said he and his wife would come to the funeral and that he might be able to post a bond for Violet. "I own quite a bit of property here. It's not worth much, but I keep hoping someday . . ."

"Are you sure you want to take that risk?" I asked.

"What risk? She's not going anywhere, is she?"

"No, but still, to put up your property as collateral?"

"Let me talk to my wife. I'll look into it. Give me a few days."

I cashed in some of my credibility chips and persuaded the judge to allow me to drive Violet from the jail to the funeral, and, even more important, to keep her out of leg shackles for the duration. He refused to budge on handcuffs though, and ordered that a deputy sheriff must follow my car and sit behind Violet at the funeral. I considered postponing the funeral until Violet was out on bail, but I didn't know when that would be, and we needed that funeral, a repository for our grief, a place where we were permitted to shut out the rest of the world and focus on the tragedy of a child's death.

The funeral was Thursday morning. The deputy's car tailed us as I drove Violet from the jail to the chapel. She wept for the whole ride, and I chewed my lip until it bled. At a stoplight I slipped a couple of Ativans into Violet's mouth, hoping to calm her down, and then I popped one myself. I was nervous that the deputy would see me putting my hand up to Violet's mouth and pull me over to investigate. But he didn't. What terrible thing could I be doing, anyway? But cops don't think like the rest of us; they're always one step ahead, scanning for trouble. I wanted to pull the car over and cry it out, take enough time to allow the whole cosmic wrongness of Teddy's death to pierce and flood me with anguish. But I couldn't. A police car was behind me and a patient and generous priest awaited our arrival.

I parked in the lot next to Our Lady of the Rosary and when I got out the sun slashed my eyes, so I leaned back in, pulled my shades off of the dashboard, put them on, and walked to the other side of the car to get Violet out. The deputy slid into the space next to mine, and he stood watch as I tugged Violet from the car. He moved toward me, as if to help. "Give us some space. Please," I snapped. He shrugged and moved back one step. He wasn't taking any chances on losing a felon up for manslaughter.

As we began the aching journey from the parking lot to the church, I saw reporters clustered on the sidewalk and two city cruisers parked in front of the church. It had been a slow news week in Port Grace and Violet would pay the price. I supported her across the church lawn, past the large wooden cross, the white plaster Madonna, and the rose bushes that did not yet bear flowers, only leaves and thorns. Reporters bore in and followed us up the steps. "Get out of here, you sick fucks," I yelled.

Marco appeared. He herded them back to the sidewalk and gestured to one of his police buddies to keep them under control and out of the way. "Very nice," he whispered, as he strode past me to Violet's other side and helped me safeguard her into the small stone chapel that adjoins the massive church. "They'll probably put that in the paper tomorrow."

I felt the deputy shadowing us. "I don't care. They are sick fucks. I'll be happy to tell them again."

"Shh." He frowned at me. He crossed himself as we paused to adjust to the dimness inside the chapel, and then we walked down the aisle to Teddy's coffin. The chapel smelled of roses and candles, stone and grief. I had convinced Violet to keep the casket closed, because I knew that looking at Teddy would destroy us all. It was covered with white tulips, yellow roses, blue delphiniums, and a framed photograph of Teddy. A large wooden crucifix hung on the back wall. Only a small scattering of people were present. Marco, Laura, and a couple of counselors from the women's shelter. Mr. and Mrs. Frank. One well-behaved reporter. A couple of older Latina women, who might have been friends of Violet's grandmother. Whoever they were they did not step forward and offer her their condolences.

I was infuriated to see Michelle alone in a pew. I steamed up to her. "What the hell are you doing here?"

"That baby in that coffin is my client," she said, as her features settled into immutable self-righteousness.

"You are a sanctimonious bitch," I said, but my words were edged with grief and she knew it. "Can't you let this go?" She didn't bother to answer, just fired a scornful glance my way, so I journeyed back to the front of the chapel and sat next to Violet. Her hands were cuffed in front of her so she couldn't even wipe the tears from her face. Somehow we got through the brief service and then Marco and I buttressed her and exited through the back of the chapel with our deputy escort right behind us. As we walked down the steps I heard an engine gunning and looked up to see a green pickup truck roaring out of the parking lot. Violet was too far gone to notice but Marco, who never misses anything, gave me a questioning look and I nodded. AJ. We drove through waves of despair to the cemetery where Teddy was buried next to Violet's grandmother. Violet was beyond crying and I was ready to start.

After the funeral I went to my office and met with a couple of clients, getting through the appointments on autopilot. I wanted to tell them, "I'm sorry. I'm not myself today. I was at a child's funeral this morning." People should just look at me and know, know that I needed to grieve, that my inner landscape was altered, that the world was not the same since Teddy died.

I think about public behavior sometimes, like when I'm at the grocery store, how we all behave in a certain expected manner. And yet I know that someone in that store is infused with tragedy—maybe a cancer diagnosis, a miscarriage, an unfaithful spouse, or a parent slipping into dementia. But if that person blocks the aisle as they stare at the overwhelming choices, unable to decide which laundry detergent, which cereal, and I cannot get my cart through though I try to rather than disturb them, they will usually look at me, startled in the headlights of my normalcy, and apologize; "Excuse me, I'm sorry," as they move their cart from my path. They rarely say "Fuck you, my wife just left me," or "Can't you see that I'm having a nervous breakdown in front of fifty-three choices of toothpaste? How can I possibly know if I want foaming action, triple protection, fresh confidence, whitening gel, or an explosion of flavor? Do I need baking soda, fluoride, fresh mint, or anti-cavity?"

And so, I slogged through the most necessary tasks, feeling worthless and lonely. Gloria was at her other job, and Marco was out interviewing witnesses for a forthcoming custody trial. Even Mr. Ziznewski was not in sight. Eventually I went home and slept for two hours, a deep and heavy sleep from which I awoke feeling irritable and groggy. I stripped off my black funeral suit, which, thanks to my nap, was now so wrinkled it would require steam pressing before I could wear it again. I dug through my clothes and pulled on plaid flannel pants and a heavy flannel shirt of a different plaid, producing a satisfying design clash. I splashed water on my face. Brushed my teeth and hair, added thick socks to my outfit, grabbed my cell phone, and padded downstairs, with Cat trailing me. Tommy was in the kitchen. Low-volume Vivaldi. A vase filled with dogwood blossoms. The smell of onions. "Where's Jake?" I asked.

"Practice. I'm making lasagna; he said he'd be home by seven o'clock."

"I'm starving." Had I eaten all day?

"There's fresh mozzarella," he said. "And some decent tomatoes." I grabbed a cutting board and put together a snack. Tommy checked out my outfit. "It's a little warm for flannel." He gestured to the window where spring was laughing in my face. It was one of those golden early evenings that push the depressed to suicide. "Rough day?"

"Horrible. Worse than you could imagine. Today was the funeral."

"I'm sorry," he said. After a respectful interval he asked, "Do you think she did it?"

"Violet?"

He nodded.

I pulled slightly away from him. "You know I can't talk about that."

"I'm not asking you to break confidentiality. Just wondering what's on your mind."

"What's on my mind? Giving her the best defense that I can. It doesn't matter to me what she did. I don't need to know."

"It doesn't matter to you? Do you mean that?"

"Of course! You've seen me defend worse cases than this. Why are you digging?"

"The paper said the autopsy report was conclusive. Doesn't that mean that she shook him?"

"Maybe someone else shook him. Maybe she did it without meaning to."

"How could someone shake their baby without meaning to?"

"They could be in a frenzy, and not realize what they were doing. Most people don't even know about shaken baby syndrome. They're frustrated and they think shaking is better than smacking the kid."

"How about walking away until they cool down?"

His icy logic infuriated me. "You know it's not that simple."

"Parents shouldn't hurt their kids. That's pretty simple."

"And kids shouldn't go to bed hungry, or be sold into slavery, or born drug addicted and HIV positive. The world sucks and you know it."

"Oh, that's helpful. The world sucks. Is that part of your opening statement?"

"Why are we fighting?"

"Because there's nothing worse than the death of a child?"

I paced to the French doors that open onto our backyard, filling the kitchen with light, then opened the doors and stepped outside. Spring was settling in with stunning predictability. Despite the vagaries of weather, nature can be counted on for certain things. Spring in the East means new leaves will unfurl, leaves that in autumn will age and tumble to the ground. Grass grows. Fireflies appear. Bees and butterflies perform their duties. Tommy had turned the sprinkler on. It wasn't hot enough to need it, but I enjoyed watching the sparkling whips of water, and was soothed by the rhythmic swirl of sound. Our lawn is so small that we trim the grass with a push-mower. A mélange of shade trees, shrubs and flowers grace the yard and frame the small brick patio where we have eaten many pleasant dinners, and some not so pleasant. Robins, sparrows, blue jays and cardinals competed for space at the squirrel-proof birdfeeder Tommy installed. He followed me outside and I turned to him.

"I figured it out."

"What?"

"The difference between you and me. You are the type of person who always keeps your birdfeeder full. I, on the other hand, would buy three or four birdfeeders, keep them all full for two weeks and then forget about them. Do you know that very few people actually fill their birdfeeders regularly? There are two schools of thought on that. One is that once you start feeding the birds you have to keep it up because they come to rely on you as a food source. The other is that it's OK to forget sometimes, because that's more like nature. Availability of food isn't predictable in nature. One day there are berries and worms everywhere. Turn around and some blue jays have taken them all. There's nothing left."

Tom looked at me like I was nuts. Tears stung my eyes. He put his arm around me. "Let's get dinner on the table. Jake will be home soon."

"I should go back to the office. I'm behind on everything."

"You won't be able to help anyone if you're hungry and exhausted. Come on, let's eat."

I came out on the other side of the meal feeling pretty good. Jake went upstairs to do his homework and Tommy leafed through the paper while I cleaned up. "*Taxi Driver*'s on tonight," he said; "and *Goodfellas.* It's DeNiro night." He knew my weakness for DeNiro, and it was easy to persuade me to curl up on the couch for the evening. I didn't know that he'd turned off my cell phone until I got out of bed in the morning and went to look for it in the kitchen. He was in the shower and I thought about going into the bathroom and yelling at him, but I restrained myself. After all, he is Tommy.

27

After the week of Teddy-grief I needed a quiet weekend with Tommy and Jake. On Saturday I worked for several hours, ran, and took care of errands. Tommy and I ate dinner at a Chinese restaurant, saw a production of the August Wilson play, *Fences,* and then stopped for coffee; so it was almost midnight when we returned to a house filled with Jake and a dozen other kids. Bob Dylan, *Blood on the Tracks,* cranked up full volume. Beer cans in plain sight. The lingering smells of pot and popcorn. Tommy and I observed with mild amusement as they saw us and calculated their options—run out the door or hold their position. The ones who knew us well, the ones who for years had been in and out of our house on an almost daily basis, rallied. "Mr. Burns, Mrs. Burns! Good to see you! How was the movie?" Someone softened the music and from the kitchen I heard, "Jake, your parents are home."

"Hey guys," Tommy said, as he perched on the arm of a chair. "What's up?"

Benny picked up an acoustic guitar that was leaning against the couch. "We were working out some songs, you know, some new ones. And these guys stopped by." He indicated non-band friends.

Jake tumbled down the stairs, discreetly followed by a girl with long brown hair, who veered into the kitchen and disappeared into a cluster of girls huddled near the refrigerator. "Pop! You guys are home early!" Jake grinned, like seeing us was the highlight of what appeared to have been a pretty good evening.

"You call this early?" Tommy said.

"No, it's just, what time is it?"

"Around midnight."

"Oh jeez, I had no idea. We were working on some new songs and I knew you wouldn't mind if I had a few friends over. Right?"

"Of course," Tommy said. "You know your friends are always welcome here. I'm worried about all this though." He indicated the beer cans being scooped into a Hefty bag as the kids shook themselves into action.

"We never drink and drive. And it was just a few beers."

"Anybody need a ride home?" I asked the group mobilizing in the kitchen.

Everyone looked at someone else to answer. "We can walk," Benny finally said with an arm-sweep encompassing an indeterminate number of kids.

"Anybody who is too far to walk or doesn't have someone to walk with? Get ready to go and I'll give you a ride." Five of them packed into Tommy's Explorer, which was a little roomier than my Jimmy, and I spent the next forty-five minutes driving. The car reeked of beer, cologne, and teenagers. I stayed quiet and listened to them chatter about surprisingly mundane subjects: a tedious chemistry teacher, the new deli that opened near school, the Comedy Central lineup.

"Goodnight, Mrs. Burns," they all remembered to say. "Thanks for the ride." When I got home Tommy and Jake were at the kitchen table, entrenched in nachos and conversation, so I went to bed. I didn't want to read anything having to do with crime, law, police, detectives, or lawyers, which eliminated most of my books, but I came across Roger Kahn's *The Boys of Summer,* which my college roommate and best friend Becky, who is a sports reporter, sent to me. I got into bed and immersed myself in the 1950s Brooklyn Dodgers. On Sunday we slept late, consumed coffee and bagels, and read the papers. Tommy swept through the international and national news, and then enjoyed a leisurely perusal of the arts and entertainment sections and the Sunday magazines. I scanned the editorial pages, local news, sports, comics, and columns on cars and health. In the afternoon we whittled away an hour at a nursery where we bought pink geraniums for the window boxes, yellow snapdragons and orange marigolds for the front yard, and coral impatiens and blue lobelia to plant in pots on the patio. Then we went home and planted them.

We ate dinner at Gino's—me, Tommy, Jake and his friend Benny. Halfway through a savory crab cake my cell phone rang. Tommy gave me the "that is really obnoxious to have your cell phone on in a restaurant" look, but when I reflexively checked caller ID it was Marco and I don't not answer to Marco. I put a hand over one ear to dim the restaurant chatter. "Marco?"

"I've got news."

"Hold on." I quickly walked to the door and outside into the twilight. "What's up?" I stepped aside to allow the entrance of a multi-generational family dressed for a special occasion.

"AJ's been arrested."

"Say that again."

"AJ's been arrested. They just brought him in."

"It's about time." I felt myself relax in places I didn't know I was tense.

"That doesn't mean your girl is out of the woods," he cautioned.

"Of course not. But it has to put her in a better position than she's in now." I rubbed my hand over the rough back of the life-sized plaster swordfish that ornaments the entrance to Gino's.

"Where are you?"

"Gino's. With Tommy and Jake."

"Call me later."

I flipped shut my phone and went inside the restaurant, lost in thought as I tried to calculate the implications of AJ's arrest. I stopped at our table and was startled out of my reverie by the tableau of chowder, Italian bread, hungry teenagers, and Tommy flushed with pleasure as he enjoyed dinner with the boys. "I have to go to the office," I said.

Tommy looked at me. "Not now, Ginger. It's Sunday night. We're having dinner together."

"I know. But it's important."

"More important than your family? Can't it wait?"

I sat down, surprised by Tommy's protest. "You're right." I poked my fork into the remainder of my crab cake, shredding it. I needed to talk to Violet. See her reaction when she heard that AJ was arrested; maybe she'd finally break down and implicate him. I reached for my phone to call Laura and ask if I could drop by after dinner.

"What are you doing?" Tommy asked.

I dropped the phone back in my bag. Turned to Jake and Benny. "So. Tell me about these new songs you guys are writing."

After cannolis and espresso we returned home. Jake and Benny got on the Internet to research a history project. "Labor unions in New England," Jake replied to Tom's query. He spotted the expression Tommy gets when he is about to begin pontificating. "It's okay, Dad. We've got it," he said. "But we'll let you know if we get stuck," he added, not wanting to hurt Tommy's feelings.

Tommy gave him a thumbs-up and turned to me just as I was picking up the phone. "Who are you calling?"

"Laura. I need to go over there and talk to Violet. Something's come up. Something big."

"Can it wait until tomorrow?"

I considered. Theoretically it could wait until tomorrow. But I was a hound dog and a rabbit just crossed my path. I shook my head. "Sorry. I've got to take care of it now. But I won't be long."

He walked away and I knew he was upset, but I dialed Laura's number anyway. "Laura," I said when she picked up. "It's Ginger. Can you put Violet on?"

"She's sleeping."

I checked my watch. Eight-thirty. "Can you wake her up?"

"I'd rather not. What's going on?"

"AJ's been arrested."

"Does that mean he did it?"

"They must think so."

"So they'll let Violet go?"

"I don't know about that. They can both be charged. Anyway, can I talk to her?"

"She's been having trouble sleeping. I wish you'd wait until tomorrow."

I backed down. "Call me in the morning. At my office. And don't tell her about AJ. I need to see her reaction."

I was restless. "Want to take a walk?" I asked Tommy. He shook his head, not looking up from the papers he was grading. I picked up my briefcase and went upstairs to the room we use as an office, although when we work at home it's usually at the kitchen table or from a comfortable chair in the living room. The office is the most sterile room in the house, filled with file cabinets and cartons and a couple of old desks. But there's a computer, and Jake was on the one downstairs. I needed to research a removal case; my client's ex-wife wanted to move to Arizona with their daughter, and he didn't want her to go. I clicked onto Westlaw, typed in my search query, and became engrossed in my work; when I went to bed it was well past midnight and Tommy was asleep, or pretending to be. I put my arm around him but he didn't wake up.

28

On Monday morning Marco took his Labor Law final exam, and I was alone in the office. At nine o'clock I couldn't stand it anymore, so I called Laura. "I'll bring over bagels," I said.

"Don't upset her," Laura told me as I deposited my offering of a half-dozen mixed bagels and a tub of cream cheese on the table. "She's fragile."

Violet was in bed watching *Blue's Clues.* She wore a flannel nightgown that must have been Laura's because it was huge on her and I don't see many nineteen-year-olds in the flannel section of Victoria's Secret. "I brought bagels," I said. "Would you like one?" She shook her head and kept her eyes on Blue. "AJ was arrested last night."

That trumped *Blue's Clues.* "AJ?"

"Yes."

"Why?"

"What do you think?"

"I don't know."

"Shaking Teddy."

She looked horrified. "No, he didn't. I told you that."

"Why are you protecting him? Are you scared of him?"

"He didn't hurt Teddy, I'm telling you."

I stood in the doorway. "How can you be sure? You told me there was a gap of time when you went out for pizza, and he was alone with Teddy. Remember? And Teddy was crying when you got back, wasn't he?"

"He loves kids. He wouldn't hurt him."

"He hurt you. And somebody hurt Teddy."

She turned back to the TV. It was time for *Little Bear.* I sat down and stayed quiet, hoping that the silence would make her nervous and she'd start talking. On the desk were some small watercolor sketches of flowers. I picked up one of a Virginia bluebell and studied it. "Who painted this?"

"I did."

"Really? It's good. I didn't know you were an artist."

A shadow of pleasure skimmed across her face. "I'm not. I've always liked to draw though, and Laura bought the paints for me."

"They're lovely. You're talented. Maybe you can study art someday." I examined all of the sketches and the watercolor kit Laura gave to her, and allowed myself a brief fantasy of Violet strolling across the Winslow campus with her portfolio and a backpack filled with art supplies. Then I snapped off the television. "Was Teddy alone with anyone besides you and AJ in the two weeks before he went to the hospital?"

"No."

"Did you hurt Teddy?"

"No."

"Then it must have been AJ."

"Nobody hurt him. They made a mistake."

"And when Teddy went to the hospital and the DCW worker asked you if you shook Teddy, why did you say 'I don't know'?"

"I didn't. I told you that."

"The police report says you did. So does the caseworker's contact sheet."

She pulled a blanket around herself. "I was scared. Doctors and nurses and police everywhere and everyone was talking and throwing questions at me. I was only sick with worrying about Teddy, so I don't remember what I said. But I never said that I shook him." She shook her head emphatically, braids snapping in the air. She was retreating so I pulled copies of the police report and the caseworker's contact sheets from my briefcase.

"Look here." I moved from the chair to the bed so I was close to her, and pointed to statements that I had highlighted in yellow. "Two different sources report that when asked if you shook Teddy, you said 'I don't know.' "

"Why are you accusing me? I thought you were my lawyer. Anyway, they're lying."

"Both of them?" I've seen police officers lie under oath and I'm sure that caseworkers occasionally alter their notes. However the police report and the social worker's statements were contemporaneous and almost identical. "I'll tell you what I think. I think AJ shook him and you were covering up for him but you hadn't figured out a story yet; they took you by surprise."

"No. What happened is I didn't know what they meant. When she said shake I thought she meant like bumping him on the crib when I picked him up. Something light, you know, an accident. Not *shake.*"

"Did you explain that?"

"I was afraid to say anything. They were mean and suspicious and I was so upset, and nobody cared that my baby was in a coma."

"Let's go back over the last couple times you saw AJ. Did he break up with you?"

She didn't answer.

"Did he tell you he wasn't coming back?"

"He didn't mean it," she said. "He gets in these moods. But he always comes back."

"Did you threaten to call his wife?"

"I wouldn't have done it."

"But he thought you might. Right?"

She nodded slightly.

"So he was angry, and when he's angry he gets violent. He beat you up when you were pregnant. He's capable of hurting a baby."

She turned the TV back on.

I tossed the picture aside and slammed the TV off. "Damn it, don't you understand how serious this is?"

"I don't want to talk about it."

"This isn't a game. Somebody shook Teddy and his brain bled until he died. You told me it wasn't you. So it had to be AJ. Don't protect him. You'll go to prison and he'll be at home with his wife and kids." As I spoke she lay down under the blanket and turned away from me. Then she put the pillow over her head. I turned the TV back on and slammed the door on my way out.

Laura was preoccupied with flowers; I didn't feel like talking, so I threw a wave her way and hustled toward the door. "What happened?" Laura stopped me.

"Nothing." Frustration filtered through my voice.

She placed her hands on her hips, over the green work smock she wore. "Why are you so hard on her?"

Was I hard on her? I looked at the baskets Laura was filling with orange, yellow and blue flowers. No ambivalence there. "I don't know what you're talking about."

She tucked a nasturtium amid some bachelor's buttons. "It seems like you don't care about her."

"It's not my job to care about her." I felt myself turning nasty, so I stopped. "Of course I care. But that won't keep her out of prison."

"Whether she goes to prison or not, she needs people to care about her."

"I can't go down that road. I'm trying to be a good lawyer for her, but that's all I've got. Fifty other clients need my attention too. She's going to have to find friendship, love, and nurturing somewhere else."

"I'm not saying you should adopt her. You just don't seem very compassionate."

"I'm doing the best I can. And I have to get back to work now."

She proffered one of the flower-filled baskets. "Happy May Day."

"May Day?"

"May baskets? Maypoles? You never danced around the Maypole when you were a kid?"

"No way. Must be an East Coast thing."

I made a home visit to a client who is a paraplegic (who says I'm not compassionate?), and gave her the May basket. Back at my office I left a message for Michelle to call me so I could find out what they were doing with AJ, and started writing a timeline for the months leading to trial. Although it was scheduled for September, four months hence, I had to attack it immediately—amass lists, indexes, references and cross-references; engineer blueprints and diagrams; chart, plot, design, organize, rationalize, schematize, contrive; create working plans, game plans, ground plans, strategic plans, tactical plans; draw upon forethought and foresight; project, propose, envisage, and delineate the contours of the prosecution's case, the State terrain, view the Big Picture, the Forest, AND the Trees.

In addition to Violet, approximately fifty other clients jammed my file cabinet. All needy, all struggling through the wreckage of shattered lives. Soon, very soon, Violet would have to be just another case, take her place among the others glaring at me wherever I turned. I needed to gain perspective, move Violet to the back burner. I allowed myself a morning of planning before she became just another client.

I considered expert witnesses. I needed a psychologist to

evaluate Violet, and an expert on shaken baby syndrome, preferably a pediatric neurologist. Probably an expert on battered-woman's syndrome. Most of all I needed a medical examiner who would punch holes in the local medical examiner's report, thereby opening the possibility that Teddy died from something other than being shaken. I wasn't optimistic about my chances of finding such a person. There was some weak research indicating that shaken baby symptoms might be caused by vaccines but so far that theory wasn't helpful in the legal realm.

Once I had my experts I had to prepare them for their testimony and cross-examination. The State would have their own squad of experts. Teddy's treating physician from St. Joe's would testify for them; they would have a neurologist explain the constellation of symptoms that are definitive of shaken baby syndrome, and probably a pediatric ophthalmologist to affirm that the type of retinal hemorrhaging that occurs in shaken baby syndrome is unique; all confirming the results of the medical examiner who performed the autopsy on Teddy. And of course that M.E. would also testify for them.

How could I conquer that? When the experts were finished, there would be no question that the act was committed; the only question would be who committed it, and who, if anyone, was present when the act was committed. The verdict would turn on credibility—Violet versus AJ, it would be a he-said, she-said trial. In a different type of case the lack of solid evidence could result in a hung jury. But a crime against a baby? The jurors would feel compelled to find someone guilty. Somebody had to be punished.

Marco strolled in around eleven-thirty bearing a box of cinnamon sugar doughnuts from his Uncle Paul's bakery. "How was the exam?" I asked.

"I aced it." He handed the box to me and I selected a doughnut.

"Good. I expect you to ace the Bar Exam too; I need you to start making court appearances. Did you leave one for Gloria?" I passed the bakery box back to him.

"Of course. I'm no fool." He sat in my client chair. "What's on tap?"

"Have you heard anything about AJ?"

"No. Have you?"

"Nothing. Why don't you go over to the courthouse and find out when he's being arraigned."

"Want me to go now?"

"Soon. When it's convenient." I took a bite of doughnut and a fine spray of cinnamon sugar dusted my chocolate-brown polished cotton jacket. My blouse was key lime. "We have to drum up some experts." My shoes were olive.

The front door closed and we heard Gloria noises: keys dropped on her desk, the coat closet being opened and a hanger removed, the light jazz station she listens to when she's working. She made her way to my office, doughnut in hand. "Marco," she said. "You know how much I love these, but I shouldn't." She patted her hips, which were a pleasant curve in her dress.

"You look great," I said. "Live it up. Have a doughnut. And where did you get those shoes?" I enviously viewed her ivory heels, which featured a lacy cutout across the top and along the sides.

"I ordered them from a catalog. I'll bring it to you tomorrow."

"What other colors do they come in?"

"Lots of them, a dozen or so; you're sure to find something you like." She considered the doughnut in her hand. "I think I will eat this. Thank you, Marco."

"For you, anything."

"What do you have for me today?" she asked.

"That custody removal case. I drafted a brief; it's on your desk. Type it up please, and then I'll look it over."

"Don't forget you have court this afternoon," she reminded me as she returned to her desk.

"Where were we?" I asked Marco.

"AJ's arraignment? Experts?"

"Experts. We can't afford to pay them, so I'm going to ask Judge Gonzalez to appoint them." When an indigent client is not represented by the Public Defender's Office, the State will sometimes pay for experts. "The State is tight with funds these days," I continued. "But in this case I think the judge will do it, if only to cover his own you know what."

Marco smiled. "Ass? Since when have you been reluctant to use a choice word?"

"I'm trying to be a nicer person. More considerate. And Gloria hates it when I use strong language."

He peered into the doughnut box and selected one. "What prompted this new and improved Ginger Rae?"

"Tommy got mad at me last night."

"I thought Tommy never got mad." He took a bite of doughnut; all of the cinnamon sugar went into his mouth and none fell onto his T-shirt.

"When you become a lawyer," I said, "you'll have to wear suits to court."

"I know that. Why is Tommy mad?"

"Last night I was obsessing on Violet's case. I wanted to work and he wanted family time."

"You need family time." He emphasized *you.*

I broke the rest of my doughnut into small pieces, scattering cinnamon sugar onto my desk and the various court notices and documents upon it.

"Back to our topic," I said. "Judge Gonzalez won't risk getting overturned on appeal, and this is a semi-hot case, so he'll toe the due process line. He knows this office can't afford good experts in a pro bono case, so I think he'll approve State appointments."

"Good plan. What else do you have on for today?"

"A visitation hearing this afternoon. A brief in the grandparent case and the appeal in the Du Bois case. Will you research grandparent visitation? The law keeps changing."

He nodded.

"And the Abbott hearing is tomorrow and Mr. Abbott has not submitted his financials, so I'm going to have a nasty conversation with his attorney."

"Want me to talk to the attorney?"

"You aren't vulgar enough."

"Then I need the practice."

"Good idea. Pretty soon you'll be as mean as me."

29

My afternoon in court was satisfying, and the vague sense of anxiety I'd felt since talking to Laura dissipated. Judge Bird picked up my cues that my client was a committed dad, not a McDonald's father, and granted him Wednesday overnights with his children, in addition to alternate weekends. She also scolded the ex-wife who insisted that when the children were with him he put them to bed too late, fed them junk food, and let them play computer games, and that if he had them on a weeknight he would be incapable of helping them with their homework and would forget to have them shower and brush their teeth.

I stopped by Judge Gonzalez's chambers and his law clerk said that he granted my request for the State to pay for experts for Violet's case. I was on my way to the prosecutor's offices to squeeze out some information on AJ when I saw Marco. He pulled me into an empty conference room. "I talked to DiCicco," he said. "Remember Violet's neighbor? The one next door who wasn't home the three times I went there? Well DiCicco did better, and reportedly the neighbor said that the night before Teddy went to the hospital AJ showed up around two in the morning and was banging on Violet's door and yelling. Apparently the neighbor peeked out and saw him, and later she heard more yelling and the baby crying."

"And she didn't do anything?"

"I imagine she didn't think it was her business. A domestic

contretemps." We looked at each other. Marco actually looked elated.

"You think he did it, don't you?" I said.

"Don't you?"

"Yeah. I do. It makes perfect sense. Is it a good ID?"

"DiCicco thinks so. The witness is a working woman. Older. Doesn't wear glasses. She'd seen him around before. The hall lights were working."

"Was there a line-up?"

"Not yet. They might just go with an in-court ID." He went off to study for his next exam and I returned to the office. Gloria's son Ellison was at the copy machine, listening to Mos Def, and copying and collating motion papers.

"Ellison. Good to see you," I said. "Where've you been?"

"Debate team. We're in the regional, so every day we've been staying after, to prepare."

"Good for you. How's the college search going?"

He rolled his eyes, probably sick to death of adults badgering him about college. A junior at a good parochial school, he had a great G.P.A., was captain of the debate team, and small forward on the basketball team, so he was getting a lot of interest from good schools. I was up on this stuff because Tommy was trying to get Jake, who was also a junior, to visit colleges, but Jake had only done the absolute minimum necessary to appease his father.

"I won't bug you," I said. "But be sure and let me know if I can help."

The phone rang. I motioned him to pick it up, and ducked into the bathroom. When I came out he was writing a message. He hung up and grinned. "That was a seventy-eight-year-old lady who wants a divorce from her eighty-three-year-old husband. She says she's had it up to here with him; he spits in the house and doesn't put the toilet seat down."

"Put it on Marco's desk."

"Hey, Ginger? You think I could be a lawyer?"

"Absolutely. I don't know if you'd like being a lawyer, but you certainly have what it takes."

"Marco says law school's tough."

"It is. But it's not rocket science; it's mostly just hard work. And you are a hard worker. You're good at debate; you'd be king of the courtroom."

"Man, I've got a lot to think about."

"You've got time. Just get through high school for now."

He smiled. "Right."

"Next winter want to help me coach the Y team? If it doesn't interfere with your own schedule?"

"I'd like that. Hey, Ginger?"

"Yes?"

"You played college ball."

"Until I blew out my knee junior year."

"Oh. Sorry. How'd you like it? Before your knee?"

"The best days of my life." I was not going to tell him how hard it was to do well in my classes and make all the practices, workouts and games. It was infinitely harder when I couldn't play anymore. It still aches to think about it. "Back to work," I said. "And turn that music down!" Our little joke. Gloria won't let him play rap around her, but when he and I are alone in the office I let him crank it up. Sometimes he turns me on to new bands that I go home and name-drop around Jake. "That reminds me," I said. "I have something for you." From the closet I pulled out an Equan Wilder T-shirt and CD from the party. I got two each and gave one set to Jake. I handed them to Ellison, who was delighted.

"Cool. Thanks a lot." He held the T-shirt up to his white button-down and I smiled at the contrast. I returned to my office and he raised the volume.

Later I called Laura. "How is she?"

"She hasn't come out of her room all day. She won't talk to me."

"How about I pick up some clam chowder and stop by?"

"That sounds great."

"See you around six-thirty."

I left a message for Tommy and Jake saying I'd be late, but not too late. Ellison brought me five copies of the motion papers. "These okay?" he asked.

"I'll look them over. Listen, we're out of sodas. Would you run over to the bodega and pick up a six-pack?"

"Yes, Ma'am."

I flipped him a ten. "Get me some gum too, please. And something for yourself."

"You got it."

I paged through the motion papers, ensuring that all was in order: the Notice of Motion, brief, client certification, attorney certification, certification of service, and assorted attachments and exhibits. The phone rang. "Ginger Rae Reddy."

"Ginger. Eduardo here."

"What's up, big guy?"

"I'm giving you a heads-up. I've been retained by Anthony Mulligan."

I paused a beat to make the connection. Anthony Mulligan. Anthony James. AJ. Of course. "How did he find you?"

"He's got a cousin works for the city. Recommended me."

"Since when can a prison guard afford you?"

"His family's helping. And his cousin did me a favor."

"This is a first for us."

"Don't worry about it. Routine business. I'll file the motion for severance. I'm assuming you don't want a joint trial?"

"No joint trial."

"Send me a copy of that paternity test when you get a chance.

By the way, my client is suspended from his job. Without pay."

"My heart bleeds for him."

"He's got a family."

"This is weird. Us as adversaries."

"It's just a job. It will all work out. It always does."

Right.

We disconnected and I walked to the window and watched Mrs. Rivera, whose yard was behind ours, pegging laundry while her two little granddaughters chased a dog around the yard. Ellison returned with sodas and gum.

"Do you have anything else for me?" he asked.

I pointed to a stack of closed files taking up valuable acreage on the floor. "File those and then you'll be done. I'll give you a ride."

"I can take the bus."

"I know. But I'll be leaving anyway. I'll even let you drive."

He finished filing and I closed up. "Do you have time for a quick game of PIG?" I asked.

"Sure. But your shoes." He looked at my nicely polished black heels.

"If I keep them on I'll be almost as tall as you," I pointed out. "It's PIG, I don't have to run." He gathered up his backpack, which was so full that he couldn't zip it up and he had to carry a thick volume. "What's the book?" I asked.

"*Common Ground.* It's for Sociology."

"Big book. How is it?"

"Good. It follows these three families through integration in Boston—a black family from the ghetto, a working class Irish family, and some Harvard do-gooders."

"Sounds interesting." Tommy probably owned it; I'd ask him about it. "I was a sociology major in college, but I never read it."

"Did you like sociology?"

"Yes. I grew up in a small town, a very narrow slice of the world. Sociology helped me understand different types of people and societies better. I think it made me a better lawyer." Me, the sociology cheerleader.

An old hoop hangs from the small detached garage at the end of the driveway, remnant of the days when Mr. Ziznewski's children were running around. They don't come around much anymore. On holidays one of them picks him up, drives him out to the suburbs where they now live and where he feels out of place. "They don't know their neighbors, Ginger. Can you imagine that?" After this past Christmas he was so agitated that he shoveled and sanded our sidewalk three times a day, reclaiming his territory. "They hire someone who comes in a truck and plows. They don't even shovel their own steps. I saw Mike pay a man forty dollars to plow the driveway and shovel the steps." He shook his head in disbelief. "Mike and Ellen go to a gym for exercise. The kids play videogames all day. They pay someone to shovel."

I scooped up the round ball I keep in the office coat closet, and Ellison and I stepped outside. "How's school going?" I asked him.

He shrugged. "Okay."

Gloria works hard to pay his tuition at St. Luke's. Her work at the insurance company is tedious, the environment sterile, but she gets good benefits. Between that and the hours she works for me, she gets by. I hope to be able to hire her full-time some day. She is a good worker, a pleasant person, and a desperately needed stabilizing force in the office.

Ellison beat me. He had P when I got PIG so I wasn't crushed. "Not bad for an old lady," he said. I flipped him my car keys. Gloria leases a Malibu that she takes to her job at the insurance company, which is headquartered in a corporate park sprawling outside of the city in an area with no access via public transportation. Ellison is allowed to drive the car evenings and weekends, but, like most newly licensed drivers, he loves to get behind the wheel. He cruised River Road to Gino's and fiddled with the CD changer while I purchased the chowder. When I got back in the Jimmy he had The Roots on full volume.

"I wish my mom would get one of these in her car," he said, indicating the CD player.

"Her plate's pretty full."

"I know, but you can get one for a couple hundred bucks. She says she likes the quiet, that it's the only time she's in a quiet place."

What Gloria gets from the silent interior of her car is probably the same thing that I get from one that is filled with music. I looked out the window and saw that Ellison was taking a circuitous route home. He steered up the one hilly area of Port Grace, commonly known as the Heights, the wealthy section of town that leads into the western suburbs. "Taking the scenic route?" I asked.

"Just getting the big picture." He swooped down to the western edge of Winslow College, and followed the perimeter of the campus to the southern border where St. Luke's, his school, sharply delineates the crossing into Pig Hollow, the city's most damaged and dangerous neighborhood. St. Luke's has more in common with the college than with Pig Hollow, architecturally and spiritually, and it is impossible not to be startled by the abrupt shift from formal brick and stone buildings softened by grassy paths and massive oak trees, into the crumbling streets of what was once a comfortable working class neighborhood, now destroyed by extreme poverty and its attendants: drugs, arson, dropouts, truants, exhausted mothers, and imprisoned fathers.

Ellison was born in Pig Hollow, and a confluence of events, circumstances, luck, and hard work enabled Gloria to get him and his little sister out of there when he was eight. They now live in a stately old brick apartment building in The Oaks, a quiet neighborhood on the other side of Bay Ave. Ellison passes through Pig Hollow every day on his way to school, because that is the most direct route by car, foot, or city bus. Every day he is reminded of where he came from, and of where he might return, if he doesn't work hard, harder than he would have to if he was not a young black man who is expected to be the first person in his family to graduate from college.

He pulled up in front of the apartment building. Large pots bursting with red geraniums flanked the heavy oak entry doors. Little girls played jump rope on the sidewalk, and a couple of seniors relaxed in lawn chairs. I handed him a bag containing a quart of clam chowder. "Tell your mom I accidentally bought too much."

"Oh yeah. Like she's gonna believe that."

"Tell her anyway."

He sat quietly for a moment. "Hey, Ginger?"

"Yes?"

"That girl? The one they say killed her baby? I know you're her lawyer. And I was just wondering." He couldn't or wouldn't finish his thought.

"What, Ellison?" I dreaded whatever was coming. Do you think she did it? How can you represent someone like that? It would be hard hearing those questions from him. But he surprised me.

"It's sad, isn't it?" he said.

I waited a few seconds, letting his question linger, honoring his insight and goodness. "Yes. It is. Very sad."

He slipped out and I slid over to the driver's seat. "Thanks for letting me drive," he said, "and thanks for the chowder."

"See you tomorrow."

I watched him nod to the jumping girls, wave to the seniors, climb the steps, and walk through the door. I sat there, in my car, for a little longer, allowing the sadness that Ellison had uncorked fill me.

30

Laura whisked the chowder into the kitchen and I walked back to Violet's room. The door was slightly ajar, but I knocked anyway. "Hey, kid," I said, "can I come in?" She was lying in bed, watching a *Law and Order* rerun. Still in the nightgown.

"Sure," she said, without looking at me.

"I brought clam chowder. From Gino's. You ever eaten at Gino's?"

"No."

"I'll take you there some time."

No response. I leaned against the doorframe. "Hey."

No response.

I turned off the TV and sat on the bed. "I'm worried about you. Laura says you aren't eating, that you're sleeping a lot. Do you want to talk about it?"

"No."

"You should see a counselor. A professional who can help you through this."

She gave me a sullen glance. "Laura wants me to leave?"

"No. I don't think so. She's just worried about you."

"I'm tired."

"Then you should probably see a doctor."

"I'm not sick."

"Come have dinner with us."

"I'm not hungry."

I rolled my shoulders, trying to release the tension. "Come sit with us. Maybe after dinner we can take a walk by the river."

"Maybe I should just leave if I'm bothering you."

"You aren't bothering me. You aren't bothering Laura. We're worried about you and we want to help."

"Nobody can help me."

"That's not true. You're depressed now. But someday you'll be able to move on; you'll build a new life for yourself."

She sat up. "That's bull. There's not gonna be a new life. I'm going to jail."

"You might not. And even if you do, you're very young." I stopped. It wasn't the time to discuss a post-prison life.

"You don't get it, do you?" she said. "My baby is dead. That's the only thing that matters. Eating clam chowder, walking by the river, making prom-girl corsages; that's not going to make me feel better, or bring my son back to life, is it?"

"No. No, it's not. I'm sorry." I gestured toward the kitchen. "I'm going to eat. It would be nice if you'd join us."

The table was set for three, with bowls of clam chowder, a salad, and tall glasses of iced tea. I responded to Laura's inquiring look with a shrug.

"What do you think?" she asked.

"She's depressed, scared, hurt, confused. Rightfully so. As she pointed out to me, her baby died ten days ago. And she's being blamed for it. And she might go to jail. Who wouldn't be depressed?"

"I'm worried she'll hurt herself."

I shrugged. "I doubt it. Anyway, there's only so much we can do. If you don't want the responsibility, and I don't think you should have it, she can go to the shelter."

"No."

We sat down. I was famished, and I rapidly downed half a bowl of chowder and demolished my salad. Swallowed several ounces of iced tea, into which I'd squeezed the juice of three lemon wedges. Laura ate slowly, her gestures revealing a childhood cultivation of refined manners.

"I'm sorry I attacked you this morning," she said.

"No problem. I need to hear it once in a while."

"Maybe I'm caring too much and was projecting my feelings onto you."

Feelings. "Forget about it. This is hard on all of us."

"What should we do?"

"Let her be for now. I'll schedule an appointment with a counselor at the women's center. I have to talk to her again. Meanwhile, I have to get her to tell me about AJ."

"You think he shook Teddy?"

"I'm sure he did. Usually it's the boyfriend or stepfather who does it. Sometimes the biological father. And there are no indications of prior abuse, no reports that Violet was ever suspected of abuse or neglect. AJ hits women. I have no reason to believe that he wouldn't hurt a child." I finished my chowder, refrained from licking the bowl, and swallowed the last of my iced tea.

Laura stopped eating. She sat with her back to the window, and the early evening light framed her loveliness and her distress. "What if it was an accident?" she asked. "And she's afraid to tell us?"

I shook my head. "There's no way. That shaking was so violent that no observer would think it was an accident. Though that possibly leaves wiggle room for state of mind."

"What do you mean?"

"Suppose you and I were watching someone shake their baby. Hard enough to cause the effects of shaken baby syndrome. Which means hard enough to cause their brain to bounce off the walls of their skull." Laura, horrified, held her hand up to stop me. "That's what happened," I said, keeping my tone cool and detached. "You never saw a shaking case when you worked for DCW?"

"No. Burns, starvation, sexual abuse. But not specifically shaking. I would remember."

"As objective observers, you and I would see the shaking as a violent act. We might not know that there was a risk of death, but it would obviously be dangerous. What we don't know is what's going on in the head of the person doing the shaking, because their state of mind is not the same as ours. Most people don't know about shaken baby syndrome, so you can't assume that the cause and effect are common knowledge. Whereas if I shoot you in the head it can be assumed that I know there is a high probability that you will die."

"So the person doing the shaking wouldn't necessarily know the risk?"

"Exactly."

"Does any of that make a difference?"

"It could make the difference between aggravated manslaughter and reckless manslaughter. Depending on the circumstances, maybe child endangerment. But those all carry prison time."

"It must have been AJ," Laura said. "That violence could not have come from Violet."

"I hope you're right."

"I'm worried that she's still in love with him. She's heartbroken that he hasn't called her. And she's even more upset since you told her he was arrested; she hasn't talked to me all day. Can she possibly think that they'll get back together?"

"He's a sick bastard." I was irritated. "She's got to get over him."

"I thought you were a big believer in redemption."

"Not the way I used to be." Time to change the subject. "I'll see if she wants to go out for ice cream. I haven't been to Silvia's in ages."

"What's your favorite flavor?"

I ticked them off on my fingers. "Vanilla fudge. Peanut butter. Strawberry. Black raspberry. Mint chocolate chip. Almost anything but pistachio or coffee."

"Speaking of which, would you like some coffee?"

"Not now, thanks. I'll grab some later. Did you know that Judge Silvia's father started Silvia's? He's the toughest criminal judge on the bench. He worked there as a kid, through college, I think. He loves to bring it up in court when he's giving a work ethic lecture."

I returned to Violet's room. "How about some ice cream? Whatever you want—a triple scoop with sprinkles on top, a root beer float, a banana split." She looked up. "Doesn't that sound good?"

She shrugged.

"Good. Get dressed."

She put her head back on the pillow. "I can't go out."

"Why not?"

"People know. Someone will see me who knows."

"That's not likely. Your picture wasn't in the paper. You don't know many people in Port Grace, do you? C'mon. You can wear my sunglasses." She was going to refuse. "Please. I had a rough day and I really need some ice cream. Laura won't go with me, and I don't like to go out for ice cream by myself."

"We'll come right back?"

"Right back."

She shuffled into some clothes. She needed a shower and shampoo, but I figured clothes were a start.

We drove to Silvia's in silence. Violet ordered a small cup of strawberry and I chose a double scoop of vanilla peanut butter precariously stuffed into a cone. We slid into a back booth, and I launched into an ice cream monologue—store-bought versus ice cream parlor, cones versus cups, sugar cones versus wafer cones. I opined that frozen yogurt and sorbets were for sissies although on a really hot night a good sorbet could hit the spot. "Is sorbet just expensive sherbet?" I asked.

Violet shrugged. She ignored her ice cream and was on the edge of tears.

"Maybe having a French name lets you double the price," I concluded. I finished my monologue and my cone, dropped a buck in the tips-for-college jar, and we headed out to the parking lot. I drove to the bay. "This is one my favorite places," I said as we walked to the end of the dock and sat with our feet dangling over the water. Daylight was bleeding into darkness, and the people who'd been fishing off the dock were packing their gear, leaving us to admire thick golden-orange streaks burning though the sky as it darkened. We sat quietly for a few minutes. "Violet," I said, "with AJ arrested everything changes."

"What do you mean?"

"I mean that you and AJ are going to be pitted against each other. The D.A. will try to get you to rat out each other."

"That won't happen."

"Are you sure? I think that AJ will do whatever he has to, to stay out of prison. He's a prison guard. Imagine what would happen to him inside. I have no doubt that he will lie to avoid that."

"So it will just be one of us? I mean could we both go to jail?"

"If one of you shook Teddy, but you were both there, you could both be convicted. For instance, if he shook Teddy and you were in the apartment, he might be convicted of manslaughter, and you of child endangerment for failure to protect Teddy. But if you were out getting pizza when it happened, and could prove it, then you might not get convicted." She covered her face with her hands. A cabin cruiser motored in, and I watched the occupants tie up to the dock. Then I took a deep breath and turned to Violet. I pushed her hair back from her face. "Talk to me, Violet," I whispered.

She shook her head. "He didn't do anything."

I drove her back to Laura's and made sure she went inside. Called home, but nobody answered. Restless and edgy, I drove to Marco's apartment, which is on the first floor of a three-family in Deer Point, two blocks from where he grew up. He opened the door, surprised to see me. "What's up?"

"I need a drink," I said.

He stood back to let me in. I smelled coffee. He was dressed in sweats and looked tired. "What's wrong?"

"Do you have any pot?"

"Of course not."

I needed something to take the edge off. I imagined pulling a bottle of beer from Marco's fridge, fitting the opener to the cap, prying it off, and that first wonderful swallow. I walked over to the pool table that fills the dining area. "Want to play?"

"Ginger. What's going on?"

I flopped on the couch. A Cuban mix was on the CD player and I leafed through the constitutional law book that was open on the couch. Marco sat next to me, took the book from my hands and placed it on the floor.

"Tell me why you're here."

And so I told him. How Violet and I sat on the dock and the sky turned from slate to navy, and the gulls shot into the water and then quieted. "I'm sick about this case," I said. "I keep picturing AJ shaking the baby, his little head snapping back and forth."

"Then he's gotta go down."

We sat quietly for a while. My cell phone rang. I ignored it. The music ended and sounds of a foghorn came through the screen. Inexplicably, a rooster was crowing nearby. I went outside and smoked a cigarette and then I drove home.

31

Tommy was curt with me, hurt by my recent erratic hours and behavior. We were slipping into the danger zone that preceded our separation, and so the following night I made a point of getting home before him and cooking dinner. He started to thaw and after dinner we pulled weeds and prepared a flowerbed. Then the phone rang. I hurried to catch it before the machine clicked on, Tommy telling me not to answer. "What if it's Jake," I said. It wasn't Jake, it was Laura.

"Violet's gone."

"What do you mean, gone?"

"She's not here. I was out all day, setting up parties, and then I had dinner with a friend. When I got home she was gone. There's no note. Nothing."

"Are her clothes there? Her stuff?"

"Everything seems to be. Give or take a T-shirt."

"She probably went for a walk."

"You think so?"

"Relax. She'll be back soon. I hung up, returned to weeding and Tom. "Laura doesn't know where Violet is." He didn't respond. I pulled clumps of dandelions, careful to get the roots. "We need snapdragons here. Yellow ones and some blue salvia."

Jake came outside with a plate of leftovers and a deck of cards. "You guys work too hard," he said, and proceeded to talk us into playing gin rummy until dark. We didn't answer the house phone though Jake's cell phone rang constantly, providing a distraction that gave Tommy and me an advantage; but somehow Jake still won most of the hands.

I did answer when the phone rang hard at five-thirty in the morning. "Should I call the police?" Laura asked. "She's not back. I drove around half the night, looking for her."

"Do you have Caller ID? Go through yesterday's calls for any you don't recognize." I heard a series of beeps as she scrolled through the numbers.

"One says Private and there's a few Out of Area's, but those are usually solicitors."

"The police won't do anything until she's been gone forty-eight hours, unless foul play is suspected. Let me drink coffee and think. I'll get back to you later."

"Sorry," I said to Tommy, who was not happy to be awake. "Go back to sleep." While the coffee dripped I ate a peanut butter and banana sandwich and flipped through the newspaper. I petted Cat, who seemed annoyed with me too. I wanted to go back to bed. But I was in my office before seven o'clock, turning on lights and listening to messages when I heard, "This is Frank George from the barbershop in Old Bridge. Please call me." I punched in the number. "She came here last night," he said. "I had your card and I didn't know who else to call. She's very upset."

"Can I talk to her?"

"She's sleeping. It was real late when she showed up."

"How did she get there?"

"Took the Greyhound."

"Have her call me when she wakes up."

I briefed Laura, who said, "I'm swamped at work and I've got a date tonight. Can you take care of it?"

Cooling off of her good-will mission. "No problem."

"I'm a little hurt that she didn't call my cell or leave a note."

"After all you've done for her."

"I didn't mean it that way. Or maybe I did."

"I'm just yanking your chain. Babysitting a teen felon is no fun. You don't hear me volunteering to take her in. Do you want her back?"

She took too long to answer. "Sure." Trying to find her Saint Laura hat.

"Who's the boyfriend?"

"Girlfriend, actually."

"No kidding. Good for you."

"Now you're going to tell me that some of your best friends are gay."

"How did you know?"

"I bet some of your other best friends are black, right?"

"Except for the ones who are Latinos and Muslims."

"Muslim friends? How very cool."

"Well, it used to be cool to have gay friends, but now everybody does it."

"Seriously, I know it seems like I'm dropping the ball. I'm not, I still want to help Violet."

"Sure. I'll keep you posted."

Violet refused to talk to me on the phone, so I swore a lot, broke a date with Tommy, and motored down to Old Bridge. This is what she told me:

The night before last, after she and I sat on the dock, she called AJ. Begged him to see her. He hung up on her and didn't answer for the rest of the night, even though she practically wore out the redial button. But the following afternoon he called her, having picked up Laura's number from his Caller ID. "I'm coming down there," he said. "We'll work it out." He didn't sound drunk or upset, so she showered and dressed pretty and fussed with her hair, hopeful that something good would come out of everything bad.

He walked in angry. "What the hell is going on? I lost my job because of you. I'll lose everything because of you."

"No," Violet said. "I told her you weren't there."

He reached out and wrapped his hands around her neck, his thick fingers squeezing, compressing. She smelled alcohol steaming out of his pores, as though he'd drunk his way through the previous night. And then he slammed her to the floor.

She tried to scream but her throat hurt and he was looming over her.

"Shut up. If you say one word to those lawyers or the police about me? I'll kill you." He kicked her like he'd kick a dog. "Wherever you are? I'll find you and kill you. I've got a gun and I know how to use it." And then he left.

She stayed on the floor for a long time. Panic blew up inside her like a grenade; she had to get out of there, so she took her flower money, walked to the bus station and caught the Greyhound to Old Bridge.

We knew that he owned a handgun and a hunting rifle—they were seized after the domestic violence conviction, but six months later he got them back. Even if he hadn't, he comes from a family of men with guns. "I saw it once," Violet said about the handgun. "In the truck, he keeps it in the compartment between the seats, with maps and CD's. He said he keeps it loaded. He said it's a fucked-up world."

She emitted fear. Fear of AJ, of guns, of the loss of Teddy, the loss of AJ—she finally understood that he was really gone, that they were both really gone, and her anguish was painful to behold. "You have to file charges against him," I said. "That's assault and a terroristic threat."

"No. No police."

"Damn it, Violet, you have to do something. He can't get away with this. He'll terrorize you for the rest of your life. Why aren't you angry?"

"I can't talk to you," she said, rising from the table. "You don't understand. He'll kill me." She left the room and went upstairs.

Mr. George came into the kitchen. "Can I get you some iced tea?" he asked. "My wife should be back soon. She's at a church meeting."

"Did Violet tell you what's going on?"

"Some. She's got a lot of weight on her shoulders."

"Maybe you or your wife can talk some sense into her. I don't even know if she'll come back with me."

"She can stay for a while."

"You sure?"

He nodded.

"Do you have a camera?"

"An old one. I haven't used it in years. Why?"

"I need you to take photographs of the bruises on her neck. At some point you might have to testify to their authenticity—that you took them, when and where. Are you willing to do that?"

"I can borrow one of those new digital ones. That'll be better than my old dinosaur."

"I'll try her one more time before I go."

"Upstairs, door on your left."

She was in a straight back chair, gazing out the window at city rooftops and church spires. I sat on the bed, and ran my finger along the wallpaper, which was patterned with faded pink roses.

"Let's try again," I said. "I'm trying to figure out the best strategy for your trial and I need your help. I can make recommendations, but ultimately it's your decision; you tell me what you want to do." She continued looking out the window, but I could tell that she was listening. "The biggest problem is the risk of AJ testifying against you at your trial."

"He won't."

"He will. You've got to understand that because we're just about down to prayer to keep you out of prison."

"It doesn't matter."

"Of course it matters. With the medical evidence and AJ's testimony, they'll find you guilty in a heartbeat. You're going to have to testify on your own behalf, and show the jury that AJ is lying. And testify against him at his trial. If you press charges on this assault it could help your case because we might be able to use it to show that he has a propensity for violence."

She pushed up the double hung window and let Old Bridge in—barking dogs, cars, sirens, the steady beat of a boom box, carousel music from an ice cream truck. I would have guessed that ice-cream- truck drivers would be afraid to have a route in Old Bridge, but that's just another racist assumption. Where there are kids there are Popsicles.

"I should go to jail."

"Don't say that."

"I deserve to be punished. Teddy's dead. It's my fault." She finally looked at me.

"Please don't say that. You can make a good life for yourself."

"I don't deserve a good life." There was no screen or safety bar in the window and she put her arm out, reaching for nothing. I stood up and looked; saw the ice cream truck parked on the street, a crowd gathering. It was early May, but I could smell summer in that white truck full of choices: Popsicles in red, white and blue or shaped like a frog with a bubblegum nose, Creamsicles, ice-cream sandwiches, drumsticks, crunch bars, Italian ices, push-ups, Dixie cups, sno-cones; choices that unlock the door to the cocoa butter scent and shine of suntan lotion, to fire hydrants and sprinklers pumping the coolest water on earth, lemonade and ice cold beer, hot kissing, street hockey, playing hooky to go to a day game and hear the crack of the bat, watch the stretch of the outfielder's arm as he runs back, back, back, the arc of the ball in sunlight, to the wall, over the wall, it's gone!

I forced myself to return to Violet. "What happened to Teddy was a terrible thing. I won't pretend that you'll ever get over it. But you do deserve a good life, and one day you will be able to look forward."

"No," she said. "I want to go to jail. I want you to call that bitch prosecutor and tell her."

"I won't do that. You have no idea what prison is like. Prison is hell."

"I'm already in hell. And I'm telling you to. You're my lawyer and you said I get to tell you what to do, right?"

I nodded.

"Then tell them I'm going to plead guilty and go to jail."

"Nothing good will come out of that; you're just saying it because you feel guilty."

She pulled her arm in and slammed the window shut. "I am guilty."

I absorbed her words and ignored them, said the only thing I could think of. "Do you want to go down and get a Popsicle?" She shook her head. I had an urge for an ice cream sandwich; I like it when they soften up and the vanilla oozes out so you have to lick it. But I sat down on that bed again and started preparing my closing argument. "You have to let go of AJ. I know he was nice to you. You felt cared for. You felt loved. But then what happened? One, you were pregnant and he beat you. Then he choked you, kicked you, and threatened to kill you. Not to mention what he did to Teddy." She shifted around in the chair as she absorbed my words, and I closed in on her. "Do you see the picture that paints of him? Look at it, Violet. AJ must be held accountable. If he hurt you and Teddy, he'll hurt someone else. Another woman. Somebody else's baby. One of his own kids. You have the power to prevent that. You can stop him."

She turned back to the window.

"Think about it."

She nodded.

"Do you want to come back to Port Grace?"

She shook her head.

I left Falls River and as I screamed down that highway, I rummaged through Violet's file until I found AJ's number and punched it in. "How dare you threaten Violet, you stupid motherfucker," I stormed into his answering machine. "Don't you ever call her again. Don't go near her, don't even think about her." Unprofessional. Unethical too, since he was represented by counsel. So I put my tail between my legs and called Eduardo. It was eight-thirty and he was still in his office. "AJ Mulligan choked my client last night. He threatened to kill her. I just yelled at his cell phone answering machine."

"How do you know this?"

"She told me, she's got bruises on her throat, she's scared, Eduardo, it really happened. He's got a gun and said he'd use it."

"Calm down. When did it happen?"

"Yesterday."

"Did she call the police?"

"No, he said he'd kill her if she did. I just found out and if I have my way he'll get locked up."

"Sweetheart. We're adversaries, not enemies."

"Sorry. It's been a helluva week. Month. Whatever. I'm on the road and shouldn't be talking, but where are you with the case? Is he going to plea?"

"Plea? That's not the plan. They've got nothing solid on him. He's got a good chance at trial and a lot to lose."

"We need to talk. When I calm down."

"Call me, my friend."

I wanted to drive right across the country to California, work in the nursery among roses and sage, wield hoses and lift flats. Drive the forklift; pallets stacked with fifty pound bags of cedar chips, cocoa hulls, fertilizer, topsoil, bales of hay. I should never have left. I could've married a biker, or better yet buy my own bike, a nice little Harley or Triumph, and at night I'd ride anywhere I damn well pleased—south on 5 to Bakersfield, west to Route 1, the Pacific Coast Highway, on the way I'd salute the Salinas pickers, cruise past Monterey, where barely a breath of Steinbeck remains, past the money that has ruined Carmel with high-end boutiques and golf courses; but Big Sur is still there, and I would disappear into fog, I would live inside the wind, with cypress trees and night birds for company. Nights I didn't ride I'd float in the pool after work, icing down raging Valley summers and sore muscles, I'd share a joint with my Dad, rescue a dog abandoned by some trailer crankhead, go to 49er's games, A's, Giants, Lakers, Kings, even the Trailblazers, follow games up and down the coast, on my girl Harley with the dog in a sidecar, and I would send the losing teams bushels of corn on the cob and armloads of daisies and honeysuckle.

32

The following morning Marco and I were conferring on a case when Gloria buzzed. "A Mr. George is on the phone. It sounds urgent."

I slowly reached for the phone. It could only be bad. "Ginger Rae Reddy."

"Frank George here. I'm sorry to disturb you again, but it's Violet, she . . ." He paused to clear his throat. "She's in the hospital."

As we spoke I stepped out into the yard, wandered to the viburnum and plunged my arm deep into the shrub, simultaneously getting scratched and releasing fragrance. "Why?"

"She cut herself and took some pills, my wife's from her surgery—she didn't take many, didn't like feeling doped-up. My wife, I mean."

"Her condition?"

"She's all right. They pumped her stomach and bandaged her wrists, said the cuts are superficial. But they won't let her out until she talks to a psychiatrist."

"I don't suppose you've heard from her mother."

"I haven't seen any of her people for quite some time."

I looked at the back of Mr. Z's house. The paint was peeling. I looked at the sky. It was blue. "What hospital?"

"Holy Angels. They know down there. About the baby, one of them recognized her name, I heard them talking. And the way they looked at her."

"Who found her?"

"My wife. Ruth. She called 911."

"So the police came."

"And the ambulance and the fire department. I feel terrible and Ruth is very upset. She's at the hospital now."

"Please don't blame yourself. She went to you because you're the closest thing to family that she has."

"That's kind of you to say."

"I'm not being kind. It's true. I'll call the hospital and check in with you later." I broke the connection and surveyed Mr. Z's yard where years ago his children scampered, his wife hung laundry, and he planted tomatoes. I couldn't think.

Marco came out looking for me. "Sit down," he said. "You look like you're going to pass out." He led me to the patio and removed the phone from my hand.

"Violet tried to kill herself."

"Oh Jesus."

"It's okay, you can go back to work."

"You look like you're unraveling."

"I'm fine. I can handle it."

"We'll work on this together."

"You don't want anything to do with this case."

"I'm beginning to understand it; I'm more sympathetic to her. She's lost everything. Her baby, her parents, her grandmother, even that dumb-fuck AJ. We know he's a monster but she's just figuring it out and she's devastated. And she didn't have much to start with. I'm getting that empathy you're always talking about."

I exhaled, dizzy with apprehension and relief. "What, are you getting your degree in psychology?"

"No, I just want in. I'm slow, but sometimes I catch up."

"Yeah, okay, we can try it that way." I tapped my finger on

the table, on the edge of a thought. Something that might actually matter.

"What?" he asked. I rested my feet on top of his boots. I wore a pair of tangerine pointy-toed pumps with impractical high heels, the footwear opposite of Marco's Sears steel-toe boots. My blouse was also tangerine, transmitting the message that beneath the beige pantsuit is a fiery individual. Somehow Marco manages a similar effect without altering his wardrobe; he does it with his eyes.

"Here's an idea," I said.

"I can't wait."

I gave him a little kick with one of those pointy toes. "What if I back off and you become the contact for Violet?"

"Why?"

"Because you are a charming guy. You emote sincerity and kindness, and I think Violet will respond to you. She's losing confidence in me."

"Emote? That sounds like a new-age techno band. Enya. Eno. Emo. Bjork. Emote. What, has Tommy been reading the dictionary to you at bedtime?"

"All right, wise guy. Start by calling the hospital, and if they clear it, go over and talk to her. See if a uniform can be there and try to get a statement from her on the assault. Then your next challenge will be to convince her to testify against him on the baby case."

"I'll need the file."

"It's in my briefcase. I'll call Mr. George and let him know that you're taking over. He's a good guy and will be helpful. She'll need psychiatric follow-up and some Prozac. Oh, and make sure the doctor records the bruises on her neck."

"And while I'm busy emoting what do you plan to do?"

"Get re-acquainted with my other clients. Maybe buy some

new shoes." I played it light, trying to recover from my distress.

Laura called me late that afternoon and I gave her the condensed version of AJ's assault and Violet's attempt at suicide.

"I let her down."

"No. You took her in."

"But I didn't want her back."

"Did she know that?"

"No. I didn't know it until she was gone."

"It wasn't your job to rescue her."

"I can't believe that AJ was here. It's such a violation."

I pictured her surveying her immaculate loft for signs of him. "Hopefully she'll press charges against him. Then your neighbors will be interviewed to discover if anyone saw him. If not, we've got another he-said, she-said."

"Want me to look for clues? Footprints, hairs, fibers, a bloody glove?"

"That would be the job of the police. Unfortunately, they can't go in until she files charges, and by then it'll be too late."

"The cameras," she said.

"What cameras?"

"We've had security cameras at both entrances ever since Octavio's loft was burglarized. He was preparing for a New York show and somebody smashed his sculptures."

"That's horrible. Did they ever catch the perp?"

"No. He thinks it was his ex-wife, but they couldn't prove it."

"The cameras work? They aren't dummies?"

"I think so. I'll find out."

I called Marco with that news. "Where are you?"

"The Holy Angels cafeteria. Getting little Miss Violet a strawberry milkshake."

"You're already getting fond of her."

"I've known a lot of girls like her."

"She likes you, right?"

"We're getting there. I figure by the time she's finished the shake she'll say anything I tell her to. Seriously though, they want to keep her here for another day or two for observation. Those bruises, her neck . . . we've gotta get that guy. He's killing her."

33

Marco cajoled Violet into filing a complaint against AJ. I gave him credit for his charm, finesse, and skills, but he was also in the right place at the right time, because whatever happened between AJ and Violet that day at the loft had provoked her; first she attempted suicide, now she was ready to turn on him. I guess it's true that suicide and homicide are flip sides of the same emotional coin.

The police got AJ on camera entering the warehouse, and Laura's phone records showed an incoming call from him two hours prior to the assault. He was charged with aggravated assault, and Violet was released from Holy Angels into the care of Mr. and Mrs. George. The following day ADA Michelle Bonpietro called me. "Let's talk," she said.

"Come on over."

"I'd prefer you to come to the District Attorney's offices."

"We're busy. How's four o'clock?"

She assented without argument, so I knew she wanted something.

"Michelle's ready to deal," I told Marco. "They've decided AJ did it. She's going to agree to reduce charges if Violet will testify against him."

"You know that for a fact?"

"It's an educated guess. The assault charge is solid. AJ isn't looking so good to them anymore. It's easier to put Violet on the scene, but statistical odds are that a man did it. And I want a chance to deal before Eduardo offers up AJ. See, on one hand, it's a circumstantial case, flimsy. On the other hand, medical experts will convince the jury that Teddy died of shaken baby syndrome, so they'll want to find someone guilty. If Violet goes to trial they'll find her guilty because she was with Teddy 99% of the time. At AJ's trial they'll find him guilty, probably of endangerment, if they believe he was there the night Teddy was shaken but didn't actually do it. If they think he did it, he's doing double digit hard time."

"You do the talking; I've never worked a plea bargain."

"I did a bunch for Eduardo. It's a game—it's kind of fun. You'll see."

Michelle, Marco and I sat on the patio, my spring conference room. I served drinks and we chit-chatted about Marco's impending graduation and the Bar Exam. We all had yellow legal pads and pens—Michelle held a silver Cross, mine was a black Paper Mate, and Marco's was a freebie from Jack's Tire and Auto. Michelle got started. "The assault case against Mulligan is strong. He's starting to smell pretty bad."

"So you want to play let's make a deal?"

"Will your client agree to testify against him in both cases?"

"I don't know. If she does?"

"I reduce the charge from aggravated man to reckless man; that's first degree to second."

"Drop the charges. You'll get two convictions on him and you know he's the danger to society, not her."

"No way."

"What's your theory?" I asked. "Are you just randomly tossing charges, hoping one will stick? You don't think they both shook the baby, do you?"

"We think he did it. But she was responsible for the infant."

"What makes you think she was there when it happened?"

"Does she have an alibi?"

"I believe she does."

"You have an obligation to notify me of any alibis."

"Don't worry. I will." I tried to distract her. "Nice pen." Must have been a gift; even after eight years her salary was probably still in the forties, not a Cross pen salary. She just glared at me. "Look," I said. "You'll never get a conviction on aggravated manslaughter; reduce it to child endangerment."

"That's second degree too. What's the difference?"

"Because for something she'll wear for the rest of her life, endangerment sounds softer than manslaughter. But it's still a tough rap. Every time she fills out a job application she'll have to check off that box—'have you ever been convicted of a felony'—and endangering the welfare of a child sounds bad. Real bad."

She shook her head.

"I'm not finished," I said. "I also want you to agree to recommend alternate sentencing—a suspended sentence with community service."

"Are you crazy? Maybe, maybe, I could recommend the light side of a five to ten for second degree, but suspended? It will never happen on a plea of manslaughter or child endangerment. She'll do time. Even if I did recommend it, and I wouldn't, no judge would go for it."

"That's because nobody reads the statutes. Take a look at 4D: 52-4 and 53-1. With the exception of murder, the court can impose a suspended sentence or one that requires probation, fines, community service, night imprisonment, treatment, or a bunch of alternates. And, in convictions of first- or second-degree crimes, where the court is convinced that mitigating factors substantially outweigh aggravating factors and the interest of justice requires, the sentence can be that of a crime that's one degree lower. For third degree or less, there is a presumption of non-incarceration unless the judge finds aggravating factors that make imprisonment necessary."

"Nobody does that." Michelle was irritated that I could recite the statutes from memory. "Certainly not in first- or second-degree crimes."

"Then it's time to start. This is the perfect case. Essentially she meets all or most of the mitigating factors and none of the aggravating. She's a battered woman. He killed her baby. The jury would be so sympathetic they'd want to adopt her by the end of the trial."

"The judge decides the sentence, not the jury."

"But it's Judge Gonzalez. I think he'd go for it. Especially with a plea."

She felt bulldozed by me, I could tell even before she said, "No. She'd be getting away with murder. She's going to do time, she has to be punished and to know that what she did is wrong."

"Do you know where she was for the last three days? Did you pay attention to where she was when the police took her statement on the assault? In the hospital on suicide watch. Why? Because she tried to kill herself. And you think she needs to be punished for her alleged crime? What can you do that would make her feel worse? She probably wants you to lock her up. She'll be facing the fact of Teddy's death for the rest of her life. In prison she'll be surrounded by people in the same predicament. But out in the world? She's going to have to find out if she can live with it."

Michelle drew precise geometric designs on her legal pad. "I've got a *prima facie* case of shaken baby syndrome against her. And you have nothing."

Mr. Z appeared in the backyard. "Ginger, have you seen my push broom? Am I interrupting?"

"No, Mr. Z, this is the perfect time for a break. I'll help you find your broom. Let's take ten."

Michelle pulled out her cell phone and started yelling at someone. Marco went inside and Mr. Z and I checked out the garage where his tools were neatly stored the way they've been for decades. No push broom. "When was the last time you had it?" I asked.

"This morning, early. I was talking to Phil the butcher before he opened. We were talking about sausages." And then, "That's it." He whacked himself on the forehead. "The kid left Phil's broom in the alley last night and it was gone this morning. Who would steal a broom? So he said could he borrow mine and he'd have the kid bring it over after closing. I wonder if he's gonna take it out of the boy's check? Said he'd send over some nice sausages too. How could I forget that? I'm getting old."

"No way," I said. "You are still the sharpest guy on the block."

I walked past Michelle and her cell phone and went inside to confer with Marco. "What do you think?"

"I think Michelle's not going to give you everything. You want endangerment and a suspended sentence. She won't go that far."

"What I want is to have the charges dropped."

"There's no chance of that."

"I know. We were talking about what I want."

When we resumed our seats I said, "I'm going to advise my client to go to trial."

She looked surprised, like she'd thought I was smarter than that. "We've got the medical evidence to convict her. It'll take the jury five minutes."

"And that's all you've got. Some states don't even allow shaken baby convictions—they don't feel the scientific evidence is enough, that the injury could be caused by something else, like a vaccine or a virus."

"That's ridiculous."

"Do a Google news search; the vaccine defense comes up a lot. I'll parade out-of-state experts. I'm very good at putting doubt in a jury's mind. You know that."

"That defense isn't recognized in this state."

"Maybe we'll change that. When the jury hears her story they'll be looking for an excuse to not convict her."

"So your position now is no deal, we're going to trial?"

"And she won't testify against AJ. You don't seem to appreciate the fact that doing so will put her at risk. I have no faith in your office's ability to protect her. Or, you can agree to endangerment and to strongly recommend a suspended sentence and I will discuss that option with her." I waited while she considered. Tapped my pen on my teeth, looked at Marco whose eyes told me nothing. My out-of-state experts' threat was a bluff; I couldn't afford it. Besides, a local jury would believe the state medical examiner, not hired guns.

Michelle spoke. "Your client pleads to Second Degree Child Endangerment. I recommend probation, not suspended sentence, and some meaningful community service. Also counseling and anger management. That's as far as I go."

"So you get a second-degree conviction, you don't have to prep for trial; all you have to do is support my sentencing statement. And we take all the risk."

"I don't even know if I'll be allowed to do that; I have to run it by my supervisor."

"Who's your supervisor?"

She hesitated. "Barney."

"Barney? Barney Rubble? How in the hell did he get to be your supervisor?"

"He's the D.A.'s nephew."

"He's an idiot." I swear she almost giggled.

Marco couldn't keep quiet. "Is his name really Barney Rubble?"

"Billy Rossi. He was ahead of us in law school—a total buffoon. I can't believe you still call him Barney," I said to Michelle. "So you haven't completely lost your sense of humor."

I looked at her pen and saw a monogram on it. She followed my look and said, "No, I can't afford it. It was a gift from my parents when I passed the Bar Exam."

"You've had that pen for eight years? Damn! You'll be running this county some day. You'll be D.A. before you're forty. Barney will be your chauffeur." She smiled. She was probably planning her campaign. She stopped smiling when I asked, "Why probation?"

"She has to be accountable to someone. Every month she'll have to report to her probation officer, who will expect her to do certain things, like get a job or go to school. And if she screws up? She goes to prison. No suspended sentence," she said. "Besides, there's no chance she'll get one, whereas there is a teeny-tiny chance she'll get probation."

"Teeny-tiny? Then when you support my sentencing statement to the judge you do it zealously."

Marco cleared his throat. "G. You're running a big risk here."

Why was he calling me G? And expressing doubt in front of the enemy? "That's what I'm telling Michelle. She's killing us with her prosecutorial prowess. But we really aren't that far apart. Right, Michelle? Marco and I will go to our client and propose the deal?"

"Let me talk to Barney. And remember this is all contingent on your client testifying against AJ on the assault and the manslaughter."

"Of course." I gestured to her pen again. "You're definitely gonna be D.A. some day," I said. "A black female D.A. You'd be the first one in the state. How cool would that be? Sometimes you're not so bad. Maybe we should have lunch together."

"Don't hold your breath."

She left to talk to Barney and I high-fived Marco. “That is a great deal.”

“It is? You’ve got Violet pleading to a second degree felony and taking an enormous risk with that alternate sentence business. Have you ever seen it done?”

“Not for a second degree crime.”

“Not even Eduardo?”

“Nope.”

“So you plan to be a trailblazer at your client’s expense.”

“Or maybe we will go to trial.”

34

Marco drove us to Old Bridge, singing along with Springsteen and acting like we were on a jaunt to the beach, not to visit a suicidal young woman accused of killing her baby. "The screen door slams, Mary's dress waves . . ." I gazed out the window and thought about Jake telling Tommy that he didn't want to go to college after graduation; he wanted to devote everything to music, to see if he could make it. "And if I don't make it in a few years," he said, "I can still go to college. I won't be an old man or anything."

"Why can't you go to college *and* play music?" Tommy asked.

"Like Phish," I contributed. "They met in college. The University of Vermont. And look at them."

"You don't understand," Jake said. "I need to live my music, not sit around analyzing and deconstructing." The pitfalls of having a father who is an academic.

"What are you thinking about?" Marco asked.

"Jake. He told Tommy he doesn't want to go to college."

"It's not the right thing for everyone, but he's probably just rebelling against his old man. Christ, how many degrees does Tommy have?" We bumped over the bridge into Old Bridge.

"Look who's talking, Mr. Police Academy graduate; B.S. in Criminal Justice; and soon to be Juris Doctorate." Old Bridge was looking shabby and depleted. Whereas Port Grace has the river path, Old Bridge's river was lined with litter—unidentifiable rusty objects, unidentifiable plastic objects, garbage bags, bagless garbage. "I think you should lead the conversation with Violet. I'll interject if it's necessary."

"You want me to emote?" I slugged him in the arm. "Hey, assaulting an officer."

"You aren't an officer anymore, remember? And nobody cares if a lawyer gets assaulted. In fact they all cheer."

Violet and Ruth George were in the kitchen. Violet was mixing cheese sauce and macaroni in a pan the size of a football field and Ruth was seasoning a vat of stew. "It's my night to cook for the homeless shelter," Ruth said. "Usually, I use the church kitchen but there was a fire and we haven't fixed it up yet. And people have to eat."

"A fire," Marco said. "When?"

"About two months ago. The insurance says it was arson. But who would want to burn an old people's church?" Bags filled with apples stood next to the door. "I got those from the A&P out in Fredericksburg, and they donated bread too; they feel guilty because they're afraid to put up a store in this town. Yesterday I made brownies, so the folks will have a nice meal."

"Can we help?" I asked.

"Maybe later you can help carry to the car. Violet, are you finished with that macaroni and cheese? Now cover it with foil and then go talk to your lawyers." Violet's wrists were still bandaged and she appeared sad but calm. "Go on in the front room," Ruth said. "It's quiet in there."

We settled into comfortable upholstered furniture, Violet on the love seat, Marco next to her in a wing chair, me in a matching chair across the room. "We talked to the prosecutor," Marco said. "And she wants to make a plea bargain with you." Violet watched him closely, her expression neutral. "Right now you're charged with aggravated manslaughter. She says that if you testify against AJ you can plead guilty to child endangerment, which is a lesser charge. And she's agreed to recommend that you don't serve any prison time." Violet seemed to grow more sad with each word that Marco spoke. "But it's up to the judge. You could also be sentenced to the maximum ten years."

"Judge Gonzalez is the best judge we could have gotten," I said. "I really think he'll consider giving you probation and community service instead of sending you to prison. But Marco's right," I added. "There's no guarantee that he'll do that."

She rubbed the bandage on her left wrist. "What would I say?" she said. "About AJ?"

"Exactly what happened," I said. "And there might be two trials. One for Teddy and one for attacking you."

"I'd have to talk at both?" She looked at Marco.

"Yes, Violet." He spoke gently. "But we'll spend lots of time getting you ready, practicing what to say, so that by the time you go in there you'll be completely comfortable."

She looked seriously unhappy, but she was still with us, not turning inward like she usually did. "I have to tell everything?"

"Yes."

She stopped rubbing her wrist and started twirling one of her braids around her index finger. Marco looked at me and I slightly raised my hand. Silence is okay, I transmitted. I pretended to read the notes on my legal pad and Marco studied some family photos. She finally spoke. "How do I know he won't hurt me?"

"He'll go to prison, Violet," I said. "For years." Enough years to forget about her? I doubted it, but we could try to get her set up somewhere where he couldn't find her. "Don't worry about him. We'll make sure you're protected."

"They can do that?" she asked Marco.

"Yes," he said, but he didn't sound confident. "If you are a witness for the prosecution and he threatens you, they have an obligation to protect you." He and I both knew that not much would be done for her. That it was a risk. The only witnesses who get real protection are in large, complicated Federal cases like drug rings and organized crime.

She massed together a bunch of braids and twisted them. The fragrance of cooking meat and onions drifted in from the kitchen and I heard Mr. and Mrs. George talking, not loud enough to understand their words, just a comforting domestic murmur. She looked at me. "You know what I told you? About that night?" She choked on her words, on her thoughts.

"The night Teddy got hurt?"

She nodded, but couldn't speak.

"Can I get you something to drink?" Marco asked. She nodded as tears soaked her face and she rubbed them with her knuckles like a little kid. Marco went to the kitchen and I heard him talking to the Georges. He brought Violet a glass of lemonade and said, "I'm going to help load the car, I'll be right back, but you guys go ahead and talk." We watched him leave the room. I admired the way his jeans and crisp white button-down fit him. Violet probably admired that too, or maybe she was thinking about what a kind person he is. Or maybe she was thinking about something I couldn't imagine. I felt like the runner-up, but I tried to coax her to talk.

"Is there something you want to tell me?" I attempted to match the gentleness of Marco's voice and to be sincere about it. "Something about that night?" I saw Marco walk by carrying the vat of stew, and Mr. and Mrs. George laden with boxes and bags and pans. A bunch of scents came our way, the barbershop smells of Mr. George, Mrs. George's cooking and perfume, night smells that burst through the opened front door and lingered after it was closed. Shaving cream, stars, onions, talc, lime, asphalt, lavender, and exhaust fumes.

She sipped the lemonade. Took a deep breath and blew it out. "It wasn't like that," she said. "Like I told you." She resumed weeping. I sat in Marco's chair, next to her. Her hands covered her face. I reached out and stroked them, and then sat beside her on the loveseat, touched her hair, smoothed the bundle of braids, and then I wrapped my arm around her shoulder and she turned to me and nestled like a puppy as I held her and rubbed her back. Eventually her sobs subsided and I saw that Marco had come back and was looking pensive. I pointed to a box of tissues and he brought them over and put some into Violet's hand. He sat down and I disengaged myself from Violet, careful to not disturb the delicate linkage that had formed between us. When I thought she was ready, I said, "Tell us." She looked over at Marco who smiled a smile that was just for her, something to warm her up. And this is what she told us:

It's two o'clock in the morning. Violet and Teddy are sleeping. Finally. Teddy's painful ear infection kept him awake and crying the previous two nights. Violet took him to the clinic that morning and antibiotics were prescribed. The pink stuff. He fell asleep around eight, woke up screaming at eleven. The doctor said the antibiotics took twenty-four hours to begin working and she could give him baby aspirin every six hours, so she gave him aspirin and a bottle, and around midnight they both fell asleep, exhausted.

She wakes up. Looks at the crib but Teddy is asleep. Her clock glows in the dark. Two o'clock. Then she hears banging, her front door pushed against the chain lock. A split second's worth of choices occur to her. Call 911. Grab Teddy and get out the window to the fire escape. Then she hears him. His force on the door. The explosion of his voice.

"Violet! Bitch! Open up." He has keys to the lock and the deadbolt, but she hadn't expected him and had fastened the chain lock like she always did when she was alone.

She gets out of bed and hurries to the door, but before she gets there he splinters the chain lock and stumbles into the living room. Grabs her by the shoulders. "Why the fuck you lock me out?" Doesn't listen to her answer. Teddy starts crying. He collapses on the couch. "Get me a beer."

She is pretty sure there isn't any beer. Teddy is crying. She goes to the kitchen. Opens the fridge. No beer. She fills a baby bottle with apple juice. Has to walk through the living room to get to the bedroom and calm Teddy down. AJ slumps deep into the couch. "What the fuck is that?" The baby bottle.

"For Teddy." She indicates the bedroom, Teddy's piercing cry.

"I told you to get me a beer." He stands up.

"I don't have any. I'm sorry." She is shivering. She'd fallen asleep in T-shirt and underwear. She takes a step toward the bedroom. He takes a bigger step across the room. Grabs her. Pushes her to the couch. The bottle falls from her grasp. "Teddy's sick." Teddy's screams filling the room, filling her head. He holds her down with one hand, pulls her underwear down with the other. Teddy screams.

"Shut the fuck up," he roars. Teddy screams. His ears hurt. The doctor had explained it all to her, how the fluid filled his ears at night from lying down, how the pressure caused him terrible pain. She liked the way the doctor took his time and helped her understand why Teddy was crying so much. She could picture it now, fluid and bacteria filling the tiny tunnel of his ear canal, the painful pressure against the delicate membrane of his eardrum.

He pulls up her shirt. Rubs her breasts hard. Unfastens his belt. Teddy's cries fill the room. Fill her head. He pulls the belt out of the loops, snaps it threateningly. "Shut that baby the fuck up."

She struggles up from the couch. Pulls her shirt down. "He's sick," she says. "He has an ear infection." She pulls up her underwear, reaches for the baby bottle that fell on the carpet.

Takes it to the bedroom. Feels his hot glare on her back.

Teddy. Sitting in his crib, pulling on the bars. Crying. Hiccupping. She reaches to pull him up, hug him, rock him, hold him upright while he drinks his bottle and the fluid in his ears drains and stops tormenting him. AJ behind her. "Throw it in there. He can hold his own bottle." A direct order. She pauses. He wrenches the bottle from her, throws it into the crib. Teddy cries louder. AJ pulls her away from the crib, pushes her onto the bed, takes off his pants, his underwear. Teddy cries. The room fills with Teddy's tears. Her head fills with Teddy's tears. AJ on top of her she conjures an image of Teddy's ear canal full of pus, and then she imagines the pus draining away, the ear clean and healthy, Teddy sucking his bottle and smiling up at her.

Teddy crying. AJ on top of her. He has an erection and then he doesn't. "That's it," he says. "I'm gonna shut that baby up." Teddy crying. AJ getting up.

She is frantic. "No, no, I'll get him. Lie down." Forces a smile. "Lie down. Rest. I'll be right back." Touching him. Making him believe her. That she'll be right back. Will do whatever he wants.

He grunts, lies down on the bed. He's drunk. He's tired. He's angry. Angry at his supervisor at the prison who reprimanded him for excessive force. Angry at the prisoners who fill his days with swill. Angry at his wife who wants a divorce. Angry at Violet for locking him out. Angry at Teddy because he won't stop crying.

Violet reaches for Teddy, pulls him up. "Shh . . . Shh . . ." Soothing little mommy noises.

He's had it up to here. "Hurry up or I'm coming over there." It's time to take a crack at someone, relieve all that pressure built up inside of him. She hears the fist in his voice.

"Shh . . . Shh . . . Shh . . ." She lifts the baby from his crib, crooks him in one arm, holds the bottle to his mouth, he pushes it away, crying, crying. "Take it, Teddy, you have to take it." She tries to jam it in his mouth. He slaps it out of her hand. He is a strong baby and she is a petite woman. He is enraged, in pain, he screams. She picks up the bottle. "Take it take it take it." AJ is getting up. He's growling he's coming over his fist is ready. She must quiet the baby before AJ does. "Take it," she says again, trying to jam the bottle into his mouth, but he turns his head, and AJ is behind her. "Take it. Takeit! Takeit! Takeit!" she hears herself scream feels herself shaking him. Finally, he is quiet. She lays him in the crib, she is exhausted. Covers him with the Winnie the Pooh quilt. AJ shoves her back to the bed.

It took a long time for Violet to get through it all. When she finished, she said, "I did it." Her voice was soft and hoarse and I wasn't certain that I heard correctly. She looked at me, avoiding Marco's eyes. "I shook him so he'd be quiet. I didn't know what else to do. AJ would have beat him. He would have killed him. I didn't mean to hurt him. You know I didn't."

"Okay," I said softly. "Okay, that's good. I'm glad you told us."

On the drive home I fiddled with the radio and tried to make conversation. "What are you up to tonight?" I asked Marco. Twisting the knob through NPR, college, folk, jazz, baseball, classic rock, all news all the time, country, oldies, hip-hop, hate talk, light rock.

He reached over and covered my hand with his. Pushed the pre-set to classical. "Rehearsal. We've got a gig at Murphy's Saturday night."

"Cool. I'll come." I rolled down the window to feel the heady sweetness of a spring evening. Stuck my head out like a dog. Just for a minute, as the plaintive cry of a cello flew out of the speakers and into the night.

"You think she's telling the truth?" he asked.

I re-entered the car and pawed through a box of cassette tapes. "Counting Crows?" He shook his head. "Marvin Gaye? Gaelic Storm? Metallica? REM? Los Lobos?"

"Los Lobos."

I popped it in. "You don't think she's telling the truth?"

"You've been so certain it was him."

"Yeah, I was, wasn't I?"

"Why is she telling us now?"

"So she won't have to testify against him?"

"Maybe she feels guilty."

"Maybe she's protecting him."

"Still?"

"Who the fuck knows?" I pulled a cigarette out of my purse and looked at it. "This sucks. AJ was supposed to be the bad guy. If this was a movie he'd be the bad guy."

"He is."

"But maybe she is too. Then who's the good guy?"

He looked at me for a long, hot second. "Sometimes there aren't any good guys."

I shoved the cigarette back into the pack. "What do you think happened?"

"How the fuck should I know? Does it matter?"

"Not really." I turned up the volume. "Fucking clients."

We were quiet for a while, listening to Tex-Mex, *How Will the Wolf Survive?* I contemplated Texas, a state big enough to get lost in.

When Marco cornered into the Port Grace exit I said, "What now?"

"Which what?"

"Violet. What should we do?"

"Ask her what she wants to do, trial or the plea offer."

"Our trial strategy will have to change. You think if she told that story to a jury they'd convict her?"

"Yes."

"Not even one hold-out, someone who would empathize with her enough for a hung jury?"

"Maybe. But then there'd be another trial. I'll call her tomorrow, lay out her choices again and we'll do what she says. If she's old enough to go to prison she's old enough to make the decision." He dropped me off at the office so I could get my car.

When I got home Tommy was lying on the couch half-asleep, listening to Neil Young and reading. I took a deep breath and sauntered over. "Hey, cute stuff."

"Hi," he said in the briefest way possible.

I pushed the book so I could see the cover. *My Manhattan,* by Pete Hamill. "You miss New York?"

"Yeah. Sometimes I do."

I pushed at his feet and scrunched onto the couch. "Put it down. I brought you a vanilla milkshake."

He rested the book on his chest. "Vanilla milkshake?" I nodded and he marked his place in the book and dropped it on the floor.

"Move over. You don't get it until you make room for me." He half sat, enough so that he wouldn't dribble. "Come on, Tommy, smile." I handed him the shake, pulled up his T-shirt, and rested my head against his belly.

"Jake will be home soon," he said.

"So? I'm not doing anything." I closed my eyes and relaxed into his body. He drank the shake and ran his fingers through my hair.

"Something's different," he said. I pulled his hand down and kissed his palm. We wrapped ourselves in the moment, in the comfort of people who have slept together a couple thousand times and still like each other.

I took the empty cup from his hand and set it on top of *My Manhattan.* "Let's go to bed."

35

I woke up at four o'clock feeling like I couldn't breathe. Pushed a change of clothes into a duffel bag, wrote a note to Tommy, and drove north toward my friend Becky's cabin in Maine. At six-thirty I called her on my cell phone and said I was on my way. Then I left a message on Marco's answering machine, because I didn't want to talk to him and I knew he'd be at the gym.

When I entered the cabin Becky was cozy on the couch with a book in her lap. The Franklin stove was burning. "Want some coffee or hot chocolate?" she asked.

"No, I'm good. You and Tom are the only people who have ever made me hot chocolate. I never make it for myself."

"What about your dad?"

"Never. The Central Valley is always hot. Nobody drinks hot chocolate there. In fact it's banned. There's a sign posted outside of town, 'Welcome to the Central Valley! No Hot Chocolate Allowed.' "

She smiled. "Can you get it on the black market?"

"Probably. I think I've seen it in the police blotter. 'Locals discovered cultivating marijuana and serving hot chocolate to minors.' I pointed to the book in her lap. "What are you reading?"

"Graham Greene. *The End of the Affair.*"

"That sounds serious."

"Well, every now and then I like to remind myself that I was an English major. That I knew how to read something besides sports stats."

"And you're still getting over Lowell."

"That too."

"How could you fall in love with somebody named Lowell?" Then Celeste burst into the room, a little girl with wavy brown hair and fuzzy pajamas with feet in them. "Come here, you," I said. She sprang onto me. She was a bundle of warmth and good smells. I sniffed her hair. "Mmm, you smell good. Do you wash your hair with strawberries?"

She gave me the look reserved for grown-ups who say stupid things. "No, silly. It's shampoo."

"Have you had breakfast?" Becky asked.

I shook my head. "I drove straight through. I had to be here."

"We're making blueberry pancakes," Celeste said. "I helped pick the blueberries."

"Then they'll probably be the best pancakes that I ever ate." I sat up. "Remember last summer when you and me and your Mom went blueberry picking?"

"No."

"Well, you were just a little kid then. How old are you now?"

"Three." She held up the correct number of fingers.

"Three! Wow! Can you eat three pancakes?"

"Of course."

"Of course." We moved into the kitchen. I poured coffee for Becky and myself, and milk for Celeste, folded napkins and placed them beneath forks. Becky ladled batter onto the skillet.

"We picked these blueberries last summer," she said. "The time you were with us. I froze some of them."

"That was a great day." I stared into space, remembering the August sun and how we ate more blueberries than we put in our pails, and when Celeste got tired, I carried her on my shoulders.

Celeste came into the room, pulling a small wooden wagon, transporting a large gray cat. "Big Tom wants a pancake," she announced.

"When we're finished," Becky said, "if there's any left he can have some." Big Tom looked over the situation and closed his eyes. He obviously had faith in Celeste.

After breakfast Celeste went off to watch *Sesame Street.* There's no cable service up there, but Becky, who is a sports writer, has satellite so she can watch all sports all the time. She and I went onto the porch and settled into wooden rockers, facing the lake and the forest. It was cold. "So, what's up?" Becky asked.

I sketched out Violet's case, omitting her confession and other confidential information. "I'm out of synch, working too much, and Tommy's mad at me."

"You're not going to mess that up again, are you?"

"I don't want to. But I keep screwing up and acting inconsiderate and pretty soon I'm so far in the hole I don't know how to begin to get out."

"Does he know you feel bad?"

"I haven't specifically told him. He knows me so well that I always assume he understands everything about me."

"You shouldn't assume that. You can be very hard to read."

Fog and rain rolled in for the day, so we stayed near the wood-burning stove and read, talked, watched the Mets crush the Phillies, dozed, and played with Celeste. After dark the rain eased up and I put on Becky's old down jacket and walked to the lake. It was calm, compared to the Port Grace bay. The night sounds were different too, the whispers of a forest. I sat on an upside-down rowboat and thought about Celeste and blueberries and the way the moon was reflected in the lake, and how if I were an artist I could spend a lifetime trying to capture light on the water. And I missed Tommy. Most of all I missed Tommy. I asked myself the big questions. *What matters? What's important? Figure it out.* I ached for Tommy, for what we had. I was sick about Violet shaking Teddy. What am I going to do? I was jammed, choking.

I pushed myself up and started walking around the lake. The pine forest was dotted with the light of cabins, and the smell of burning wood filled the air, mingling with pine needles and damp earth, moss, rocks, and fresh water. A black dog streaked past me. Halfway around the lake I started to calm down as my panic was absorbed into the night. I looked across the lake at the light from Becky's cabin. I was reminded of something, and after a while I realized it was Miles's painting of the lake, the first time I met him, that day in the hall outside of Laura's loft when Teddy was still alive. It felt like years ago, but it was less than two months. My longing for Tommy and Jake overwhelmed me and I stood there feeling it cover me like fog. Tears came to my eyes when I thought of Tommy and how he would have woken up that morning and found me gone again.

When I got back to the cabin Celeste was asleep and Becky was in her chenille robe working on her laptop as Richie Havens sang softly in the background. She looked at me. "Did you get everything figured out?"

"Not even close. It's all Tommy," I said. "I can't lose him again. Without Tommy and Jake . . ." I couldn't bear to take that thought to its conclusion.

"Why are you so upset about this case?" she said. "Why are you letting it destroy you?"

"I don't know. I don't know what to do."

"Let justice take its course. You've got to do your job, but it's like a river. You've got the oars but you can't control the current. Right?"

That's why Becky's a writer. Her sports metaphors are awesome. I sank into the couch and looked at the Franklin stove. Even though I couldn't see its flames I knew they were there; I could hear them and smell them. Feel the heat. Let justice take its course. Becky was right. It was so complex and yet so simple. Let justice take its course.

36

The next morning I was on the road early. Halfway home I stopped at a diner, edged into a booth, and called Tommy while I waited for my breakfast. No answer. "I'll be home soon," I said to the answering machine. Then I dialed Marco.

"Where are you?" he asked.

"On my way home. Didn't you get my message yesterday?"

"Yes. Which you left when you knew I wouldn't be there. I can't believe you just took off without telling me. You had court yesterday and I couldn't make the appearance because I'm not licensed yet. Not to mention everything else you dumped on me."

"I forgot about court. I thought it was an office day."

"We need to talk."

I pulled into the driveway and waved to Mr. Ziznewski, who was sweeping the sidewalk. I wasn't up to a conversation with him, so I slipped through the side gate into the backyard. It was a cool morning but the sun was shining. Tulips bloomed near the patio, as did the viburnum, whose intoxicating scent filled the air.

Marco was on the patio, seated, legs stretched out in front of him, face tilted toward the sun. He wore black cop shades, black T-shirt, jeans, and black work boots. I expected to see a gun clipped to his belt; he gave off that hard-ass vibe that some cops cultivate, and some just naturally have.

"Hi," I said.

"I'm wondering if it's a good idea for us to be partners."

I felt like he'd poked me with a cattle prod. Stunned. Sick. "What are you talking about?"

"I know you're used to being my boss . . ."

"Have I ever treated you like that?" I interrupted. "Like I'm your boss?"

"Not exactly. But it's your show, you make the decisions."

"I give you plenty of responsibility. Cases and problems where I leave the decisions up to you."

"That's not what I mean. It's not the cases. It's more about . . ." He searched for words, put his hand up when I started to tell him what they were. "Let me finish." He sat up straight, removed his shades, and carefully placed them on the table. "You're self-centered. Unpredictable. I never know when you're going to take a case and let it run you into the ground so that I have to scramble to cover your butt. You ignore me, you ignore your husband, and you run off whenever you feel like it."

I was devastated. "You really think that?"

He nodded. "You're incredibly generous too. That's your basic nature. But there's this thing you do—everything seems fine and then something gets to you and you spin out; along the way you hurt the people who love you. And frankly? You expect too much of me."

"What do you mean? I thought you wanted to take on new cases, grow, expand?"

"Not the work. Emotionally. You count on me to be a rock. And I've got my own baggage to deal with."

"You're the most stable person I know. Except maybe Tommy."

"Wrong. Don't expect that of me. Or Tommy. It's not fair."

I stood up and walked around the small yard, twisted off a clump of viburnum. "Smell this." I held it out to Marco.

"Sometimes I miss California," I added for no particular reason.

"I'm sorry to be so hard on you. You know I love you. And I think you're a great lawyer and a great person. It's too much for me though. You expect me to always behave in a certain way, to never be vulnerable or confused." He looked at me dead-on, daring me to look away. Tears heated up behind my eyes.

"I'm sorry. I'll pay attention, try to change." I rubbed my eyes, cleared my throat. "But what are you talking about, baggage?"

"A lot of things. But especially one that I just can't shake. Remember when I told you that one of the reasons I left the force was because I enjoyed the power too much?"

I nodded.

"I didn't figure that out on my own. Something happened."

I waited.

"I punched a suspect. He was cuffed and I was pissed off. It was easy to take it out on him. I quit because I knew I'd do it again. And again. It felt good." A lawnmower started up next door. I leaned close to him so I could hear. He made a frustrated gesture. "You see me as this straight-arrow solid citizen. But I'm not. I'm damaged goods, just like you. And you've got to understand that."

I was silent, taking it in, watching the sparks fly off of him. "I'm trying," I finally said.

"And so am I. I struggle every goddamn day of my life to be the kind of person I want to be. But I'm still so far from it."

"Jesus, Marco. You are much more evolved than I am, ethically speaking. Don't be so hard on yourself."

"See. There you go. Why can't you see me for who I am, and not just who you need me to be? Didn't you hear me say that I hit someone and enjoyed it?"

I shivered. "You did it once?"

"Yes. But I knew I'd do it again. And I thought about my

mom and my sister, and I was so fucking lonely."

I reached for his hand. "This is totally frightening."

He held on tight. "Just tell me you'll think about what I said."

"I will. I promise."

I left work early, took care of some errands, and slunk home to get chewed out by Tommy. Jake was sprawled on the couch watching *The Godfather.* "Where's your Dad?"

"Don't know. Food shopping, maybe?" He yawned.

"How was your day?"

He pressed the pause button. "Good. How was yours?"

"Okay." I wanted to ask him if Tommy was mad at me, but figured it wasn't fair to involve him. "Watch your movie," I said. "I'll go do laundry or something."

When Tommy walked into the kitchen I was scrubbing the grout between the tiles on the counter and listening to *Beggar's Banquet* on my iPod. He dropped the grocery bags he was carrying onto the table and looked at me.

I pulled out the earbuds. "Aren't toothbrushes great," I said, holding up the one I was attacking grout with.

"I hope that's not mine." He unloaded the bags without further comment and I returned to my task with headphones off in case he wanted to talk. He folded the empty brown bags with precision, slid them into the broom closet and left the room without another word. It was worse than getting yelled at, so I abandoned grout and pursued him. He wasn't upstairs, but from our bedroom window I saw him on the patio, reading. I practiced what I would say. "Work's been really tough." But he wouldn't want to hear any excuses. "I'm sorry I went to Becky's without discussing it with you." But that wasn't the only issue. I've been such a jerk. Too egocentric. Downright shameful in fact, for someone with a talent for finely calibrated legal arguments. I sat on our bed and looked under Tommy's pillow, where earlier I had placed two round-trip tickets to Austin during the week of the big music festival, as well as a car rental confirmation for a Ford Mustang convertible and a note saying that we would search for the best tacos in Texas, and that this was the first of a series of road trips we'd take together. It would make him happy. I settled on a simple *I'm sorry* as a good place to start. Then we'd see which way the river flowed.

Epilogue

The remaining weeks of May graced me with a calm interval at work, as the embattled couples of Port Grace were rendered penitent by that generous month of nest-building and flower-blooming. Marco graduated from law school and we printed business cards and stationary declaring our partnership. I've been spending so much time with Tommy that I think he's starting to get tired of me.

In June we were slammed with a heat wave that fueled domestic strife and bar fights. Judge Gonzalez had a heart attack and Violet's case was assigned to Judge Silva, the most hard-nosed judge on the criminal bench. She went before him to enter her guilty plea to second-degree Child Endangerment. He waved off my perfectly sculpted argument for probation and sentenced her to seven years in state prison. With good behavior she'll be out in four and change, and will be less than twenty-five years old. Laura is talking about starting a vocational program at the women's prison, training them to do flower arrangements. She says she's going to visit Violet every week.

Violet didn't testify against AJ because he never went to trial. He pled guilty to third-degree Child Endangerment, which is a second-degree crime only for the person who has responsibility for the child. The assault charges were dropped and he was sentenced to three years. "How the hell did he work that?" I asked Marco. Marco asked around and found out that AJ had cut a good deal—he gave up the name of a corrupt guard who was smuggling drugs into the prison. He was sent to a country club federal prison populated with white-collar criminals and former police officers, and he could be out in two years.

Was the outcome of Violet's case an example of justice? You could ask twelve people that question and get twelve responses. Concepts of justice tend to be subjective. What I do know is that Violet hit the pavement even before she entered the judicial system. Whatever happened the night that Teddy was shaken? That was the night when she started serving her sentence.

ABOUT THE AUTHOR

Jennifer Louise Jefferson is an attorney who lives in Massachusetts with her husband and three sons. She worked on domestic violence and child abuse and neglect cases in the New Jersey Family Courts for six years. Visit www.JenniferJefferson.net. E-mail Jennifer@JenniferJefferson.net.